HAUNTING THE EARL

HAUNTING THE EARL

A NOVEL BY

GEORGINA NORTH

This is a work of fiction. Characters, names, places, and events are the product of the author's imagination or used fictitiously.

Library of Congress Cataloging-in-Publication Data

Names: North, Georgina, author.
Title: Haunting the Earl: A Novel / Georgina North.
Description: First U.S. edition | San Diego: Pepperberry Press, 2025.

Identifiers: LCCN 2024926073 (print)

ISBN 978-1-959794-11-0 (paperback)
ISBN 978-1-959794-10-3 (hardcover)
ISBN 978-1-959794-08-0 (ebook)

Cover design by Jennifer Therieau

For Lou

1

'Is this what you like? That spot, there?' Valentine Ainsley, the Earl of St Germain, hummed with happiness at his discovery. 'Yes, I thought you might. If you wish for more, you must be a very good girl and keep your claws off my trousers.'

The mischievous black creature spared him a dismissive glance from her perch on his shoulder, the thrum of her purring growing loud enough to drown out any further scolding.

'This is what your future holds then, is it?' inquired his sister Franny, coming through the doorway of his library. 'Speaking to a cat because you've elected to grow old and alone with no wife?' With a pointed look at Pip, she added, 'The dear can't understand you, you know.'

'Perhaps that's what makes her the more superior creature.' Saint didn't mean it. He preferred an educated lady with a few thoughts rattling around her brain. 'But as it stands, Pip understands quite well, don't you, biscuit?'

Saint had found the tiny thing under a bush—cold, frightened, and malnourished—after catching the faint sound of a hoarse, desperate squeak. He'd only meant to see her health restored before sending her to join the barn cats. But then Pip had bumped her little head into his cheek when he scooped her up, and curled into the crook of his neck.

Franny settled herself on the settee and melted into the cushions with such unadulterated delight, Saint felt he ought to leave the two alone. He noted her travel dress, which was not the riding habit she wore when merely coming for several hours, as she sometimes did, their homes being not so many miles apart.

'Have you come by carriage?' A note of wariness threaded through his voice.

His sister tipped her head back, closed her eyes, and answered with a noncommittal groan.

'Should I assume you've already asked the housekeeper to make up a room for you?'

Disregarding his question entirely, she said, 'I think perhaps four children was too many.'

The gentle shake of Saint's shoulders when he chuckled startled Pip. He was prising her claws from the fabric of his coat, laughter still on his lips, when the butler appeared.

'Mr Marsden for you, my lord.'

Saint nodded, and his sister straightened herself,

sending him a quizzing look, just as his long-time solicitor stepped into the room.

Mr Marsden's nervous gaze landed on the kitten.

'Leave your fear behind. It's only my clothes the adorable minx ravages.'

Keeping a cautious eye on the tiny creature, Marsden greeted Franny before setting a chair near Saint's and speaking without preamble. 'There's a buyer for Sylvancliffe.'

'Saint!' Franny cried out, her fingers gripping the edge of the settee and compelling her forward. 'You can't. It was Papa's favourite house.'

Saint ignored his sister's outburst. 'We have our answer then.' When Saint first approached his solicitor about selling off the property, the two men discussed whether the old manor's notorious reputation would help or hinder the effort.

During the previous lord's lifetime, the estate near the Norfolk coast was famed for lavish weeks-long parties, which had prompted three elopements and one divorce more scandalous than all the elopements combined. The house remained for posterity the site of several of England's most persevering mysteries, including the disappearance of Lady Cecilia Walker on a fine October day. For Saint, despite the benefit of adulthood, it was also a place filled with spectres, echoes of his father's disappointment, and their final moments together.

'I'll leave the terms for your review,' Marsden said, rising. 'But I took the liberty of letting the gentleman know he could expect a counter within a fortnight.'

Saint nodded and watched the solicitor go, wondering that he didn't feel more relief.

Once the door closed, Franny turned to him. 'Why now? I know you didn't love the place the same as I did. No one would fault you for that, when your last visit came to an end with Papa's death, but it's been an age, and not every moment spent at Sylvancliffe was miserable for you. Do you recall that sennight you wished to sleep at the beach under the stars? Your mama saw that a bed was constructed for you on the sand and made several footmen sleep there, too.' A sentimental smile touched his sister's lips.

He remembered that night with perfect clarity, and the peace he felt when no longer confined by the walls of Sylvancliffe. He also easily recalled the sour smell of life decaying around him every time he entered his father's chambers. Saint's three older sisters had been devastated by the loss, but they hadn't been present to watch each new day claim more of the man, until all that remained was a slip of ashen skin wrapped around bones set in the shape of a body.

'It's time. Long past. If I'd sold it sooner—' Saint swallowed the rest of the sentence, wishing the words unsaid after a beat of silence spent under Franny's canny stare.

'Edward is fine,' she said.

'And we are lucky it is so.'

Saint's younger brother had visited the house on a lark with some friends from school. They'd drunk a bottle of gin, gone for a swim, and Edward had nearly drowned when a current pulled him under. It was a jarring and unpleasant reminder of Saint's own mortality, of his need to find a wife and sire an heir. The very idea of marriage made him feel like a child all over again, thrust into a role he could not avoid and for which he was ill prepared.

'Certainly—but you blame some deficiency of your own—one which does not and never has existed. Edward has a generous allowance and little else to think of beyond his own whims and inclinations, besides having a fool's store of pluck. I haven't begrudged him that and neither have you. His behaviour is merely a reflection of his age, not some imagined weakness in his character or yours. How is it *I* find myself lecturing *you* on the rash and reckless exploits of young men? Really, Saint. Being your sister is exhausting.'

This was easy for Franny to say when she wasn't the one who constantly heard their father's voice, rife with disappointment. He picked up the packet Marsden had left, then set it right back down.

'The air around you has grown positively stifling. Have a house party—at Sylvancliffe. See if it's not at least a little diverting.'

'No.'

Franny shook her head. 'If it weren't for our passing resemblance, I'd hardly recognise you these last months. I don't know who would. The brother I've known and adored for so many years has gone off, and in his place left some piteous creature whose main diversion is fending off cat claws.'

Saint tipped up his head, casting a bothered look at the ceiling. His sister wasn't wrong, but nearly losing Edward had unearthed sharp-sided questions about his ability to be a worthy husband and father, when his own example of such was long buried. The doubts he felt when searching for answers had settled upon him like a heavy fog.

'My capacity for amusement has not diminished. Wouldn't you agree, biscuit?' He brushed a hand over Pip. She knocked her head into his palm, requesting scratches behind her ears.

'Making such a statement detracts from the sentiment of the statement itself, does it not?' observed a third familiar and dear voice.

'Hazelhurst, old chap. Was I expecting you?'

'No,' replied the duke. After kissing Franny on the cheek, he took the chair left vacant by Marsden, a little scowl knitting his brows together. 'My wife had the audacity to call me a distraction. Told me I was making it near impossible for her to finish her current painting.'

Saint let the tail of a smile curl his lips. 'Were you?'

Hazelhurst drew out the inspection of his nail beds. 'Perhaps.'

Saint's body shook with his roaring laugh. Pip, fearing a long fall from her perch, sunk her blade-sharp claws into the fabric of his coat. He reached across his chest to stroke the narrow space between her eyes, his shoulders still bouncing.

'You marry a woman as beautiful and talented as my wife and then tell me you don't wish to spend every moment in her presence.'

'Oh, do give us a hint of the subject,' begged Franny. 'I adored her *Woman at Water's Edge* and have yet to forgive you for stealing it out from under me at the Academy last season. Excessively unfair of you to hoard your wife's work, you know. On second thoughts, I don't care what she's painting. Tell your lovely wife I want it, and I'll pay her whatever she wishes.'

'I doubt your husband is in support of such a declaration or that Hazelhurst is here to do his wife's bidding.' Saint turned an interested look upon his friend. 'But how is it you end up here in my library—a day's ride from your own home?'

'I told Vivienne if she felt I was such a distraction, I would take myself off forthwith, not just from the room or the house, but from the whole county.'

'And she called your bluff?'

'She called my bluff.' Even as Hazelhurst said so, his petulant voice couldn't mask the mischief in his eyes or the lopsided grin tugging at his lips. 'Now, why are you defending your person?'

Saint's shoulders pulled taut. 'Sylvancliffe. I'm selling it. Franny wishes to have a party on account of me being intolerably boring.'

'And because it's the least we can do to honour Father's memory, if you're determined to be rid of the house. A part of me always thought we'd return one day.'

'None of us is looking to go to war again so soon, but I don't disagree with Franny,' said Hazelhurst, with a look of apology.

Saint glowered at his oldest friend. 'Traitor. Issuing the reproofs has always been my responsibility, and I find it much more comfortable that way.'

Franny clapped. 'A party, then?'

'Mind, I've no interest in competing with Lady Caroline.'

'Of course not. Just a few close friends, an eligible young lady or two.'

'Franny,' he said, with a note of warning, but his sister's attention was already drifting from the conversation.

She stood, waving off his concerns with a sharp flick of her wrist. 'We'll compare lists over dinner.'

Before Saint could reply—or smarter still, change his mind—she disappeared into the hall.

'What?' He was acutely aware he was being examined by the man to his left.

'Only wondering if some of your reluctance to return to Sylvancliffe, in addition to the obvious, is because you thought the manor haunted as a child.'

'It *is* haunted.'

Saint's oldest friend was the only person in the world who knew how terrified he was of the place. Even before his father passed away, the house had frightened and overwhelmed him—the eerie sounds of life in the middle of the night, the sensation of being watched when he moved about, the feeling the house could swallow him up, as it did Lady Cecilia some twenty-odd years ago.

The duke held him in a steady stare but maintained a declarative silence.

'I know you much too well to be fooled into thinking you've no more to say on the subject,' Saint said. 'Out with it, old chap.'

Hazelhurst compressed his lips, the corners turning down. 'The only ghost at Sylvancliffe, I think, is your father's.'

Even at such a distance, Saint felt the oppressive atmosphere of the house begin to crush him.

'Saint?'

He could hear Hazelhurst say his name, but all he saw when he looked towards his friend was the image of his father, prone and ghoulishly pale in his bed. Eyes closed, every breath rattling in his lungs.

'You begin to worry me, Saint.' Hazelhurst stood and was coming round to where he sat.

Saint managed to put up a staying hand, even if it betrayed him with its slight tremor. 'Fine. I'm fine.' He forced the words out of his closed throat, each one scratching on its way out.

'You can refuse Franny's request, you know. Seems more pleasant than living in a perpetual state of dread, no?'

Saint heard the hint of sarcasm in his friend's voice. 'Shows how little you know my sister.'

Hazelhurst laughed. In truth, he knew Franny almost as well as Saint himself did, the two men having been friends for more of their lives than not. He was certain Hazelhurst understood why he was going through with his sister's scheme, but said regardless, 'I owe her so much.'

Franny had a decade of wisdom on Saint and, of his three elder half-sisters, had taken on the greatest share of mothering him, Edward, and Edward's twin sister Ellena, when their mother grew too sick to do so herself. Saint had been in school for some years by the time Franny married, but he'd spent his holidays with her and her husband, a quiet man of means Saint quite liked and who balanced out the force that was Franny. If she wished to have a party at Sylvancliffe before he sold the place, he wouldn't deny her that after all she'd done for him.

'You may not enjoy yourself,' Hazelhurst said, 'but in the end I suspect you'll be glad you went.'

Saint tapped his fingers in rapid succession on the arm of the chair to keep pace with his thumping heart and eyed his friend with open scepticism.

Hazelhurst lifted a shoulder in that nonchalant way of his. 'Things never look half as bad with the benefit of a little time and space. You've had twenty years.'

'Your wife has made you sensible, and I have yet to decide whether or not I appreciate this new quality in you.'

'What effect will a wife have on you, I wonder?'

Beyond springing more worry and responsibility, Saint couldn't begin to imagine.

The duke rose from his seat. 'It's past time for me to get the dust off. Billiards before dinner?'

Saint nodded, and Hazelhurst left, shutting the door behind him. Memories filled the silence of the room. Only once before had he made to visit Sylvancliffe. Despite assurances from the steward all was well, he'd felt obligated to see the estate for himself. He'd sent a letter ahead announcing his arrival, spent several nights sleeping at inns, and made it as far as the iron gates blockading the long, winding drive to the house. They shuddered open, their old hinges howling like a barn owl, and he'd broken into a cold sweat. Overhead, carrion crows had cried out a warning. The road was devoured by the trees, just as he would be if he went on. Even his horse had stalled, unwilling to take another step.

With an uneven nod, Saint had thanked the gatekeeper and turned back. When he passed the carriage carrying his luggage on the lane, the coachman accepted the new direction to return to Belmont Hall without betraying the barest hint of surprise.

It was impossible for Saint to untangle a future trip to Sylvancliffe from his recollections of the past. All at once, he was in the small rowboat with his father, smiling, happy, the July sun golden on his skin. He pushed the hair off his face, the strands warm to the touch—a perfect moment he lived again and again during the interminable march of time after his father's death. The days before that fateful moment had been filled with expectations too heavy for a child's narrow shoulders to bear; the days after sunk in fear of being alone in the world, or so it felt to a boy acutely aware of how little he knew of the role he was expected to fill.

A quick cramp pierced Saint's side, and he pushed a hand hard into the slight dip of his waist. The other he ran over his face, the moisture at the corners of his eyes surprising him. With a ragged sigh, he pulled a sheet of paper from the desk drawer and began a letter of invitation.

2

The sensitive skin around the nail on Anabel's right ring finger grew more tender the longer she picked at it. She couldn't decide what was worse—the discomfort or the bit of skin she couldn't quite get. If she didn't stop soon, her mother would notice and take to dipping Anabel's fingertips in vinegar, as she had done when Anabel was in the schoolroom.

She drew the pained fingertip to her mouth, hoping to stifle the irritation. It throbbed against her teeth and tongue. Her brother Frederick glanced at her from across the table, the barest lift of his brows a warning. With a little grimace, she tucked her whole hand between her thigh and the chair on which she sat in the cosy family breakfast parlour at Woodruff Abbey. She looked at the roll on her plate, fluffy pieces torn and buttered and slathered in jam, and realised with a wet swallow she could only sit on her aching hand for so many minutes if she had any desire to eat her meal.

From under her lashes, her eyes swooped towards her mother at one end of the table. Mrs Boyton was the model of a proper English woman—refined, elegant, capable of smiling, but with the laughter bred out of her. Anabel was just well-mannered enough when in society to avoid being thought a hoyden. She loved gossip, and laughing till a stitch pained her side, and the chaos of a full house, except that only two of her eight brothers and sisters remained at home—her eldest brother and a sister still in the schoolroom.

She nipped her lip and freed her hand—the whole of it an unbecoming shade of red from the pressure of her weight upon it—and picked up a piece of the roll. In her ears, the loud sound of her own chewing, the rustle of a newspaper as her father turned the page, the soft clucking of her mother as she read a letter from Anabel's eldest sister, Althea.

'She asks that I might send you to her at my earliest convenience. One of the children has a cough,' said her mother, passing her a creased sheet.

The lines on the pages were crossed and crossed again. Anabel covered her face with the paper and rolled her eyes. Her eldest sister loved nothing so much as being virtuous in her economy, despite having married a man who could buy her an entire paper mill.

'The way she writes over her lines, it's impossible for me to make any sense of her missives, as you well know.'

Anabel couldn't recall a time when reading had been easy for her, the way bits of letters seemed to disappear or rearrange themselves on the page.

Mrs Boyton took a slow sip from the delicate cup in her hand, set it upon the saucer, dabbed her lips, and sighed. 'A husband worth having has no interest in a wife so willing to display her dearth of understanding and diligence, dear. You expose yourself and your family to mockery every time you draw attention to your deficiency.'

'It's not as though she's put an advertisement in the newspaper, Mama,' interjected Freddy.

'She may as well do if she means so to go about it. Only think how damaging such a thing would be to her prospects—to her younger sister's when she makes her come out—if every eligible gentleman discovers she lacks the intelligence and refinement a suitable match must possess. Having the rest of your sisters married is my only consolation. No one can question whether *their* understanding is excellent, *their* minds much improved.'

Anabel had heard some variation of these words for fifteen years or more. Still, a rhythmic throb began to beat her temples. The muscles in her neck tensed, tightness pinching her shoulders and pulling tight along her spine.

When she was only beginning her tenure in the schoolroom, Anabel had told her mama how hard it was to see the letters as they were written out. Mrs Boyton was already preparing one of the older girls for her first season and had time only to scold Anabel for not trying harder—

after all, all her other brothers and sisters excelled in their lessons, so what reason could she have for not doing the same, unless she was dim-witted?

Once Anabel entered society, she let people think little more than air filled the space between her ears, rather than be labelled a fool and suffer the shame of being regarded inept and insufficient because the words on a page didn't flow through her mind as easily as they did for everyone else.

A weak, resigned breath drifted from where her mother sat. 'If only you would apply yourself.'

Whether she were speaking of Anabel finding a husband or bettering her reading skill, it mattered not. The table fell silent. Anabel, with casual regret for stuffing another piece of roll in her mouth before she'd finished the first, forced down the too-large bite and reached for her coffee.

The door to the breakfast parlour opened. The butler entered and paused at Freddy's side, extending a silver tray upon which a missive waited, prettily and patiently. The clink of her brother's setting down his fork onto his plate was loud in the relative silence of the room. With a face void of expression, he took the letter. Anabel's mother spared it little more than a cursory glance—she was much too polite to inquire after the sender—but Anabel squinted, tipped her head, and tried to make sense of the inky black letters, which were both too far away and written too closely together for her to read, even if the task had been an easy one. There was a quick, sharp crack as the letter opener separated wax from paper.

Her mama requested more tea. Her father turned another page. The old clock that had belonged to her great-great-grandfather ticked a steady beat.

'Well?' inquired Anabel, with undisguised impatience.

'Well, what?' Freddy, accustomed to his sister's restive character, did nothing more than lift his gaze from the page to meet hers for a mere moment.

She watched his eyes shift back and forth as he read through the contents. 'Come now, Freddy. I don't ask much of you.' He snorted, but Anabel ignored the unpleasant sound and continued with her plea. 'Do say you'll relieve this morning of its tedium.'

'As it's my letter...Had you anyone to correspond with, you could alleviate your own boredom.'

Anabel winced, although she didn't think he noticed. The only people with whom she maintained a regular correspondence were her dearest friend, Vivienne, the new Duchess of Hazelhurst, and the one sister who took to heart the struggle Anabel had making sense of words put to the page.

'Who sent it?'

'Again, my letter.'

'Very well. I suppose I'll just have to guess.' A dangerous lilt of false innocence tipped up her words as she seized the opportunity to repay her brother for teasing. 'If it were from one of our many brothers or sisters, you would say so.' Freddy continued to ignore her. She swept a gaze right towards her mother and left towards her father before pushing forward. 'Perhaps Miss Benson's—' his gaze shot up, his glare bright with a warning, 'uncle has something he wishes to—'

'We're invited to a house party,' rushed her brother, his voice a little too loud in the quiet room. 'At Sylvancliffe.'

'Sylvancliffe?' Anabel couldn't keep the amazement from her voice. 'Where Lady Cecilia disappeared?' Her stomach fluttered with anticipation. There was little she loved so much as gossip and intrigue. The opportunity to explore the infamous house herself, prowl for clues, perhaps even solve the mystery of the poor woman's unknown fate—

'For a fortnight in October. Before St Germain sells the property.'

Anabel's heart lurched. Caught in the thrill of possibilities, she'd overlooked the salient fact that a house party would, naturally, be hosted by the owner.

She had known—and loved—Valentine Ainsley, the Earl of St Germain, since she was just a tiny thing hiding in a tree, trying to get a better look at the handsome friend her brother had brought home. At six, she hadn't climbed very high nor concealed herself very well, and it took years for her to realise he'd known she was there all along. The stories he'd told of princes and princesses in faraway lands while he and Freddy fished had all been for her entertainment. After she lost her balance and landed in a heap on the ground, it was St Germain who carried her back to the house when her brother insisted she was well enough to walk, despite her rush of tears and the matching red blooms on her skinned knees.

In her mind, St Germain lived as an example of the best of men, defined by kindness and self-possession, possessed of good manners and good humour, and owning a sensible, discerning mind. The older she grew, the more she learned of the world and the men in it, the more pleasing she found him. St Germain, however, was entirely unaware of her enduring *tendre* and had never shown more interest in her than what was due a pleasant acquaintance—or in her case, the younger sister of a friend.

'He invited the both of us?' She stretched across the table and made to snatch the page. Although she was still a foot too far away, Freddy whipped the letter behind himself.

'Sit down, Anabel,' admonished her mother, while building the perfect bite of egg and bacon on her fork.

Anabel fell back in her chair, her attention fixated on her brother.

'You're as shocked as I am,' commented Freddy dryly. 'Although Saint has had the advantage of only seeing you on your best behaviour.'

She pursed her lips, mocking his own expression, and set down the slice of white peach she held pinched between her fingers. What she'd already eaten had begun to churn dangerously in her stomach. Two weeks was an impossible length of time to spend in company with St Germain when one had a secret to keep. Anabel could accept never being more to him than a shadow at the backs of the people he truly cared for, but she could not bear his disgust or pity should he discover her shortcoming. She tucked both hands under the table and picked at the raw edge of her cuticle.

'Perhaps it's best if Freddy attends on his own.'

Mrs Boyton, stirring sugar into freshly poured tea, glanced up. 'You will give me the benefit of knowing what is best for my children.'

'I'd really rather not go, Mama. You said yourself only minutes ago how terrible it would be should my shame be exposed.'

'No doubt you'll contrive some way to manage when the respectability of your family depends upon it. Perhaps you'll finally catch the eye of some eligible gentleman.'

'From whom I'll be forced to hide my lack of natural intelligence. How charming a prospect. For one concerned with ensuring such a thing never leaves the confines of the family, your desire to see me wed seems a trifle inconsistent.'

'What care have I for consistency?' replied her mother, between silent sips from the porcelain cup in her hands.

Across the table, Freddy shared a commiserating look. Their mother never failed to point out that no man of proper rank and worth wished for a wife who could hardly read.

'What of Althea's request?'

'Your sister will understand.'

Anabel's brain and heart grasped for some other excuse. 'And I'm to travel north to see Aunt Mary in November.'

'Mary wrote yesterday. She's decided to sail to Spain

for the winter.' Mrs Boyton tsked. Along with tardiness and raspberry preserve, she couldn't abide boats.

Anabel looked at the wall of print behind which her father was hiding, wishing for rescue yet knowing there would be none from that quarter of the table. Freddy set down the letter to pick up his knife. Her mama began speaking of some item of gossip in the scandal sheet, and Anabel stared at the remnants of food on her plate, the knots in her stomach preventing her from eating anything more.

She excused herself and slipped away from the table in unassuming and dignified silence, walking with every appearance of calm through the corridor and up the stairs. Her chin was held high, her neck long and elegant, her shoulders rolled down and back. She glided past the portraits hung on the wall of the hall and ignored the hard stares of her ancestors. Often, she censured them for the displeasure upon their faces, but in that moment, she felt a twinge of camaraderie.

Outside the entry to her room, she paused just for time enough to say a silent prayer it was free of maids going about their work. Then she pushed in. The space she'd occupied the whole of her life was empty, quiet, and the rush of her own relieved exhale surprised her. After closing the door snug behind her, she strode towards her bed—her quick gait devouring the distance in very few steps. At the edge, she filled her lungs with a great breath, dropped face first into the plump mattress, arms limp at her sides, and bellowed with the might of someone twice her size.

She was still in the prone position, her face hot from breathing into her sheets, where she'd made a little pocket for her nose and mouth, when her lady's maid came in some time later.

'Goodness me,' exclaimed Harriet in her low, matter-of-fact voice. 'Do you need the physician or ought I to sneak you a glass of your father's brandy?'

Anabel groaned, then said, 'I'm going to a house party,' although the words came out muffled beyond under-standing.

Harriet clucked. 'I suppose you'd rather just suffocate, then.'

Anabel could hear her maid bustling about, and after several more minutes pretending it was entirely possible for her to lie there and expire of dismay, thereby relieving herself of all forthcoming travel plans, she flopped onto her back and covered her face with both her hands. The noise she made was somewhere between a sob and a sigh, but when she finally removed her hands from her face, there were no tears. She stared blankly overhead, imagining herself a damsel trapped in the highest tower in all the land, waiting for rescue that would never come.

'Freddy and I are going to a house party at Sylvan-cliffe,' she said finally.

'You love house parties, Miss Ana,' replied Harriet, managing to sound both confused and reassuring. 'And invited to a one such as that!'

Anabel frowned. She enjoyed house parties with her brothers and sisters—people from whom she didn't have to hide. 'Being able to visit a place of such notoriety is no small thing, I suppose.'

'Exactly so. Is not the prospect a thrilling one for you, Miss Ana?'

Anabel felt certain such a scheme, despite its merits, was not enough to overcome her fear of exposure and the constant reminder of what could never be hers. She couldn't say as much and so scrunched her lips to one side and remained quiet.

'How nice it will be for you to wear the gowns you lately purchased in London,' remarked Harriet, disappearing for a moment into the dressing room. 'And none of that dowdy wool you wear at your aunt's.'

It was true Anabel hated exchanging her finer things for her practical things, despite how much she enjoyed her cosy visits with her aunt Mary. However, the mention of London only served to remind her of what she couldn't have. Despite all the years she'd been out, she could count on one hand the number of times St Germain had led her in a dance. Between them there were no lingering caresses, no long looks. Anabel couldn't even recall a perfunctory compliment, and she was certain had he ever said something in praise of her appearance, she would have catalogued it for all eternity.

Worse still was her one disastrous attempt to flirt with him at Miss Kent's picnic during the previous season by pretending to be awkward with a mallet and terrible at pall-mall. He was a patient instructor and every bit the gentleman. Much to her disappointment, not a soul looking on would have observed anything untoward in his manner, even with his arms wedging her close to him as he showed her how to swing. Anabel became so frustrated she hit the ball well, as she was quite capable of doing. St Germain nicked her chin and said, 'Well done, you.' Her fingers cramped so tightly where they wrapped around the mallet, she'd wondered if it would splinter in her grip.

'I think I'll take a walk,' she announced, forcing herself upright on the bed.

'Nothing like fresh air and the last of the summer sun to assuage your doubts and revive your spirits.'

Anabel paused in front of the mirror. She was blessed with thick, loose curls, but her hair was Venetian blonde—a far cry from the rich brown and black locks in fashion—and her hazel eyes were neither dark enough to be mysterious nor so light they might mesmerise the beholder. For the first time, she wondered what St Germain saw when he looked at her, if he discerned anything at all beyond the very ordinary features of her face. Not that it mattered. Not when she was ill-suited to be any man's wife, especially one as dear as St Germain and deserving of a partner who would share his burdens, not add to them.

She took the shawl Harriet held out to her and left. After spending an hour or more watching the mother ducks and their ducklings go about their day near the lake at the edge of the property, Anabel returned to the house feeling reconciled to the trip, if not eager. But by the time September had ambled to a close and she stepped into the carriage bound for Sylvancliffe, the door biting at the hem of her dress as it closed, the only thing on her mind was whether she might be sick on the ride. The carriage lurched forward, and she put a hand to her stomach, forcing down a bitter swallow. She could walk the whole length of England and still know this with certainty: nothing could be more unbearable than passing a fortnight in continual dread that the man she secretly adored might discover the awkwardness and folly that lay hidden within her.

3

'Let us consider turning around,' said Saint, casting his best impression of a disinterested look outside as drenching rain bellowed at the windows of the carriage.

The day had dawned quite fine. The first stretch of travel had been completed under the subdued warmth of October's autumnal sun, with soft light filtering through the mosaic of changing leaves and spilling its glowing golden hue over the countryside. But as rolling hills and river valleys gave way to woodland, and they drew nearer to the coast where Sylvancliffe was located, angry black clouds had swept in.

'If the coachman has no complaint, then neither should you.' Franny's words were even, although she was worrying a handkerchief between her hands. 'Furthermore, with so little light left, we're better off pushing ahead.'

Saint flipped his watch cover open, then snapped it closed. Open. Then closed. It was only half two, but the dismal weather blocked out the sun, and a gloomy night nipped at their heels. 'We are going to drive off a cliff, mark my words.'

'If you cross paths with the man I've long recognised as my brother, I'd very much appreciate you returning him to his body. In the meantime, sir, you may rest easy. We are nowhere near a cliff, as you well know.'

In the corner, his younger sister Ellena snickered but obscured the sound with a cough when he settled a murderous stare upon her.

'Aside from our great distance to any such source of calamity,' began Franny, studying the rain shivering down the carriage window, 'if we were to tumble and perish, you would leave behind nothing but dashed hopes and broken hearts. I, on the other hand, will have orphaned my dear children—'

'Their father remains in good health, unless you've something else to share with me.' Not for the first time, Saint wondered about the pattern of his life, how different the days might've looked had his father lived another five, ten, or even twenty years.

'And what good is that?'

'As his name and wealth keep you and your family in comfort—a great deal, I'd say.'

'You take a wife, beget some children, and then you may have an opinion.'

The cold, tight grip of dread choked Saint's attempt at a

response. He was a child all over again, facing the prospect of too much responsibility, too soon.

Pip stood in her travelling basket on the seat across from him. She arched her back in a generous stretch before pawing at the soft pile of blankets until they were exactly as she wished. With an untroubled sigh, she curled back down and was asleep in an instant. He was jealous of her contentment.

'Was it necessary to bring that little creature?'

''Tis often how I feel about your children.'

Franny lifted her nose to the ceiling and gave a little sniff. 'There's no need to be peevish.'

'I'm not.' Saint heard the sulkiness in his own voice, which only made him more irritable.

A thoughtful silence descended upon the carriage. The coil of foreboding in Saint's stomach curled tighter as they drew closer to Sylvancliffe. Despite more than two decades having passed since he'd visited the place, he had memories of each bend and turn that brought him there. The fractured yew trees along the roads, cracked and broken by a violent summer storm. The smell of salt from the ocean, carried on the tail of a breeze. The scream of a threatened fox.

His sisters' voices rose and fell around him, but their words were muffled under the sound of his thumping heart, and the more he tried to moderate the feeling, the worse it became. Even as a boy, he was afraid of little else besides this house. When one inherits at nine years old, one loses the luxury of childhood fancies. Spiders, snakes, beasts, bullies—he'd no time for them. He had no time to worry over 'what if' or 'could be', not when the responsibilities of a great house and a great name were his to honour and protect, to keep together when circumstance made it all too easy for everything to fracture.

The narrow lane to Sylvancliffe twisted like a serpent, wrapping him up tight and suffocating the scream burning in his lungs. Gone were the yew trees. In their place, a colonnade of maples had sprung. The dense canopy of leaves refused even a peek of the ominous sky above, and the steady pelting rain was replaced by frantic drops.

They rode deeper into the belly of the wood, and Saint could feel the air pulse around him with the same steady rhythm of a heartbeat.

It seemed impossible that in the middle of nature, so content with its own company, there would be space for a house. Saint didn't know which was worse—waiting for the manor to come into view, or the certainty that it would. He let his head fall back against the velvet squabs and closed his eyes. He remained so until he heard a quivering 'my goodness' uttered by Ellena, who had never before visited Sylvancliffe. The carriage had left the hungry wood behind, and ahead, the house stood like a sentry, guarding the bay just beyond.

A quick shiver cascaded from the base of Saint's neck down his back, and he was too late in suppressing the small shudder.

Sylvancliffe stood tall, imposing, impenetrable in its authority. The high-pitched gabled roof, the round tower protruding from the corner of the house, and the way parts of the façade seemed to fade from view reminded Saint of those homes built during the French Renaissance. Ivy spun up the grey stone and curled around the paned windows, strangling the view in and out. To either side of the entry grew deep pink chrysanthemums, menacing in their cheer. Outside, a tidy line of servants were standing under black, melancholy umbrellas.

The ladies were quick to seek shelter within, but Saint lingered, his eyes searching the exterior for something—a crack, a weakness, a set of lifeless eyes tracking his movements.

Inside, no dust plumed up from his boots as he walked. No great cobwebs wafted overhead. No blood-red paper peeled from the walls. But relics from his father's time remained: the faint smell of brandy and tobacco, woven for posterity into the hanging tapestries; an old suit of armour in front of a window embrasure, a lookout manning his post. Saint needed all his fingers and all his toes to count how many times he had mistaken the steel guard for an intruder once the sun had dropped below the endless line of trees and darkness enfolded the front hall. His young heart would skitter to a stop; his breath would catch in his throat, stifling his cry. His feet would root where they stood, while he waited, waited, to be snatched, kidnapped, maimed, murdered.

Along the far wall, paintings of earls past watched as the small party stripped off their coats and hats and gloves. Saint was studying the man he knew to be his grandfather, long dead by the time Saint had arrived in the world, when a great clap of thunder rattled the Adam-style urn on the side table and sent his shoulders jumping to his ears.

'My left knee has been aching since Tuesday last,' said Grimm, the butler, handing their discarded outerwear to several footmen. 'I'd say we've got four, perhaps five days of this wet weather ahead of us, my lord.'

The housekeeper, Mrs Crane, nodded. 'Mr Grimm's knee knows to expect Poseidon's wrath even before the sky itself does. Once his old bones even portended—' She cut herself off. 'Never mind that. You don't wish to hear old tales when you've only just arrived.'

Saint opened his mouth to press the housekeeper, then instead said 'Pip, come,' when he saw her tail sticking out from under a sideboard.

The kitten's downy black rear wiggled as she tried to extricate herself, her paws scrabbling for purchase on the black-and-white marble floor. When her head emerged, something brown was clutched between her small, powerful jaws. A dead sparrow.

'Heavens!' Mrs Crane gasped, a hand flying to her heart.

Ellena thrilled. 'The adventure begins. You ridding yourself of the house just when I've been introduced to the delights within the walls is quite cruel.'

Saint stepped towards Pip. At the same time, she scampered nearer to show off the gift she'd found for him and dropped it at his feet. There was something wrong about the bird. The shape of its body, its glassy eyes.

He bent and picked up the sparrow, holding the thing between two pinched fingers. 'A child's toy.' The body was made of brown and white felt, greying from dirt and age, and likely filled with wool. The beak, a piece of wood, and its shiny, dead eyes, two small black buttons.

Grimm cleared his throat. 'The furniture was moved away from the walls when we prepared to open the house, and the rooms are swept daily.'

Everyone's eyes drifted to the butler. Saint swayed. The terror pressing inside his chest left little room for air. Pip stretched up his leg and released a tiny, demanding squeak. He waved the little bird at her before tossing the thing. She clamoured after the toy, the scrape of her claws echoing in the grand entry and down the yawning, silent hall.

Mrs Crane laced her fingers together. 'Well, where there is a question, there is an answer to be found. In the meantime, I'll take the ladies up to settle them in their rooms. Lady Frances, Lady Ellena, you'll follow me.'

Saint watched his sisters ascend the staircase and disappear after the second landing, his anxious mind grasping at the last remnants of comfort as they slipped away. A small cough brought his attention back to Grimm.

'This way, sir, if you please.' The butler gestured in the same general direction as the ladies had gone.

Saint nodded and allowed himself to be led away. Time stuttered and dragged as they approached the room he would occupy during his stay, but the pace of his heart quickened until he couldn't separate one beat from the next. Standing behind Grimm outside the closed door, he was conscious of the faint trembling of his limbs, and when the butler ushered him inside, he couldn't discern whether he was floating or fainting.

'Are you all right, my lord? You look a trifle pale.'

Grimm took Saint by the elbow and steered him to one of two couches facing one another in front of the gaping fireplace.

'Fine. Perfectly fine. If you could send up my valet.'

The butler bowed out of the room, closing the door behind him. Saint dropped his face into his hands, pressing his fingers and palms hard into the clammy flesh of his forehead and cheeks. He had been shown to the lord of the manor's chambers, the same suite of rooms in which he'd watched his father's spirit leave the body that had tethered the man to earth for seventy-two years.

He looked up, bringing his blurred gaze to focus on the bed where his father had drawn his last breath. Flinging himself from the couch, Saint searched frantically for a waste basket, locating one near a small writing table just in time to cast up his accounts. It was lucky he'd not been at all hungry that morning. He removed the handkerchief from his inner coat pocket and swiped it across his mouth, the bitter taste of bile and black coffee lingering on his tongue.

Wilde, the valet, entered to find his employer dependent on a nearby wall for support, head tipped back, hand over his eyes. 'My lord?'

'This room will never do. Find another. Attics, for all I care.'

'Certainly, sir. We need not go to such extremes, but you may expect to be situated nearer your guests.'

Saint would sleep outside with the owls and crows and eerie coos of a woodland coming awake while the rest of the world went quiet before he stayed one night in his father's old room. 'Truly, Wilde, it matters not. You may find me in the billiards room when my things have been unpacked.'

He left his valet, shoulders inched up to his ears. Beads of sweat gathered in the dip of his upper lip as he approached the corner of the corridor, fearing his father's ghost might be lingering just on the other side. The thought was both foolish and irrational in equal measure, yet his stride slowed and he found himself rooted where he stood.

He pulled in a laboured breath and forced it out, then put one foot in front of the other, his steps silenced by the plush runner stretching from one end of the hall to the other. Candlelight flickered and twitched as he walked past the elegant wax tapers in their resting places among the many sconces lining the wall, their intricate filigree work and the gargoyle bases an ornate design of a time gone by. The quiet crackle and hiss of fire eating up the wicks landed like sparks in the blood pumping through his veins.

A door slammed somewhere near. Saint jumped, his quick, deep bellow of surprise echoing down the corridor.

'The wind, my lord, is the real mistress of the house,' said Mrs Crane, coming through a door just behind him. 'I daresay you've long forgotten its peculiarities, but you'll be quite used to them soon enough.'

Her words, no doubt meant to soothe, sank like a rock

tossed in a pond and settled in the pit of his stomach. Saint parted his lips, but couldn't tell by the muscles pulling on his face if he achieved the smile he was hoping for or more of a grimace.

She came up next to him. 'May I be of service?'

'Not at all. I'm for the billiards room.'

'Down the stairs, fourth door on the left, if you stand in need of the reminder.'

Saint thanked the housekeeper, forced himself not to think how peculiar she must find him, yelling like a boar in the hall, and proceeded to knock the balls on the billiards table around without aim until Wilde retrieved him to dress for dinner.

Franny carried much of the conversation at the table, having many happy memories of Sylvancliffe from her youth, which she was pleased to share with Ellena. Saint could not hear her over the quick staccato rhythm ringing in his ears as rain pelted the windows. From somewhere faraway came the faint growl of thunder. He watched and waited for a flash to bring light to the darkness outside.

'Saint?'

He was entranced by the storm rolling in, but when Franny repeated his name, he turned his attention to her.

'I was asking if you recall the autumn we were here with Papa and your mama when that wild tempest uprooted all those yew trees. Cook made some wonderful chocolate with cinnamon and cloves, and we drank it in Catherine's room, on the floor near the fire, with Lydia, too. You were too scared to sleep alone, so we all piled into the bed and fell asleep listening to Lydia read. ''Twas the last time we four were together here. Catherine married the following spring,' she added with a wistful sigh. It had been a handful of years since any of them had seen their eldest sister. Catherine was married to a diplomat and had been living on the continent for some time.

Saint took a sip of his wine before saying, 'I do.' His two-word reply satisfied her, and Franny directed the rest of her sentimental soliloquy to Ellena.

For his sisters, Sylvancliffe was a retreat from the bustle of London and a change of scenery from their own home. The coastal estate was a place where they spent their days walking in the cold, soft sand along the shore or squeezing together in the phaeton and riding out to the little village situated a few miles from the house. But for Saint, those long days had unfolded not in the name of pleasure but duty. While other little boys were still playing at being highwayman or pirates, his lessons had begun almost before he could remember. Between reading and arithmetic and geography and French, he was reviewing estate ledgers and being quizzed by his father on everything from farming to family history.

When Saint snuck down to the beach instead of meeting the tutor who travelled with the family, his father found him—his father always seemed to find him. No matter where he went, he was always under the man's expectant gaze.

Saint and his sisters did not separate after dinner and spent only a short while in the drawing room, the ladies choosing to retire early after the day of travel. Wilde met Saint in the hall and showed him to another room, several doors down from the one where his father had lived and died. But if he had hoped the change would usher in a peaceful night of rest, he would have been severely disappointed.

A different bed, a different hue of wallpaper, a chair in one spot instead of another made no difference. Nothing could scrape away the memories of a house etched so deeply into his bones.

4

Anabel fidgeted on the carriage seat as she and her brother entered the county where Sylvancliffe was situated. Her nerves were unwilling to settle as she had been urging them to do with each mile that brought her closer to St Germain and further from her own happiness.

'Are the stories true?' she asked, hoping to distract herself from the fate she could not escape by focusing on the mystery surrounding the estate.

'What stories?'

'Don't be ridiculous, Freddy. Just because you don't repeat gossip doesn't mean you never hear it. *Everyone* knows about the parties the previous earl used to host at the house.'

'I don't know how. Saint's father has been dead twenty years. You yourself were little more than a babe.'

Unlike her brother, Anabel thrived on *on dits,* on

observing others and collecting information. Some people believed preserving a dignified silence forced those around them to speak. Anabel found prattling a much better alternative. It put people at ease, comfortable in their superiority.

She replied to Freddy with a little lift of her shoulder. 'Talk of fabled parties and unsolved mysteries will always endure. It's a shame St Germain is parting with the house. I could never give up a place of such notoriety if I were in possession of it. Do you suppose Lady Cecilia Walker was murdered and buried somewhere on the grounds? With hundreds of acres to choose from, one could spend forever looking for her body.'

'Anabel!'

'Well, what else could explain her disappearance? All of her things were left behind. What woman would go anywhere without her hairbrush, toothpowder, and a change of clothes at the very least?'

Freddy rubbed a hand over his brow. 'How are you even thinking of such things?'

'Who doesn't, from time to time? I once spent an entire hour in a drawing room listening to Miss Peele talk about the party from which Lady Cecilia disappeared at which Mr and Mrs Peele had been guests. Miss Peele is certain her mother knows something but thinks her father is preventing her mama from speaking out, because of the way the woman shifts in her chair every time her husband enters a room. Except there isn't a member of the *ton* who doesn't know Mrs Peele's discomfort arises from Mr Peele discovering his wife's cicisbeo was doing more than attending her to the theatre in his absence. And anyway, everyone said the Pulham girl who came out this last year is an exact copy of Lady Cecilia, so naturally people speculated Lady Cecilia was the girl's mother but had to give her up because she refused to come out of hiding. As far as what she would be hiding from—'

'If Lady Cecilia is in hiding, then she can't very well be dead and buried, can she?'

Anabel's eyelids flitted as she fought the impulse to roll her eyes. 'Of course a man's brain is only capable of holding one thought at a time.'

'And a woman's only capable of catching salacious gossip without the benefit of critical thinking.'

They stared one another down, a scene familiar to those who knew them best.

'While on the subject,' Freddy began, his tone a touch high-handed for Anabel's liking, '*do not* go snooping about.'

She blinked. 'Apologies, brother, I do not take your meaning.'

'I'm certain you do. There ought not to be a need to warn you off such uncouth behaviour as rifling through possessions in the ownership of another, traipsing the halls at night, inserting yourself where you do not belong.'

Anabel reached into the basket at her side, feeling around for something to eat. 'And yet…'

'And yet, I know you, Ana.'

'How pleasant it is to be lectured by *you* about *my* behaviour.' Their mother might feign ignorance about Freddy's rakish ways, but Anabel never had and never would. She loved her brother but didn't always care much for him as a man. 'Small wonder you haven't found a woman willing to marry your charmingly imperious person.'

'There are plenty of women willing to accept my proposal, only none I've cared to ask. Regardless, bachelor sounds so much better than spinster, does it not?'

Anabel narrowed her eyes and tossed a small chunk of the cheese she'd been nibbling at him. He cried out when it pelted his cheek.

'Lord, Ana, that could have been my eye.'

'If only my aim were better than my reading comprehension.'

Freddy gave her a dark look and settled into silence with his book, leaving Anabel to watch the rugged countryside of the coast unfold beyond the window.

Eventually, the carriage slowed to a stop before an enormous wrought-iron gate. Beyond, the gilded glow of maples and bright bursts of red rowans beckoned. When the path was opened before them, the leaves on the ground yielded to the carriage wheels with a hiss and sough.

The fat raindrops that had splattered the carriage eased into a spectral mist, and the doleful clouds above were no match for a determined sun. Lambent light dappled the wood as they rolled through. Birds emerged once more from the shelters where they had withdrawn and cooed in greeting. Anabel let down the window to breathe in the fresh scent of damp earth. Autumn, with its unrivalled beauty and atmosphere of mystery—the way it bridged vibrant summer with dormant winter; the way falling leaves marked the passage of time; the ethereal light seen only for a few months each year—was her favourite season.

Sylvancliffe came into view, breathtaking in its ivy shawl. Against the deep green, well-lit windows glowed, and Anabel could almost feel the cosy warmth wash over her. For a moment, she was able to forget where she was or why. Until the little figures standing outside the house grew in size as the carriage approached.

St Germain's fair features were set off by the dark stone and wet vegetation.

Anabel put a hand to her stomach as it dropped. She had seen him as recently as four months ago, before everyone left town, but somehow he had managed to grow more handsome between June and October.

Within the confines of her warm skin, the muscles and sinew and nerves holding her together tightened, and the bones caging her heart hardened. After so many years hiding how she felt—first because she was a silly schoolgirl, and then because she wished to avoid the awkwardness which inevitably accompanied unrequited feelings—doing so had become second nature. The sensation of her body wrapping up a secret had become as familiar to her as the sound of her own voice.

They came to a stop, and Freddy alighted from the carriage first. A footman appeared at the open door to hand Anabel down. St Germain was looking at something beyond her, but she was watching him approach and missed the step. In the space of a heartbeat, he was there, catching her arm before she landed in a heap of wool in the dirt drive. But her foot slammed into the ground, soaked from the day's early rain, and sent a splatter of mud across her skirt and his fine cream-coloured trousers.

The flush that stole up her neck and over her cheeks was swift and hot and disappeared almost as quickly as it came. Anabel had largely given up on blushing, or rather had become inured to the feelings which often gave rise to such a thing, after years of being teased by her brothers and sisters for her continued war with the written word.

Sweat gathered in her palms with no regard for the chilled air. She chided her mind into some semblance of order, telling herself that when she looked up, she would see nothing more than an attractive man—not the man who'd held her heart since before she knew to protect it.

With a regal lift of her head, Anabel brought her eyes to meet his warm brown pair, noticing in spite of herself how they sparked with laughter, the effect softening the sharp angles of his face.

She ought to say something, to acknowledge her misstep with an apology, to thank him for preserving at least some of her dignity, but she couldn't untangle herself from his gaze. Time dragged the moment out, and Anabel felt with perfect conviction she could have lived her life preserved in those slow seconds when his attention was all for her.

From somewhere behind him came a delicate coughing sound.

'Yes, well.' He cleared his throat and removed the hand he still had wrapped around Anabel's arm.

The feeling of loss was startling and immediate.

Despite the thick wool of her travelling dress, the skin beneath grew suddenly cool when freed from his touch.

Franny came forward, wrapping Anabel in an affectionate embrace and placing a matronly kiss upon her cheek. ''Tis unbearable you should look so fetching after travel,' she said, taking Anabel's arm and steering the small group towards the entrance to the house.

Ellena asked after Anabel and Freddy's parents and the journey to Sylvancliffe, while Franny spoke in detail of the activities which might be enjoyed during the party—archery and lawn games, musicales and theatricals, a day at the seaside, if the weather would only listen to her scolds. Anabel nodded along, resisting the impulse to throw a backward glance over her shoulder, where St Germain trailed.

When they came through the large wooden door, she was captivated by the gothic details in the house: the grand chandelier sending candlelight skittering across the black-and-white marble floor; the stone arches over corridors leading guests to greater adventure; the old suit of armour at the window adding a touch of whimsy. In the air, a masculine scent and hint of mystery. Sylvancliffe was elegant in its age, welcoming in its splendour, and not for a moment did Anabel doubt the house held many secrets.

She looked around in wonder, her fingers fumbling at her neck with the frog fasteners on her pelisse.

'Allow me.'

Her whole body tensed at the warm timbre of St Germain's smooth, deep voice—or perhaps it was his nearness—but her hands fell away, yielding to his request. She needed to say something—any words, in any order—to distract from the way every inhalation smelled of the soap he had used that morning, woody and a little sweet, like the forest at dusk.

'Your home is charming.'

He paused and peered up from his task, pinning upon her a queer sort of stare.

'Wet weather has never done more for a façade,' she added, a chuckle accompanying her words. The slight sound quivered. She hoped he didn't notice. 'It positively dumps at my aunt Mary's, but Westmere Lodge doesn't get to tuck itself behind a verdant ivy veil. Instead, the ceiling in my favourite parlour leaks, no matter how many times it's been repaired. This county has the best trees, too, don't you think? The pretty poplar and beech and maple.' By the end of her meandering speech, Anabel's voice was both faster and higher pitched than normal. She stared at his cravat, nervous of finding an expression upon his countenance somewhere between confusion and thinking her fit for Bedlam.

In an even and perfectly serious tone, he replied, 'Yes, the trees are the root of local pride, I believe.'

Her eyes snapped up. His lips were quirked to one side, and his eyes crinkled at their corners. He freed her of her outerwear and handed it to a waiting footman. There was a sudden lurch under her breast. For a fleeting moment, she caught a glimpse of what life with St Germain would be like. Her mind understood the impossibility of such a thing, but her heart still had the temerity to ask *why not me?*

5

Nearly a dozen people circulated in the drawing room before dinner. The atmosphere was one of expectation, of genteel excitement and anticipation underscoring the gentle murmur of conversation. The scene could have been one from any party in London—young ladies draped in exquisite gowns, cut to show off their figures with each graceful movement; men clad in white silk waistcoats with intricate embroidery, in rich purple and blue and green velvet coats, and with expertly folded cravats, white as the snow which would not fall for another month or maybe two.

Except unlike rooms in the great houses of London, papered and furnished again and again by hostesses given over to the whims of fickle fashion, Sylvancliffe remained untouched by the years gone by. The walls were still adorned with the luxurious silk damask that had once been the same rich green as the ivy spiralling up the stone walls outside. Elegant upholstered sofas were arranged for conversation around an ornate Persian rug. As a boy, Saint used to trace its intricate pattern with his eyes, following one curved line into another until he lost his place entirely. Candleflames tripped and bounded and danced in the crystal chandelier overhead, a favourite piece of his mother's. At the windows, heavy-fringed curtains were parted to let in the last of the dwindling daylight.

Saint allowed himself a moment to stare out into the advancing darkness, his mind flashing to the last night he'd spent in the house. The last night of a life that bore any resemblance to childhood. On the following day, Saint had ridden behind the wagon carrying his father's body to Belmont where it would be interred in the crypt, each mile drawing him nearer the life of estate owner and head of his family.

The faint brush of something against his leg startled him. Saint looked down to find a fluffy black tail waving and winding along his calf. He stooped to run a hand over Pip's back. The motion always soothed him, as did the thrum of her steady purring. With a thick swallow, he stood once more and turned back to the assembled company.

Franny was flitting from one small group to the next. She bestowed her most winsome expression upon Sir Marcus, with whom he had only a slight acquaintance and who had been invited at the request of his friend Roberts. Lady Catherine Marrow received a kiss on the cheek. The woman was a confidant of his sister's; however, he was certain she'd only been invited for the sake of throwing him in company with her niece, Lady Hester—lovely and refined, but his conversations with her never imbued him with the desire to repeat the experience beyond polite obligation.

His gaze trailed in Franny's wake as she went on, until it fell upon Miss Boyton. She had been in the periphery of his life for fifteen years or more, but he hadn't ever taken the time to appreciate her wide, radiant smile, the kind that could pull a man to her side in an instant. The thought took him unawares, and a frown flitted over his features when he tried to trace its origin.

Miss Boyton was in conversation with her brother and Ellena. She smiled at something Freddy said, but her lips were pinched where they met and her expression was strained, unlike earlier when she'd spoken to Saint of the house and the trees. The memory pulled a furtive chuckle from him.

'Our tastes have always run parallel,' said Antony Glassbrook, coming to stand alongside Saint. 'She's quite lovely, is she not?'

'Who?' he asked, feigning ignorance.

The other man smirked. 'The woman you've been staring at the last minute or more. You've known her for many years. Perhaps you've grown accustomed to looking at her charming face.'

Saint felt a scowl tugging his brows and smoothed it immediately. One of the best things about his long-time friend was also the worst, depending on the day and conversation, and whether one was the subject of his scrutiny. As one of the most sought-after barristers in the country, the man was discerning to a fault and possessed one of the keenest minds in England.

'Well done,' complimented Glassbrook. 'You're much too handsome to mar your countenance with something so common as lines.'

'I'd not thought myself your type,' Saint replied, with a lazy drawl.

His friend laughed, a much richer sound than his natural elegance would have suggested. 'I've only the one type, my good fellow: beautiful. Which you are, with those possessing brown eyes, and a jaw so sharp, I fear it would cut me if I came too close. But you may consider yourself safe from me, or at least from advances to further my own interests.'

'Heavens. Can't say I at all like what that implies.'

'No, I didn't think you would. You, my dear friend, are going to be one of the unexpected pleasures of this house party.'

'Antony.' The one word rang low and reproving, but Glassbrook beamed with satisfaction.

'Ah, my sister beckons,' he said, and left the conversation without further comment.

Glassbrook's remarks only added to the hum of uncertainty that had swelled in Saint's chest from the moment he agreed to the house party and had never left. He stared briefly at his friend's back as the man walked away, before his gaze jumped from guest to guest until it once more landed upon Miss Boyton. No matter where he tried to send his focus, his eyes fell back to her. She slipped to the edge of the room, a hint of mischief in her slow, unbothered movements. For several seconds she studied the wall. Then she began to run her hands lightly over the wood panelling. At a distance, it almost appeared as if she were inspecting the seams with as keen an eye as she could manage in the limited light. Curiosity pulled him to her.

'Is there some way in which I may be of service to you, Miss Boyton?'

Her hand stilled at chest height for a beat before continuing. She looked behind her shoulder at the same time he moved nearer her side.

'You could tell me where I might find the trapdoor—or is it doors?—if you please.'

'Trapdoors?' he repeated, a little baffled.

'Surely this place has been keeping secrets since it was built.' His shoulders stiffened, but if she noticed, she didn't remark on it. 'Trapdoors, hidden passageways, moving pictures, a gust of wind whistling through the hall when all the windows are closed.' Her voice dropped as she spoke, and a dimple he'd never before noticed peeped at him when the tips of her lips curled up in amusement. Her hazel eyes, a little too large for her face, were earnest, although a roguish gleam lurked in their depths. 'Surely, there must be one trapdoor or secret passageway at the very least in this old house.'

He stepped towards the wall and raised a hand as if to press a hidden release. 'You're standing on top of it. Shall I send you directly down to the dungeon to keep the old bones company?'

She squeaked and hopped sideways.

'Don't say your courage has failed you already.'

'Courage has nothing to do with it. This happens to be one of my favourite gowns, and I've no wish to sully it with bone dust, dirt, and grime, as it seems unlikely any of your staff are sweeping out secret passageways with the same regularity as one might clean the drawing room.'

Her statement drew all his attention to the dress she wore, eliminating from his mind any other thought besides how becoming she looked. The satin was the colour of champagne, and fleurs-de-lis of thin gold thread swirled in the translucent puffed sleeves, setting off the soft glow of her smooth skin.

She was looking at him expectantly, but the only words on the tip of his tongue were *beauty, pleasure, magic*.

'I beg your pardon, Miss Boyton.' He took a deep breath and gave a deeper bow. 'Sylvancliffe possesses no trapdoors, no secret passageways. In outward appearance, the house possesses all the characteristics of a manor plucked from the pages of the gothic novels my sister reads, but I'm afraid that is where the similarities end.'

'Pity.'

The word drifted over him on her wistful sigh.

'Then again, nor are you a tormented hero haunted by his past, or I a damsel in distress.'

A high-pitched ringing pierced his ears, and his mind went blank. He stared, wondering if she was truly the lady he'd known more than half his life or some apparition conjured by the house to haunt him.

'Well,' she said, when he failed to collect his wits and form a timely response. 'You may believe your statement to be true, but I think the house will have its own opinion on the matter.'

He watched her retreat to the far side of the room—his eyes catching on the perfect curve of her neck, the dip of her waist—uncertain if it were fear licking at his heart or something even more terrifying.

6

Anabel flounced away, pretending to herself that she didn't care whether his stare lingered on her back or not. She knew, even if he was watching her go, which he very likely wasn't, that turning around would only confirm her imagination was playing tricks on her, convincing her the gaze that had raked over her had been pleased with what it discovered. Her fanciful mind wished to ignore what she knew to be true: St Germain looked at her the way someone might glance at a blank sheet of paper resting upon a desk or some other unremarkable sight, like an empty bench in a park.

Squaring her shoulders, she joined the other young ladies where they stood gathered round a little table; the small stack of books upon it earned a wary glance. To one side of Ellena was Lady Hester Blackwell, daughter of the Duke of Norland and niece of Lady Marrow, with whom Anabel shared a cordial acquaintance. On the other, Hero

Glassbrook, a serene young lady she had come to consider a friend two seasons past.

Anabel only had half an ear to the conversation happening around her when Lady Hester said, with her usual self-possession, 'Not all things lost wish to be found.'

The philosophical bent of the comment caused Anabel's brows to inch up. 'Has something of yours gone missing? Perhaps we can form a little search party.'

The young lady absently fiddled with a delicate gold locket hanging round her neck. 'We were just discussing whether or not the vision Hero saw earlier was the spirit of Lady Cecilia. For my part, I don't think the woman is dead, or she wasn't when she was last here, at any rate.'

A thrill of exhilaration shot through Anabel, and several questions crowded her brain. St Germain's answer had not deterred her in the least. A manor like Sylvancliffe—gusty, obscure, enigmatic—was rich in secrets. Somewhere behind a trick panel, under a trapdoor buried beneath a rug, in a secret room accessible only by a hidden stairway, were clues that would unravel the truth of Lady Cecilia's unsolved disappearance.

'When was this?' Anabel asked.

Hero shook her head, as though she wished to demur, but after a short moment, much to Anabel's satisfaction, she answered, 'I'm sure it was nothing. As I was leaving my room, I noticed an odd sort of shadow at the end of the hall. The dwindling light was streaming in through the far window, strained through the branches of the maple outside. I watched the umbrage dancing on the floor for several seconds. When I looked up, it was as if the shadows grew with my stare and stood before my eyes, forming the loose shape of a woman. The sight was so unusual it caught my breath, and then—of course now I wish I hadn't—I blinked. Hard. Whether I was willing myself to believe what I was seeing or convincing myself otherwise, I'm still unsure. When I opened my eyes, the shadows once again resembled something much more familiar.'

'It seems obvious Lady Cecilia had a lover here, does it not?' asked Ellena. 'Perhaps he's the one who murdered her. Or maybe they were promised to one another, and all these years she's been begging for release so she might finally rest in peace.'

'Poor Lady Cecilia,' Hero sighed.

'Lady Hester,' began Anabel. 'Did I hear you correctly—you don't think Lady Cecilia perished?'

The young woman tilted her head a little to the side and examined each lady standing around her with a guarded expression before answering. 'No. The sinister is much more diverting, particularly in such a setting as this, but my heart tells me Lady Cecilia had a much happier ending than any of us are willing to believe.'

Hero put a hand over her heart. 'I do hope you're right.'

Anabel was less certain, but more interested than ever to resolve the woman's disappearance.

The other ladies were murmuring their agreement when Freddy appeared to escort her into dinner. Since she was neither titled nor wed, she found her name on a place card closer to the middle than she cared for. To one side of her was

Hero's older brother, a notable Corinthian who sailed his own yacht, kept his shirt points as sharp as his wit, and who had gained recognition as a barrister at some of the most scandalous trials in court. On her other side was Roberts, whom she'd known nearly as many years as St Germain.

'I hope the weather was fine for your travel, Miss Boyton.'

She turned her head and smiled at Mr Glassbrook. 'Quite. Thank you. It appears my brother and I were lucky in that way.' As she said so, a distant rumble of thunder growled in the background.

'I'm partial to a fierce storm—sweep the leaves from their trees, churn the waters at the shore, rattle the windows and my heart.' Mr Glassbrook clutched his chest for dramatic effect, a playful glint in his eye.

'Careful, sir,' she replied, with false seriousness. 'The ladies at this table may mistake you for a romantic.'

'Have I lost all credit with you so soon?' The gravity of his words was belied by the twitch of his lip.

'Hardly that. Although I do question whether a man with intimate knowledge of the most salacious crim-con cases would be capable of holding something so trite as romantic notions in his head.'

His eyebrows drifted up in surprise. 'You, Miss Boyton, are a cynic masquerading as a respectable young lady.'

Anabel took an unhurried sip of wine. 'And a gossip. You wouldn't want to forget that. I plan to ask you all about the Acker–Edwards trial. We'll see which of us is better at extracting information over the fish course.'

Mr Glassbrook's delighted laugh was the kind that made those around him feel they had accomplished something special by bringing forth the sound, and Anabel smiled into her spoonful of creamed asparagus.

Without any desire to do so, she found herself looking towards the head of the table. St Germain was leaning in a little, listening intently to Lady Hester, who was undoubtedly the kind of woman his family wished to see him choose for a wife. It suddenly seemed the most probable thing in the world, that their two families would wish for the match, and Lady Hester's presence must be confirmation of such. He made some response, his seat too far to hear what was said, but his words were accompanied by a devastating grin, or at least it was to Anabel because it wasn't for her—never would be for her.

A painful tug of awareness pulsed in her chest. This very same scene had played out countless times—her watching him from a distance, wishing she might be the one to command his attention. Yet she would remain always just beyond his notice—not quite invisible, but a fleeting vision lingering in the corner of his eye and fading before he'd ever seen her clearly.

AFTER DINNER, instead of the men and women separating, Franny insisted on dancing. ''Tis the best way to acquaint ourselves with those with whom we are unfamiliar,' she had declared, with the éclat of one handing down a proverb and disregarding the fact that all the gathered guests knew each other to varying degrees.

'Something has put your nose out of joint,' Mr Glassbrook said, leading Anabel to their places for the set forming.

Despite her best efforts, it had been impossible for Anabel to recover her spirits entirely, even when Mr Glassbrook regaled her with every detail of the Acker–Edwards trial he was able to share.

'Not at finding yourself partnered with me, I hope,' he added, when faced with her continued silence. 'Although the responsibility for such rests upon our hostess. No doubt her instruction to begin with the same partners with whom we were seated at dinner was to avoid any embarrassment among the company, when there are so few members of the opposite sex from which we may choose.'

The country dance began. He reached out for her hand and, as one, they turned and stepped in the same direction.

Finally, Anabel spoke, the forced liveliness in her tone dulling the spiky edge of her words. 'Because all the men would wish to secure their interest with the duke's daughter, leaving the rest of us to linger on our rejection and reflect on our own ill fortune, that we have come into the world mere misses? Terribly unfair that someone should be born to rank and fortune *and* also have her choice of partners for the first. Perhaps you might consider drafting a bill giving precedent to untitled ladies of respectable fortunes, let us say one Wednesday a month at Almack's. We don't have the luxury of being *that* choosy, after all.'

His keen eyes sparked with appreciation before they

parted to weave round the others. When they were once more returned, he said, 'You need a Member of Parliament, not a barrister, which I suspect you know. Is your request then a veiled grasp at a compliment? No, I don't think it is. Still, I will not gratify you by stating how artfully arranged your curls are or how you are in no need of aid to have your own choice of men for the first.'

Anabel couldn't stop the muscle in her lip from quivering as she repressed a smile.

'Subsequently, the possibility arises you buried your own knowledge in the hope I might introduce you to some upstanding Member of Parliament. A savvy manoeuvre, Miss Boyton, but surely you know St Germain sits in the House of Lords. In which case—'

His sentence came to an abrupt end. He was staring at her, head cocked, eyes narrowed in interest, a posture he maintained even as he turned. Anabel stretched down a hand for his, the space between their arms making a 'V' as they promenaded around each other.

Mr Glassbrook issued a quiet, tuneless hum, and said, almost too discreet to be heard, 'I begin to understand the lay of the land.'

Her chest swelled with an anxious breath, but she tipped her chin upward. 'I can't say I follow.'

'A very credible denial. How fun it would be to have you on the stand.'

'If someone who has had little more than the length of a dinner to become acquainted with me can read my thoughts, I am quite doomed. Pray, tell me if it's true. I'll secure rocks to the hem of my dress and walk into the sea.'

The song came to an end. She and Mr Glassbrook bowed with the others and applauded Franny's playing before he led her to the side of the makeshift dancefloor.

'When success in one's chosen career is predicated on correctly interpreting wayward gazes, detecting even the smallest irregularities in a person's breathing, and noticing tells, like picking at the skin around one's nail, one gets rather good at it. How may I be of service?'

'You're absurd, Mr Glassbrook.'

'Ah! Our *objet d'amour* looks this way. Lean in,' he instructed, tilting his head closer to hers. 'Now, a fetching smile if you please, and do *try* to be convincing.'

The conspiratorial wink was too much for Anabel, and a reluctant, amused curve shaped her mouth.

'Better than I hoped, Miss Boyton. At a distance, this will appear a victory in a hard-fought battle for your regard.'

'What a peculiar creature you are proving to be, sir. I wonder if I may come to regret indulging your quirks,' she replied, only half in jest.

'You may trust yourself with me, if promises from gentlemen hold any weight with you. In point of fact, you remind me of my elder sister. I've just the two—Hero and Bella—and Bella has been in India with her husband three years gone now. I miss her, and the fun we used to have, terribly.'

A wry crook tipped the corner of Anabel's lips. 'You used to flirt with your sister to make other men jealous?'

Mr Glassbrook's eyes rounded, then he tossed his head

back and howled, drawing the notice of every person present.

'Lady Hester is a very fine girl, but you, Miss Boyton, are a gem.'

'And you, I think, are whimsy personified. I haven't the slightest clue what to make of you.' She teased him to deflect the swell of emotion in her breast at the compliment he delivered so sincerely and despite deciding she liked him very well indeed.

He bent at the waist, a bow far more gallant and respectful than the moment required. 'Your servant.'

She laughed again at his inanity, but the merry sound died on her lips when St Germain stepped up to her side. He was tall and lithe, and the way he moved commanded attention.

'Your next, Miss Boyton?'

Her head jerked in something like a nod, an erratic movement to match the beat of her quickened heart. Mr Glassbrook stepped away to find another partner, slipping her a subtle wink as he departed.

St Germain guided her to the place across from him, his warm, masculine scent catching on the breeze of the movement.

Lady Marrow took Franny's place at the pianoforte. The first notes of a Scotch reel quieted the swell of chatter. The limitations of the room kept the dancers nearer to one another than typically called for, and Anabel couldn't tell if it was the fire burning in the hearth causing a flash of heat to surge through her or the nearness of St Germain's body to her own. She gave a small shake of her head and chastised herself for behaving like a schoolroom miss.

With a lift of his brow, St Germain looked poised to comment on her odd gesture. She spoke before he could. 'What a fine party you have assembled, my lord.'

'Are we so formal with one another? I had not thought so, not after so many years.'

'Says the gentleman who addressed me as "Miss Boyton".'

His lip quivered just enough to betray a hint of amusement. 'Do house parties number among your favourite diversions?'

'Extravagant meals, the finest champagne, a chance to wear one's favourite dresses and jewels—what's not to enjoy? In addition to the opportunity to take in new scenery, new faces. Even in limited company such as this, I'm poised to leave with friendships which I was not in possession of when I first arrived.'

'You and Antony Glassbrook looked quite taken with one another. I had not realised you were so familiar.'

There was a stiffness to his speech, or so her imagination would have her believe.

'Is intimacy not one of the aims of a small house party such as the one you are hosting? Dancing, too? Should one have the wish to do so, the same could be said of Ellena and Roberts, or Miss Glassbrook and my brother, or, indeed, you and Lady Hester.'

'Miss Boyton, are you in a league with my sister? I begin to think so. If you next tell me no man is immune to the practised charms and startling eyes of a duke's daughter, I will know so.'

Anabel wished to match his humour, but her thoughts splintered when she considered whether he was using her to avoid a matchmaking sister, partnering her as a gesture to his friendship with Freddy, or simply being an attentive host. When their dance ended soon after and they parted ways, Anabel breathed out a ponderous sigh. Although whether it was one of relief or disappointment, she couldn't tell.

7

Saint rolled one way and then the other, tossing the bedclothes from his body, then yanking them back on. He blinked, rubbed his eyes, and again opened them to stare out at the plasterwork on the ceiling far above the bed where he lay, all the while telling himself it was only the quiet of the house—this house—that unsettled him and not at all whatever impulse sent him straight to Miss Boyton's side after her dance with Glassbrook.

On the table next to his bed, the candle flame flickered. Fluid shadows danced across the walls, making it look as if the intricate motif of the rich blue wallpaper was undulating with life. Pip's basket, situated near the fireplace, was empty.

With a little shake of his head, he leaned to blow out the candle, then paused and held in the breath meant for the flame. Feeling more than a little silly, he fell back into the downy pillows, the bright pulse taunting him. He ran a hand along his jaw and up his cheek. He was being absurd, by any measure of the situation, and had no need to sleep with a lit candle as he'd often done as a young boy, harbouring an intense fear of the dark.

Many years had passed since the last time he'd refused to sleep until the governess putting him to bed sent for his father, so the man could look under his bed and check his wardrobe and dressing room for things too scary to name. But even as he told himself, very logically indeed, that there wasn't anything to be afraid of, especially in a house full of people—his own house by rights—before he knew what he was doing, he had folded himself over the edge of the bed. Upside down, wary eyes searching, he scanned the dim space carefully, half expecting to discover a monster hidden between the slats.

Satisfied, Saint flung himself upwards and released a little groan as all the blood rushed from his head. His body listed a moment before he straightened. He swung his gaze right, left, right, left. Then, on an impulse, he launched himself from the bed, and, after a moment of hesitation, marched to the wardrobe on the far wall. Pausing, he inhaled deeply, grasped the handles, and whipped the doors open.

It was empty, of course, and he scoffed at his own inanity, feeling foolish beyond measure. Still, rather than returning to the bed, he went to the dressing-room door, where most of his clothing and trunks were stored. With a confidence he didn't quite feel, he pushed in, releasing a little chuckle that sounded a touch hysterical around its edges when no spectre floated out from between his coats.

'Pull yourself together, Valentine Matthias Ainsley,' he said to the stifling silence, punctuating the sentence with a sharp exhale.

He climbed back into the bed, dragged the bedclothes up to his waist, and turned to blow out the candle. With a breath held in his mouth, his lips forming a perfect 'O', he heard it. A quiet scratching, like someone dragging a stick on the stone floor. Every hair, even the very fine ones on his brow, stood on end as the sound grew louder. His throat closed, squeezing out the last bit of air, and his heart was doing its very best to run away as the scratching rose to a crescendo, passing just outside his door and continuing down the corridor. His bones trembled where they joined, leaving him feeling he might come undone at any moment. Nevertheless, he peeled back the counterpane, forced his bare feet to the ground, and reached for the banyan robe draped over the bed.

Putting one foot in front of the other, he came slowly to the door. His hand shook upon the handle as he opened it. In the low light of the hall, the shadows stretched and quivered, turning the mundane and familiar surroundings into something strange and sinister. Without the warmth of a fire to keep out autumn's chill, a cold draught whispered against his skin.

Saint padded in the direction in which the noise had travelled. He quickened his pace as the sound floated further and further away, overcome by a sudden feeling that it was better to see the awful thing than to be left conjuring nightmarish images in his own mind. Just when he'd marshalled his courage: silence. His body jerked to a stop. In the absence of all other sound, his shaking breaths were deafening. He waited, nerves frayed and limbs trembling, for some ghoulish apparition of his father or Lady Cecilia to appear before him. Seconds passed, slow, terrifying, relentless.

Suddenly, he was assailed not by the hushed scrape he'd been chasing, but a tormenting *tap, tap, tap.* The haunting beat was so faint, he could almost convince himself it wasn't there at all, but for the steady interval at which it invaded his ears. He broke into a run and was nearly at the top of the stairs when he slammed into something slight. Or rather, he tumbled into it, taking a jumble of cotton, satin, and silken hair to the ground with him, billows of fabric muzzling a feminine shriek.

Saint barely noticed, a dozen thoughts competing for his attention. *The sound had been a trap to lure him from his room. He was surely about to be murdered by the ghost of Lady Cecilia. Would anyone find his body? Did this have anything to do with the stuffed bird*? And on his mind tumbled. On instinct, he'd wrapped his arms around the other body as they fell, but he hadn't realised he was still holding on until the spectre tried to speak.

'My airways,' the lady rasped out. 'You're crushing them.'

Confusion fogged Saint's mind. He pulled his head back and found a pair of concerned—and very much alive—hazel eyes staring back at him. They widened, the lady's expression transforming into one of impatience and mild panic, without a trace of murderous inclination about it.

'Oh, good god! My apologies, Miss Boyton,' he cried,

rolling onto his side next to her, the full length of his body a hair's breadth from her own.

She gasped, putting one hand to her chest and one to her stomach, and sucking in a lungful of air. Saint glanced heavenwards and searched for the will to move away from her. Instead, he turned his head and brushed his nose in the soft, tousled strands of her hair. He swallowed a breath full of lilac and the intoxicating aroma of musk, then lifted a finger and carefully wound it around a few golden threads.

Miss Boyton jerked and made a sharp turn to regard him with a suspicious gaze. The quick motion freed her strands, but his finger was still raised. He flicked the tip of his nose, adopting as bland an expression as he could muster.

'A spot of dust.'

Her focus dropped, and she ran her tongue over the seam of her lips. His skin prickled with an uncomfortable heat. Every thread of his clothing seemed to tighten, constricting the breath he attempted to draw.

'I see.' She cleared her throat. 'Why were you running? Have the spirits in the house come out to play?'

Saint bit the inside of his cheek, unwilling to admit he was following a phantom sound that had long since been consumed by the bowels of the house. 'Nothing so exciting, I'm afraid. Just a casual bout of night terrors.' He gave an exaggerated sigh and an irreverent grin, hoping his jest would satisfy her.

Her delicate features flickered with curiosity and a hint of mischief. 'Very well. Keep your secrets to yourself.'

Neither had yet moved. He watched her, overcome by the intangible sense of what might be, as though the future had already laid some claim to his thoughts. Even in the near-dark, Saint could see a deep ring of colour hugging tight to the iris of her eyes. They were a hazy mix of green and brown, like a leaf caught between the seasons. The image of her peeping up at Antony Glassbrook at dinner, of her smiling and laughing with him, overtook Saint in a sudden jealous rush. His shoulders tensed. He rolled them against the hard floor, ignoring the dull bite of pain in his bones as he did so.

'Your turn, Miss Boyton. What are you doing out of your rooms at this hour?'

A teasing smile pulled at the edge of her mouth. 'Something went bump in the night.'

Saint worked to keep his expression neutral, even as his mind spiralled like dry autumn leaves seized by a whirlwind, and tried to pry his tongue from the roof of his mouth.

'New place, new sounds. I could not sleep and thought to retrieve a book from the library.'

Saint's strained exhale was his first indication he'd been holding his breath. He wished to ask if she were sincere in her first answer, but his mouth refused to form the words.

She stirred at his side, his nascent yearning an echo in the slight space creeping between them. He pushed himself to standing and offered her a hand. Together, they found their balance. Her skin was soft and cool from the chill in the air.

'Your hand is cold.'

She nodded but wasn't looking at him. Her focus lingered where his fingers wrapped around her own. Saint would have given his every material possession to know what she was thinking—if she too felt how right, how natural a thing it was, the clasp of their bare hands. He reached for the other and folded both of hers between his, giving her fingers a rub and blowing gently on them, like a man possessed.

'Thank you.' Miss Boyton sounded cautious, a touch uncertain even, and reclaimed her hands.

Saint missed the feel of her immediately.

'If you would be so kind as to point me in the direction of the library, I'm sure I can manage to find my way.'

'Allow me.' He motioned for her to go ahead, his other hand floating at the small of her back for an indulgent second before dropping to his side. She studied him out of the corner of her eye but kept her conclusions to herself, much to his dismay. In the space of several minutes, the ache of terror in his chest had been replaced by something hungry and desperate.

They walked in silence down the stairs, Saint wrestling with the unfamiliar and unexpected surge of longing for Miss Boyton, a woman he'd seen at hundreds of balls and routs and dinners over the years. Never once had he looked down a table or across a room and experienced the awful burn of envy for the man with whom she was speaking, the way he had that night.

After passing several closed doors, he guided her through one near the back of the house. There were no curtains on the bare windows, and he knew in the daytime one could see a crest of sparkling blue sea where it peeped from behind the treeline. In the dead of night, the view was nothing more than an endless black expanse.

'Is there something in particular you wished for?'

She moved in front of a shelf, scanning the titles. He came next to her, to stand close. Too close. The sleeve of his robe brushed her wrapper, and a thrill shot up his arm.

Miss Boyton rose on her tiptoes and stretched for a slim volume.

'Here, let me.' Saint extended a hand, the movement tipping his body a little into hers. His palm grazed her knuckles as they fell away.

He heard the sharp intake of air as she stepped a little to the side.

'Did you accompany me to the library with plans to seduce me? Or because you're hoping I'll protect you from whatever it was from which you were running?'

Amusement brightened her countenance, and all Saint could think of was taking her right there on the chaise. He tucked his hands behind his back, clenching them into fists before flexing his fingers.

'I begin to wonder if it's you from whom I need protecting.'

A funny little laugh bubbled out of her.

He was reluctant to move, to relinquish the odd intimacy of the moment and give up the nearness a quarter-hour in her company had taught him to crave, but he gestured towards the door nevertheless. 'Come. I can't very well leave you roaming the halls, nor would it do for us to be caught alone. I'm certain you have no wish to be forced into matrimony.'

A flash of emotion pinched her features, so fleeting he nearly missed it and couldn't even begin to identify what it was.

'A husband who can reach things from higher shelves is certainly a boon,' she said, waving the volume of poetry between them. 'What more could any young lady wish for?'

Hearing the word 'husband' slip from Miss Boyton's lips dislodged something inside him, something both needy and afraid.

She made for the door, and he followed without reply. Saint strained to catch any unusual noise in the hall, but he heard nothing, not even the creak of a floorboard or a branch brushing along a window. At the door to her room, she asked whether he'd prefer her first to check under his bed for any monsters. He choked on the breath he'd taken and gave a little cough before opening her door and nudging her inside with a quiet 'Goodnight' and an easy grin to pair her mischievous one.

Once more in his own room, a ragged breath shuddered through him. Monsters or no, Saint knew he wouldn't sleep at all.

8

Anabel wielded conversation and charm like a shield. To the best of her memory, she had never before been left bereft of words. The night prior, however, every moment in St Germain's company made stringing a sentence together more challenging than the one that came before, and teasing had felt like her only defence to his nearness.

She suspected the odd noise outside her door, the one that sent a trill of excitement through her, had been the same thing to pull him from his room. But when she danced near the subject, he'd made no response, showed no reaction, and so she said she'd been on her way to retrieve a book. He wouldn't, she hoped, seek her opinion on the one she borrowed.

Over and over she analysed his presence in the hall and his curious words in the library. She played through their exchange in her mind until faded grey light peeked through the curtains and her head throbbed—an awful sensation which had not abated by the time she left her room for breakfast. She tried not to look at the ground outside her door, to imagine her form stretched close to his, or how the flicker of candlelight gave the appearance of fire floating in his brown eyes, rich and inviting, but tinged with a faint trace of strain.

She took quick stock of the breakfast parlour. Tall arched windows overlooked lush green lawn and a scatter of beech and poplar trees. The angle at which the windows were set gave the room the appearance of being curved, and the alcove this created hugged the large round table at which St Germain sat with both his sisters, Freddy, Hero, and Mr Glassbrook.

Anabel wandered to the sideboard and filled a plate before making her way to join the others. Freddy abruptly rose from his place next to Mr Glassbrook. The feet of the chair scraped hard along the wood floor, the sharp noise cutting short the casual conversations of the morning.

'Take my seat, Ana.'

She cocked her head in bemusement and swept a quick look over the many empty places from which she might choose. 'Thank you, Freddy, but that's hardly necessary.'

'I insist. Your eyes being sensitive to light, you will be much more comfortable facing away from the window.' He motioned for a footman to retrieve his plate and stood behind the chair, in expectation of her taking it.

Anabel considered for a moment if the sound she'd heard the night prior was a spirit coming to possess her brother. Never in her life had she ever expressed such an odd complaint as the one he assigned to her. She walked in slow steps round the table, noting the interested rise of Mr Glassbrook's eyebrows when she approached his side.

Freddy pushed the chair in as she sat before moving to an empty one across from her and next to Ellena. The hum of idle chatter swelled once more. She stared blankly at her brother, who went on tearing into his toast with enthusiasm and giving no indication he'd done a very odd thing indeed.

'Curious,' murmured Mr Glassbrook in a low voice. 'Tell me, does this sensitivity also prevent you from staring directly into a blazing fire? Snow on a sunny day? Two eyes of polished amber, shining and mysterious like they're lit from within by a thousand stars?' He hid a smile behind his coffee cup.

Under the table, Anabel drove the tip of her shoe into the side of his. He sputtered on the sip he was taking.

'Has anyone seen a handkerchief with my initials embroidered in the corner?' asked Sir Marcus Seward, coming into the breakfast parlour on the heels of Roberts. 'I had a stack of three sitting neatly on a chest in my room, but this morning there were only two.'

Anabel took a bite of brioche and, under the guise of studying her plate, let her eyes slip towards St Germain to gauge his reaction. She wondered if the missing item, the noise she'd heard, and his presence in the hall the night before were at all connected and thought he appeared a trifle tired. The fork he'd been raising to his lips stalled, only for a second, the movement slight enough anyone else might overlook it.

'Is it possible you miscounted?' suggested Hero in her gentle way. Anabel noticed her friend was once more in a flattering shade of soft pink, not unlike the dress she'd worn down to dinner. 'Or perhaps you placed it in a coat pocket without recalling doing so. I often misplace things in such a way.'

Sir Marcus shook his head, a tinge of colour flaring on his cheeks and ears when he spoke. 'It's silly, but I always fold and stack them just so before bed. My grandmama made them for me before she died. One has my initials, one the family motto, and one a pretty little grouping of bluebells like those prolific at my father's estate.'

'Which is missing?' asked Freddy.

'The bluebells. It was the topmost.'

'Grimm.' St Germain called his butler. 'Let Mrs Crane know. The staff as well. It can't have got too far.'

'Especially in this weather,' Franny added, casting a disheartened glance at the closed window, which was, at that very moment, being lashed by a torrential outpouring of rain. 'I'd a whole day of outdoor amusements planned, but the sky appears determined to thwart us. How about dominoes once everyone is finished?'

Ellena groaned. 'I hardly woke in time to break my fast and you wish to put me to sleep again?'

'Cribbage?' Franny tried.

Sir Marcus offered up chess, or backgammon, or consequences.

'Ah! I've got it!' exclaimed Roberts, dropping his fork onto his plate with a startling clang and immediately grabbing it again, immune to the winces around the table.

'Charades, but we mime instead of speaking. All the rage in France.'

Beads of sweat gathered between Anabel's shoulder blades. The game, as she knew it, involved unravelling the complex language of written riddles. 'How does such a thing work?'

Roberts thought a moment before he answered. 'If we use a riddle book, I suppose we would solve the clue independently and act out the answer for everyone else to guess.'

In her mouth, Anabel's tongue felt so thick it was difficult for her to swallow even a sip of her coffee, and she wracked her brain for any plausible reason she might excuse herself from the game.

'Although,' continued Roberts, 'I was previously at a house party where, for simplicity's sake, we wrote words on strips of paper cut for the purpose.'

Every muscle in Anabel's body was pulled taut by hope and fear. When St Germain directed a footman named Charles to cut up a half-dozen sheets of paper, the breath caught in her lungs freed itself and she sagged in her chair. She looked up over the cup held between her hands. St Germain was eyeing her with a closed expression. Her fingertips were white against the porcelain. She wondered if he'd seen her relief—or worse—her alarm.

Franny stood, signalling to those gathered around the table she was ready to relocate to the smaller drawing room at the front of the house, overlooking the drive. Beyond, the trees seemed to eat up the lane. In the wet grey rain, the road away from Sylvancliffe all but disappeared.

The footman returned with paper, three pens, and as many pots of ink, and set them on a small table. Behind him, another carried a large decorative bowl.

'We've come down not a moment too soon. What's all this?' asked Lady Hester, entering together with her aunt.

St Germain greeted the pair with a short explanation before questioning if Roberts had any rules for the group to follow.

'The game is all about miming. No speaking of any sort. As for the things we are to guess, I'd suggest nothing too complicated. It's jolly fun to shout out answers, but after a minute or two, one feels rather foolish if no one has guessed correctly.'

'Who will go first?' Ellena asked.

'I say Franny,' offered Freddy. 'As our hostess. Then whoever calls out the right answer can take the next turn.'

Everyone nodded in agreement and lined up to use the pens and paper. Franny wrote with decisive strokes, Lady Hester with a delicate air of panic, and Sir Marcus used up so many minutes, St Germain imposed a time limit. Hero looked a little confused, Freddy thoughtful, and Mr Glassbrook worked the pen with the devil in his smirk. For her part, Anabel selected from words she knew she could compose with minimal effort: an animal—cat—and an emotion—pensive. Panic at having to make quick sense of other people's writing had just begun to swell in her breast when mischief got the best of her. She did not commit to paper the next phrase that crossed her mind, but a cheeky grin played about her lips when she returned to her chair. Should she have a turn, she knew what she would act out, regardless of the clue.

One by one, after folding and depositing their pieces of paper into the waiting bowl, everyone settled on the couch in front of the fireplace or else on the chairs gathered nearby.

Franny withdrew a creased slip. She peeked at the contents before quickly refolding it, her features pinched with dismay.

'Goodness.' She opened the paper once more, studying the words as though they might have changed in the seconds since she'd last looked, and then set it on the mantle. Much to the unrestrained delight of those playing, the party's hostess acted out a cow grazing in the meadow, a feat which took several iterations and cost her nearly all her dignity.

Both Freddy and Hero shouted out the answer at the same time. Freddy ceded the second turn with an elegant dip of his head. Anabel's lashes fluttered as she reined in an eye-roll. Had it been she who yelled out the answer, no doubt Freddy would have jumped from his chair before Anabel even realised what was happening.

The next correct guess was her own. Anabel rose to take her turn with her chin lifted and a mischievous glint in her eye.

Her gaze found St Germain, who lingered a little apart from everybody else. About him, an air of casual indifference. He had not bothered to call out a single guess for his sister or for Hero.

Making a show of swimming her hand around in the bowl, Anabel whipped out a piece of paper. She glanced at the clue, creased her brows in mock study, and crumpled it tight in her hand.

St Germain came forward from the part of the room where he'd sequestered himself and stood next to the sofa, cautious interest flickering across his features the longer she stood there.

She took a deep breath and opened her eyes as wide as they'd go, her mouth too, as if she were screaming into the room. On her face, what she hoped was an expression of unmatched fear. She threw her arms about in frantic, flailing motions and moved in a zigzag pattern around the open space in front of where everyone was sitting.

Her focus never wavered from St Germain. The tip of her tongue peeked out of her mouth in what she hoped would be taken for determined concentration, but which was really a failing attempt to hold back the laugh rattling around inside her. She knew by his simmering expression he'd worked it out.

'Ghost!' someone cried.

'Possessed!' yelled another.

'The Castle of Otranto,' guessed Freddy.

And then, cutting through the din, two words said through a slow, secretive smile. 'Night terrors.' He spoke to the room as a whole, but his fiery, determined look was only for her. 'Perhaps we ought to be pocketing the slips of paper when we win, an easy way to keep score.' Each word drew him nearer her person, his steps unhurried and deliberate, a hunter stalking his quarry.

Her skin prickled with a shiver.

He pounced.

She cried out and flung her hands behind her back with the paper still clutched within her grip, just as he attempted to snatch it away. The reaction was instinctual—it mattered not at all if he knew she'd made up the clue simply to tease him. She met his sly gaze with a shallow, half-gasping giggle. He snaked both arms around her, blindly searching for the scrap of paper.

His hands grazed her bare arms, her wrist, her fist, the paper she was set on protecting nearly forgotten. Her heart quickened. He was so close, her breasts grazed his chest with each erratic breath. His proximity forced her to tip her head back. She was studying his jaw, sharp as a razor's edge, when his eyes found hers. They dropped to her lips, suddenly dry and parted. At her back, some of her fingers had trapped a few of his—or maybe it was he who'd caught her hands.

'Would anyone else care for more coffee?' Franny's unruffled voice pierced the dead quiet of the room. She bid the footman bring a fresh pot, and Charles hurried out without further instruction.

Anabel could feel the hard stares of every person in the room fixed on her and St Germain, still tangled up in one another. She struggled to force down a rough, painful swallow. Then, with half-averted eyes and a slow, careful step, she extricated herself from his hold.

St Germain attempted to clear his throat, stifling the raspy sound with a fist to his mouth. 'Coffee would be just the thing, Franny.'

'Your surplus of enthusiasm suggests you've already had plenty.'

Anabel returned to her seat, careful not to look at any one guest in particular.

'Assuming you were not hasty in your charge,' Franny quipped to her brother, 'it would be your turn to draw a clue, unless Anabel chooses to correct us presently.'

Everyone shifted to look at Anabel once more. For a quick second she debated saying someone else had yelled out the right answer, but the idea of watching St Germain perform was too great a draw.

'Go on, then.' She bit her lip to keep from smiling but couldn't repress the muscle quivering in her cheek. 'We are all on the edge of our seats with anticipation.'

There was a quick squint of his eyes, but he went to the bowl and plucked out a clue without argument.

Charles entered with the coffee, and everyone seemed content enough to throw themselves once more into the new bustle of activity.

Anabel accepted a cup from Franny, grinning into it when St Germain grudgingly pretended to paw his ear, and spent the rest of the game trying to excise from her mind the feeling of his arms wrapped tight around her.

9

Interest in the game began to wane after the same few people proved superior at guessing. The rain had stopped, although great swathes of clouds remained peppered in the sky, occasionally plunging the room into darkness or casting peculiar shadows at odd intervals.

Franny suggested everyone do as they pleased with the unexpected break in the weather, and Roberts was the first to act, declaring his intention to exercise his horse. Freddy and Glassbrook attached themselves to his scheme. Saint loved a short, hard ride, but what he needed was fresh air and a quiet moment to gather his wits.

Lady Hester was the next to excuse herself, hiding a yawn behind her hand. There was something mismatched in the gesture—the sound or the lack of breath drawn in or how very awake she appeared. Ellena wished to run an errand in the village, and Miss Glassbrook mentioned letters she had to write. Miss Boyton remained oddly silent.

In the commotion of people going one way or the other, and with a last sidelong glance in her direction, Saint slipped away to retrieve his journal from his room, then exited the house through a door off the library. He'd begun filling blank pages soon after his father died, at the suggestion of a tutor. Occasionally, he would make note of something he came upon when out for a ride or walk, but most often, the journal served simply as a place to hold emotions that had nowhere else to go.

He left the formal garden behind and entered the large copse of maples, their semi-bare branches closing around him like skeletal limbs. Briny air blowing from the sea filled his lungs, and each gust rattled the withering leaves, their swirling song a lullaby he recalled from long ago. Although the rain had stopped, the atmosphere around him remained heavy and damp, and light forcing its way through the canopy cast a spectral glow on the path. The birds had not yet returned to the perches they'd abandoned in the storm, their absent song an eerie, silent grief.

Saint watched the path where he walked. The tree roots seemed to shift in the dirt, rising at a moment's notice to trip him if he didn't mind his step. Somewhere among the trunks, a twig snapped. He paused and cast a quick look around, ignoring the passing thought that if he shouted, there might be no one to hear him.

It was only half a minute or so before he picked up another trail, this one much narrower and without so definite an origin as the one leading from the garden through the woodland. A moment later, he found himself within a stone's throw of a small cottage, its original purpose buried with the earls of generations past. The wrought-iron gate surrounding the small garden screamed on its hinges when he pushed it open.

When he was very young, he and his mother would sneak off to this cosy out-building. He couldn't remember why his mother loved the cottage, only that she did. She would read to him, or they would play games. It was the only place on the property where Saint felt at ease—the only place from which his father wouldn't wrest him back, something for which he was sure he could thank his mother. The inside was all exposed wood and smooth grey stone, furnished with old, oversized pieces his mother had selected from the attics and had brought down for her own private use.

The cottage had lost the musty smell which had plagued his senses the first time he escaped there, but he opened one of the far windows, despite the biting autumn air. After placing his journal on a small round table next to his favourite chair, he went to the decanter he'd had Grimm set out on a sideboard. He poured two fingers' worth and drew a brimming sip into his mouth, letting the woody, sweet liquid settle on his tongue before swallowing it and setting the glass next to the journal.

At the fireplace, he retrieved the tinder-box off the mantle and squatted down to arrange the kindling, all the while wondering if there were enough brandy in the whole of England to make him forget the heat of Miss Boyton's body pressed snug against his. The way her curves rounded around his hard planes, the way holding her was a natural constant, like the steady march of time, to the point he forgot himself in a room full of people.

Since returning to Sylvancliffe, he'd slipped away to the cottage several times to find a moment of peace, to escape whatever had been lurking in the shadows of the house the last two decades or more. He'd never imagined also being haunted by a vexatious scamp with a laugh in her brilliant eyes.

Saint had known Anabel Boyton since she was a little thing in the schoolroom with paint on her dress and more hair running free from her braids than constrained by them. The image, complete with an impish grin showing her missing two front teeth, arrived in his mind unbidden, and without him being able to place exactly when it was from, or if it were merely a composite of sundry trips he'd made to the Boyton family home.

However the little girl in his mind wasn't dashing through the open fields at Woodruff Abbey. She was scampering down the same shoreline Saint had frequented as a boy, the one running parallel to the sea that edged in Sylvancliffe. When he closed out the world around him, he noticed the girl's hair was light, with only the barest hint of red, similar to Miss Boyton's, but her eyes were darker —like his. He rolled his shoulders and brushed a hand over his brow, attempting to rid himself of a memory that was all figment and no truth.

Hardly a day in her company, and Anabel Boyton—imp, terror, overlooked beauty, had—

'Boo!'

The noise emitted from Saint's throat was somewhere between a howl, a curse, and a guttural scream. When he jumped up and knocked the top of his head on the ledge of the mantle, it was most definitely a curse.

'Devil take—!' He broke off on wheeling around to see Miss Boyton standing in the doorway. Both hands covered her mouth, but laughter still slipped through her fingers and tears spilled down the rise of her cheeks. The very sight of her quelled every sensation of fear.

A wicked smile curled his lips. 'Don't worry, I'll tell your brother where I've buried your body.' He darted towards her, and she let out a little shriek of her own before turning and fleeing up a path different from the one by which he'd originally arrived—a path he knew led to the topiary garden, which was exposed to the entire east side of the house. Anyone looking out of a window might see them. And yet, as the trees thinned and opened to a gentle slope of green, he knew he would not stop pursuing her till she was his.

He was closing in.

A chuckle, or something like it, floated over her shoulder between her panted breaths, and he considered whether she belonged in Bedlam, and he together with her. The slight downward grade of the hill propelled him forward, and he was just near enough to grasp her wrist when it swung back. Her long stride faltered, and her feet slipped out from under her. Before Saint could fully regret his decision, she crashed towards the ground, taking him down with her.

She landed halfway on top of him, the sharp bone of

her shoulder slamming into his stomach with the force of a large rock dropping into a pond. He could feel her ribs expanding and contracting at a rapid pace as she tried to regain her breath, while he willed the air back into his own lungs.

He winced at the pain radiating through him when she rolled onto her back, her head still resting upon his body, leaves somehow impossibly entangled in her hair of Venetian gold. How little he truly cared about sore ribs and a bruised back when she was there, lying nearly on top of him, in the kind of intimate sprawl reserved for lovers during a private picnic. The hand twitching at his side with longing dipped into her wild tendrils. In the quiet of the moment, her inhale was as clear as a clarion call, telling him he'd already gone too far.

'Are you—are you picking twigs from my hair?'

There was no mistaking the note of disbelief in her tone, and he said, as blandly as he could manage when his heart was perilously near bursting, 'Not only have you ruined one of my favourite coats as well as my peace, but you've enough foliage in your hair for the magpies to build a nest. Would you prefer I leave the vegetation untouched?'

Miss Boyton seemed to consider the question. 'Well, I suppose it depends on how fetching I look. Green brings out my eyes, but orange, even though it *should* be very becoming with my warm colouring, always reads a bit sallow when put up to my skin. Shame, really, I'm quite fond of the colour. There's something happy about it, don't you think?'

'Your humble servant, ma'am,' Saint drawled, working loose a sliver of grass, which he then presented to her. 'Say the word, and I shall return it to your jumble of curls.'

'I still have curls, then? What a pleasant surprise. Poor Harriet tries her best, but even her decades of experience cannot outwit our lady Mother Nature. Quite the beast when she wishes to be.'

'I may have been too generous with the description.'

The exchange gave Saint an excuse to wrap a heavy, limp lock around his finger. He wondered at the softness in spite of the wet weather taking a toll.

Her spirited laugh startled him. Tucked tight to his side, he could feel the little tremors of her body running through his own.

'Never in my life have you issued me a compliment,' she said. 'I find it impossible to believe you'd choose this moment to begin being charitable with your words.'

His brows knit in confusion, but the question in his mind remained half formed. Miss Boyton reached up to investigate the state of her dishevelled hair, her hand going still when she brushed along his, buried in her strands.

Saint suddenly felt hot all over.

He jerked himself up, thrusting her off as he did so. He felt a little guilty as she scrambled to right herself, patting her head where he'd yanked away his hand and brushing out the skirts of her dress.

He allowed himself one sweeping, hungry gaze while she was distracted before offering an abrupt, 'Good day, Miss Boyton,' and stalking back to the cottage to retrieve his journal and search for his equanimity.

10

Anabel stood, mouth hanging open, feeling even more bewildered than she must look. She watched St Germain stride back to the cottage, replaying the last hour in her mind.

When she slipped from the house, her only intention had been a walk to clear her mind or scold it back into submission. Her imagination was making her question what she knew to be true: a gentleman such as St Germain would never find worth in a woman like herself. Her own mama said so often enough.

She had meant to find her way to the beach, maybe even take off her half-boots and let her toes curl in the soft, cold sand. Perhaps catch furtive lovers in the midst of a secret rendezvous, or else come upon smugglers running spirits onto the shore, although this was admittedly unlikely given the time of day. But then she'd heard the distinct squeak of an iron hinge protesting its use, and the thrill of uncertainty had compelled her to take another path.

Anabel had regretted her choice once she fell, landing on top of him. His muscled chest propped up her head. In her ear, the steady thump of a heart that would never beat for her.

For a brief spell, she invented a life where the moment was real between them—normal, even. A moment where his love matched her own, where he might be hers to rest against, where they discussed who to invite for the festive Christmas season, and whether they would host a ball for Twelfth Night.

She was still living inside the life she couldn't have when he'd cast her off.

St Germain had long disappeared into the treeline, but Anabel remained rooted, staring into the shedding boughs of the maples a minute more before the cry of a magpie brought her back to herself. She pulled the hood of her cape to cover her hair and made for the house.

Her earlier headache, which had begun to abate after her second cup of coffee, returned with great force, the space from temple to temple pulsing with acute pain.

Wishing to avoid any awkward encounters with the other guests, Anabel was relieved to find the door of the conservatory at the side of the house unlocked. She tread swiftly and silently across the room, pausing midway to cast a searching look about when a cool draught tickled the little hairs on her neck.

Outside, leaves quivered on their thin branches as the wind passed through the trees.

Second-guessing herself, Anabel retraced her steps. The door was closed tight. She stared down at the elegant curved handle, her mouth scrunched up to one side.

'Well, then,' she said, on an exhale.

The empty space made no response.

Her breath fogged the glass door, and she used the edge of her sleeve to wipe it clear. Movement outside pulled her attention from the task, the heel of her palm growing cold through the fabric of her dress where it rested on the pane. Just inside the treeline, a red-cloaked figure was bobbing swiftly between the trunks.

Anabel squinted. 'What?' The word came out sharp, confused, and clouded the glass.

With short, agitated movements, she wiped away the steam. Whoever, or whatever, was gone. Still, her eyes remained pinned on the woodland.

In the sky, a cloud settled over a piece of the sun like a mourning veil. The persistent gloom made the shadows in the wood twist and writhe with life. A chill slithered up her spine.

Then she saw it.

Obscured by branches and boles and scattered leaves, a pale face was watching her from under a beaver hat.

She jerked back. Blinked. The face was gone. Too much distance spanned between her and the wood to discern any notable features, although she was certain the one watching her had been a man and suspected the cloaked figure was a woman.

In her mind, a thousand questions formed in an instant, but her search for answers was cut short. A thin sound, like air slipping between two lips, reached her ears.

She whirled around. Not another soul was present. She walked the perimeter, chasing a whisper, and ended in the centre of the conservatory. The noise seemed to exist only in the atmosphere of the room. Hugging her cape tight to herself, she made one full, slow circle.

'Anabel?'

She swept around in a flash, the hood of her cape dropping. 'Ellena. Hello.'

'Goodness! Your hair.'

Instinctively, Anabel lifted a hand to pat her soggy, wilted curls. 'The weather. I've just come in from out of doors.'

An expression of interest sharpened Ellena's pretty features. 'The grounds are lovely, are they not? Where did you walk out?'

'The woods, mostly. I'd intended to make my way to the beach, but the trees had other plans.' She gestured vaguely to her hair. 'I came in this way hoping to spare myself the embarrassment of being caught in such a state. Your afternoon has proven less troublesome, I hope.'

'Indeed, but diverting nevertheless.'

Something in Ellena's tone, or maybe it was the gleam in her eye, caused a knot of tension to settle between Anabel's shoulders.

'Don't let me keep you.' Ellena stepped to one side, clearing the way for her to exit the room. 'You're anxious to set yourself to rights before dinner.'

Anabel mustered a tight smile, pulled her hood up once more, and departed without a look back.

Several hours later, in a dress free of grass stains and locks brushed into order, Anabel entered the drawing room before dinner. Immediately, she lost the fight with her eyes, which seemed to track St Germain of their own accord.

'I've just had the most marvellous idea,' announced Franny, garnering everyone's attention. 'We are all friends, are we not? Let us do away with formal arrangements when we sit down to dine and place ourselves where we please. Dinner will be a much cosier affair.' She turned to the footman and asked him to remove the name cards before Grimm announced dinner.

'Interesting choice of words from our hostess.'

Freddy was standing next to Anabel. She hid her surprise, having not the slightest idea how or when he'd taken his position.

'In what way?'

'I cautioned you against sneaking about. I'd not thought to warn you off public displays of whatever the hell that was during charades.'

Anabel raised her chin. 'If you've a problem with St Germain's behaviour, you may find him just over there.'

'His sense of propriety and decorum has never been in question.'

''Twas nothing. A spot of fun gone too far.'

'That's not how it appeared to me.'

Grimm entered then, and Freddy offered his arm to Anabel in silence.

In the dining room, she scanned the seats, desiring only to be far away from her brother for the meal.

'Anabel!' Ellena beamed from her place to St Germain's right. 'Sit next to me.'

She released Freddy's arm, her legs feeling like two tree trunks rooted deep in the soil as she took slow steps towards the empty chair.

'My sister was right—was she not?' Ellena said. 'How much easier for us to enjoy one another without speaking across the table.'

'Certainly,' agreed Anabel, watching a footman fill her wineglass.

'You and my brother are of a like mind.'

In her periphery, Anabel felt St Germain staring, but she refused to look his direction. 'Considering the many years we have been known to one another, that's not so surprising, is it?'

'Not at all. He, too, was out for a stroll, unless my mind deceived me. It was from an upstairs window I saw him coming in from the woods.'

Anabel choked on the sip of wine in her mouth, the liquid burning as she swallowed it down.

'How odd your paths should not cross.'

'Not at all,' Anabel replied, a touch too quickly, wishing to snuff the fire she felt kindling under her. Unfortunately, she spoke at the exact moment St Germain said, 'They did.'

For the first time all evening, her eyes met his. She was

taken aback by the crinkle of amusement lurking at their corners.

'I only meant there are several footpaths,' she explained, unclenching her hand where it rested in her lap. 'Our encounter was brief. Little more than two ships sailing past one another, really.'

Ellena tipped her head to one side. 'Only you didn't mention it when I saw you in the conservatory.'

'I hadn't thought your brother's presence on his own grounds worth noting, is all. Nor did I wish to relive further mortification at being caught with hair fit for the birds and little else.' She waved a deprecating hand and longed for the conversation to change course. Inside her mouth, the tip of her tongue found the sharp point of her incisor, and she focused on the discomfort rather than the twinge of panic swelling in her breast to be under such dogged scrutiny.

'Nature has never done so much for a young lady. Between the becoming flush of her cheeks and the lustre of her bewitching hazel eyes, it would be near impossible for anyone to instead attend a spot of foliage making a home where it ought not. Although green *is* a fetching colour on Miss Boyton. Do not you agree, Ellena?' said St Germain, sipping his wine as might a man who wielded a sword with no more care than if he held a hairbrush.

She refused to look down at her dress, made of silk satin a rich shade of bottle green.

Ellena murmured her agreement, her penetrating stare drifting between them. Across the table, Mr Glassbrook and his insolent brows were looking on with interest.

Anabel dismissed the absurd statement by preserving an unconvinced silence and spearing an artichoke bottom with her fork. He was making a point, she assumed, after she'd claimed never to have received a compliment from him.

For the rest of the meal, however, she offered perfunctory replies when spoken to, pushed her food around her plate without taking a bite, and tried not to dwell on how his words pressed up against something inside her or why she felt as exposed as if she'd come down to dinner in nothing but her shift.

11

A cold mist threaded through the boles of the wood and prowled low along the edge of the formal gardens.

The guests who had come down to breakfast scattered afterwards, everyone at liberty to spend their morning in the way that would give them the most pleasure. Anabel had never considered reading an act that brought her joy, which is how she found herself sneaking out of the house with the volume of poetry she'd selected the first night tucked snuggly under her arm.

She paused a moment at the fountain. In its centre was a woman wearing a gossamer gown and holding a large shell upon her shoulder, from which the water sprayed. The detail in the marble sculpture was so fine, the draping of the dress and the longing on the woman's face so life-like, Anabel's chest burned with emotion.

Leaving behind the constant rush of water, she slipped

into the secret garden, following the serpentine path between short walls of green until she came upon a bench that was rather out of the way.

With a quick look in each direction, she pulled out the book and flipped to a page with fewer lines than most of the rest. At the top, the title: 'A Hymn To The Moon', by Lady Mary Wortley Montagu.

'Thou silver di—deit—deity of sec—secret night.' Anabel stumbled through the first line, feeling a little silly reading aloud to herself. Once more she scanned her surroundings to be sure she was alone. 'Di—rect my foos —' She took a deep breath. 'My foospep—foot—footsteps th—to—tro—' In one swift, furious motion, Anabel slammed the book down on the hard stone. Pain radiated through her hand and up her arm.

She growled, the belligerent noise cutting through the quiet calm of the day, and pressed the heels of her palms to her eyes. With a sigh equal parts determination and resignation, she picked up the book and opened it once more.

'Tro—Through the woodland shade.'

She forced herself to finish the entire poem. By the end, a sheen of sweat sat between her skin and her dress, and dozens of tiny wet circles warped the page where tear after frustrated tear had landed. After blotting her cheeks and the paper as best she could with her sleeve, she set the book aside and stared at the ground, seeing nothing but St Germain's soft gaze from the night before.

'Ana?'

She drew a startled breath. Autumn's crisp air filled her lungs, and a cold burn coursed through her. She straightened a little and faced her brother, tucking as much of the book as she could under the skirt of her dress.

'Walk with me?'

'Oh, I—' Her voice snagged on the word, drawing it out till it became too meaningful a sound.

'Have I interrupted a clandestine tryst?' Despite the playful, exaggerated way he swung his head from side to side and bent to look under the bench in mock search, there was a palpable edge to his speech.

Anabel stood, one hand reaching out to take the arm Freddy offered, the other snatching up the book.

'What have you there?'

She lifted a nonchalant shoulder. ''Tis nothing.'

'Ana.'

With his free hand, Freddy tried to reach around both their bodies. On a huff of indignation, she waved the collection of poetry in front of him.

'A book?'

'Goodness, Freddy, why don't you try to sound more surprised?'

'That's not—of course, I'm a little surprised—but—' There was a careful pause. 'Whatever for?'

Anabel swung up her hand to nibble at her nail, only to realise she couldn't do so without also stabbing herself with the corner of the book.

'Is this because of what Mama said? She doesn't truly think you dull-witted. Surely you must know that. Wouldn't parade you about town if she believed you a lost cause.'

Mrs Boyton marched Anabel about when in London

because that's what a mother did to her unattached daughters, whether or not the daughters were half so eligible as the matches sought for them.

'I would never dare search for logic in Mama's mind or machinations. House parties such as this are the hardest place for me to hide my—to hide—and I just thought, well, I may not be clever or a suitable bride, but perhaps…' Her thoughts tangled like a skein of yarn. The more she tugged at the knot in her mind, the more entwined it became, until she was utterly confounded.

They had strolled beyond the cover of the secret garden. Anabel heard the continuous murmur of water spraying before she saw the statue.

'What of Glassbrook?'

She tipped her head. 'What about him?'

'He's kind. You two seem to enjoy each other's presence. He's unlikely to be as—as critical, if that's your concern.'

'Because he flirts indiscriminately and is as known for his antics in the courtroom as without?' She gasped. 'This is why you insisted I take your seat at breakfast, citing some ridiculous lie about my eyes being sensitive to light.'

The gentleman himself was approaching, preventing her brother from reply.

'Glassbrook!' Freddy called. 'How serendipitous we should cross paths. I must return to the house, but my sister expressed her wish to walk down to the beach. Might I importune you to provide her with an escort?'

Mr Glassbrook offered a gallant bow. 'Nothing would give me more pleasure.'

The bottom of Anabel's eyelids twitched against the glare she was withholding. Freddy didn't meet her hard stare as he detangled their arms and scooted her towards the other gentleman. He then turned on a heel and hurried away at a pace she'd only ever seen him employ when avoiding a woman with whom he no more desired to maintain a flirtation.

'A touch heavy handed, but I suppose matchmaking falls to the purview of matrons more often than not. I'm flattered, regardless. Tell me, Miss Boyton—or should I refer to you as my betrothed?—how is it I've become your brother's choice for you? Beyond my disarming charm and dashing good looks, of course.'

Anabel's annoyance with her brother evaporated in an instant. 'What a goosecap you are! Your future wife has all my pity. If you must know, it's your coquettish reputation.'

Surprise flashed across his face.

'Not what you were expecting to hear? No, I didn't think so.'

'I'm convinced there is more to the story. The question is whether you will tell me.'

Anabel lifted her nose to the air when she felt Mr Glassbrook's perceptive gaze studying her and declined to gratify his curiosity.

'No?' he said. 'No. Well, I won't push, but there is no chance you escape this conversation unscathed. What was that exchange last night over dinner between you and Saint? Did our plan work? Was there a passionate assignation?' He clapped in delight, the motion pinching her hand between his arm and ribs.

'I've no intention of marrying you, sir, but how dull my days will be when our paths do not intersect so very often. I beg you moderate your excitement. St Germain and I came upon one another while enjoying a bit of air. Independently, mind. Nothing in the least amorous about it.' Warmth crept up her neck, slow and accusatory.

'Yes. Two ships passing, was it?' A discontented murmur accompanied his words. 'Leave it to me.'

'You need not—'

'Brother! Anabel!' Hero came from around the corner of the house, St Germain at her side. 'Our host was kind enough to show me his favourite stretch of beach. Have you been yet, Anabel? It's magnificent—the white sand; a low rugged cliff that drops into the clear water, turned murky from the storm; the way the trees suddenly just open to a never-ending view. Now, if only the rain will hold off long enough for me to begin painting.'

'Let us not waste a moment,' Mr Glassbrook said. 'Come, I'll help you gather your supplies.' He disengaged Anabel from his side, holding her hand out toward St Germain. 'May I commend Miss Boyton to your care?'

'Always.'

Anabel didn't trust herself to look at either man: Mr Glassbrook because he would discern every emotion playing across her countenance, even those she couldn't name, and St Germain because she was unsure which emotion she most desired to see upon *his* face. The latter took her hand and tucked it tight into the crook of his arm, his fingers lingering on hers for a spell before dropping away. He turned them down a little path which looped around the fountain near the house.

Silence hung in the air between them, but the morning was full of life. Songbirds sang to one another overhead, and the melodic sound of unrelenting droplets breaking the water's surface again and again scored their meandering pace. In her ears, the frantic thrum of a heart beating hard at the boned cage in which it was kept.

'Did you sleep well?'

Anabel peered at St Germain with mild uncertainty. 'I did. And you?'

'Indeed.'

'Shame. I'd rather hoped for a more exciting report: the fire in your room mysteriously went out, or the spectre of Lady Cecilia paid you a visit, or the wails of a woman locked in the attic prevented your slumber.'

'A woman is held captive in my attic and you believe my primary concern is how well my guests have slept?'

She raised one shoulder. 'Any worthy host would be concerned. By the bye, each time I've found myself alone with you, I've also found myself under you. Ought I to be concerned about ending up on the ground once more?' She only heard the words once it was too late to eat them up. A flash of heat lashed at her chest, cheeks, the tips of her ears.

St Germain swiped his free hand across his forehead and ran a finger between his throat and cravat. 'It was you —' his voice was hoarse, and he rasped on a tentative cough— 'who fell upon me yesterday.'

'Because you grabbed me like a ruffian.' Anabel was doing her best to tease him, but recollecting there was a lean, strong body beneath the layers of his clothing made it difficult to fill her lungs, much less think.

'And how I've paid for my boorish behaviour. Even Wilde, the best valet in England, isn't certain he can salvage my coat.'

'Then how fortunate you've not invited the gossips here. A man known for his fashion would never live down such a thing as grass stains on his coat.'

He chuckled. 'No. Only think of what happened to poor Mr Allen the time he dared show up to the Lieven ball in the wrong shade of yellow for his complexion. I've seen him in public only thrice since. Two of the morning papers *still* speak of his disastrous blunder.'

Anabel whipped her head his direction. 'You,' she gasped, 'are a gossip!' She hadn't thought it possible to feel more affection for him, but the discovery delighted her.

'I confess there is little else I enjoy reading over my morning coffee more than the gossip pages.' He looked down at her, his handsome features relaxed by a playful grin.

The breath she took burned her lungs, not unlike when her maid pulled the laces of her stays too tightly.

'Your turn.'

Her lashes fluttered in confusion. 'Beg your pardon?'

'A confession. I enjoy gossip. You…' St Germain left the end of the sentence open for her to fill.

Anabel's stomach churned. 'I…' *am a half-wit.* She scoured her mind for something, anything, else. 'I…ah!' A small smile crept across her face. 'You recall Miss Kent's picnic last season and demonstrating for me the proper way to swing a mallet?' He nodded. 'Well,' she caught her bottom lip between her teeth. 'I am quite proficient in pall-mall. Have been for many years.'

St Germain's mouth fell open. Anabel couldn't help herself. She let free a peal of laughter.

'I don't—' His confused chuckle joined hers. 'Why would you accept my help, then?'

Because she ached for his attention and was foolish enough to play a dangerous game with her emotions which she would never win.

'It was my hope that by keeping us both occupied, your determined friend and my stubborn one might work out some of their differences.' A lie. Harmless, however, unlike the truth. She settled a broad, cheeky smile upon him. 'Naturally, I take all the credit for their union.'

'There it is.'

She gave a low, questioning hum.

'Your dimple. One of the many things I've had the pleasure of discovering about you since your arrival at Sylvancliffe.'

His unwavering gaze held her in place, and she could scarcely draw in the air she needed to survive under its weight. For the briefest moment, she thought she might perish where she stood—wished for such a thing, even, to avoid the sudden flutter of acute discomfort and uncertainty. His first compliment put paid to her comment. Issuing a second bewildered her.

'How are you finding the poems?'

A crease formed between her brows.

'The book in your hand. The one from the library, I believe.'

Anabel glanced down, surprised to find the thing still in her possession. 'Yes. Right. Of course. Quite moving. I've always held a deep admiration for poets and their ability to make us feel so much with so little. A few words placed in just the right order and a kingdom is forsaken, the moon within arm's reach.'

'Indeed. My own admiration extends to the woman seeking to improve her mind by reading.'

She bobbed her head, but her eyes could not reach his. A raw ache bloomed in her chest.

The caw of a magpie provided some relief, something else on which she might focus. She lifted her head and scanned the tree standing tall, its weathered branches scraping the house and several upper windows.

'Do you see that?' She gestured towards the orange and gold and green canopy above.

St Germain answered in the negative.

'The flash of white.' Anabel cocked her head and squinted her eyes. 'If I were as inclined to wagering as your friend the duke, I'd bet that's Sir Marcus's missing handkerchief.'

12

Sitting in the drawing room after dinner, in want of occupation beyond the exceedingly dull card game being played between herself, Hero, Lady Hester, and Ellena, Anabel wondered if perhaps Lady Cecilia had simply perished of boredom. Even Pip was spread long, belly up and eyes closed, on a sofa.

The events of her morning proved the most exciting of her day. She and St Germain had not been successful in seeking out Sir Marcus once returned to the house. That gentleman, in point of fact, was not seen by anyone until he presented himself at the correct time when everyone gathered to dine. His absence was of some small interest to Anabel, but she had been prevented from thinking further on the matter by the arrival of Ellena and Franny in the hall. The younger woman insisted on showing Anabel the purchases she'd made on her errand to the village, including a length of ribbon she'd intended to wear to dinner but whose colour she no longer felt certain of.

Presently, Anabel cast a bored, furtive glance round the elegant space, silent except for the persistent crackle of the fire and hiss of cards gliding along one another: Franny and Lady Marrow were sipping port near the fire; St Germain and Freddy were playing chess while the other gentlemen watched.

Searching a moment for some conversation, she said brightly to Lady Hester, 'That's a very beautiful locket.'

A faint sweep of pink dusted the lady's cheeks, and she touched the oval of gold hanging from her neck. 'Thank you. A gift I cherish.'

The foursome lapsed once more into quiet until Hero spoke. 'Did anyone hear Mr Roberts speaking at dinner of some ruins he came upon while out for a ride?'

Anabel had spent the duration of the meal mired in the bogs of her own mind.

'You must be speaking of Blackthorn Court,' chimed Franny from her place of repose. 'Quite haunted, you know. When we are graced with a fine day, we may make a merry party to visit the place. It will be a great adventure, which I know you young people are fond of.'

The word *haunted* piqued Anabel's interest. Sir Marcus's handkerchief had turned up, but she had yet to determine what had been in the hall her first night, nor had she come any closer to discovering what had happened to Lady Cecilia. She had found herself growing increasingly desperate for distraction and wished everyone might retire for the night, so she may prowl about the house searching out clues.

'A diverting scheme sure to please.' Mr Glassbrook's casual tone drifted through the room. 'Near my own family's home, there are the remains of an old abbey. Centuries ago, it was the beating heart of the county, but it fell to ruins after a string of unnatural deaths, when the House of Stuart reigned.'

Anabel looked up from her cards to track his movement from where he'd been standing by the other gentlemen to a chair near the mantle. He dropped into the seat, tugged the edge of his sleeve as if preoccupied, and leaned back, letting his legs stretch in front of him.

'One nun,' he went on, 'I can't recall her name—perhaps Sister Agnes, or maybe it was Agatha. Hero, do you remember?'

Hero tossed her cards down and left the table, crossing closer to her brother. 'Agnes, I believe. She was the one who oversaw the cooking of all the meals and was accused of poisoning dishes.'

'Oh dear,' fretted Lady Marrow, taking a generous swill of her port.

'The sister proclaimed her innocence, of course,' continued Mr Glassbrook, in a lowered voice. 'She reminded her peers she was a woman of God, but it mattered not. Without any other explanation, and motivated by the desire to explain away the inexplicable, Sister Agnes was held responsible for the six bodies buried.'

A piece of wood in the fireplace popped, the sudden, violent sound eliciting several small cries from the women.

Despite the lick of an angry flame, a chill settled over the room. Anabel wandered to the couch on which Franny was settled and stood behind it, to better see Mr Glassbrook and listen to the story.

'There was another nun, one who Sister Agnes had accused of heresy. Sister Agnes claimed to have seen this lady pouring something from a vial into a pot of stew. Her complaints were given no more consideration than the pleadings of a deranged and desperate woman, and she was afforded no trial. The abbess was a hard, harsh woman who believed only God could dole out forgiveness.'

Freddy and St Germain finally abandoned their game of chess, the latter filling the empty space next to Anabel.

'Around the back of the abbey, a new refectory was being built. As punishment for her alleged crimes, Sister Agnes was walled up, still alive, during a full moon. God would spare her life, the abbess said, if the sister were truly innocent of the crime.'

Anabel's skin turned to gooseflesh when the superfine material of St Germain's coat brushed her bare forearm. A whisper of space separated his hand from hers, where it hung idle in the folds of her dress. The slightest shift…Her fingers tingled.

'It is said her restive spirit wanders the ruins at night, her mournful wails blending with the howling wind. Those who dare venture during the full moon speak of feeling icy draughts tickle the fine hairs on their necks, and a chill that seeps so deep into their bones, hours spent in front of a fire cannot warm them.'

St Germain had gone very, very still beside her.

'Worse still, they say, is a noise you will never forget. A noise that has driven some people mad, the way it wheedles into their brain and follows them long after they've left the ruined abbey. A harsh, persistent scratching sound, like nails on stone clawing their way back to the living.'

Like the sound Anabel had heard two nights prior. A chill murmured at her back in a silvery voice, teasing secrets only known by the heartbeat of the house. The room descended into a state of profound disquietude. Shadows cast by the fire grew in length, and candle flames trembled on their wicks, the light itself recoiling from the tale being told.

In one small, swift motion, Anabel grabbed St Germain's hand and whispered, 'Boo.'

He jumped, startling shrieks from half the guests. An uneasy ripple of laughter followed, slowly giving way to genuine amusement.

'You, Miss Boyton, are the worst.' But he said so through the quirk of his lips.

Saint remained sitting in his study hours after the house had gone to sleep. The fire had burned down to embers, bright heat pulsing over cracked remnants of wood. In his hand, a glass of brandy, which he churned but didn't sip. He stared past the black tips of his shoes, blind to the fine pattern woven into the rug. An enchanting face and mischievous countenance crowded every corner of his mind.

The faint scrape of an old latch being opened intruded upon his thoughts, uninvited and unwelcome. Saint stiffened. His hearing sharpened, and he listened for something more—hushed voices, careful footfall, the rustle of someone or something moving through the corners of the night.

He pushed up from the chair and approached the door connecting the study and the library, which stood a little ajar. The action savoured strongly of trepidation, and he dug the tips of his fingers into the hard muscle of his chest, hoping to ease the pain of his racing heart. After a lengthy and fruitless effort to pull in a calming breath, he wiped the cold sweat gathering in his palms on his breeches and slowly edged open the door just enough to peer into the library.

It was empty, but something moved in the dark—a shape, a shadow, a spectre—on the terrace just beyond the French doors. In a few quick strides, he crossed the room and seized the handle. He stared for a moment at his hand where it gripped the cool brass. He recognised the flesh as his own, the flex and tense of his tendons, but his body was cautioning him from going further, and a flare of warning went off in his mind.

He set his jaw, squared his shoulders, and swung the door wide. A soft cacophony of sound met him as he stepped out into the gloom: the hoot of an owl in the trees; the rustle of leaves in a brittle wind; the chatter of animals readying to survive an uncertain winter. When his vision had adjusted to the blackness, he saw a feminine figure taking quick steps over the stretch of lawn between the house and the treeline, reddish golden hair falling down her back.

Saint was faintly aware of the tension in his core uncoiling, and impulse carried him further from the house in Miss Boyton's wake. Still several paces behind her, he called her name, trying to balance a whisper with a shout.

She stopped and turned, pausing at the edge of the wood.

'What in the high heavens are you about?' he asked, when he'd caught up with her.

Her hair was loose, and a few shorter strands curled about her face. A deep blue fur-lined velvet cloak draped her body. She held it closed at the chest with her hand, but the silk of her dressing gown peeped through.

'You cannot just march out into the dead of night by yourself.'

'I'm not. You're with me.'

'I am n—' Before he could refute her claim, she'd taken off again, and he had little choice but to follow. Her stride was quick, and he trotted to cover the distance between them. 'What are you doing out here at this hour? Do I even want to know?'

She cut her movement short and spun to face him. 'What are *you* doing?'

'I heard a noise in the library.' It was an honest answer, but he questioned whether he would have tailed after the cloaked figure if it had been anyone but her.

'And so you followed me?'

'To ensure your safety.' He shifted from one foot to the other.

She regarded him with an assessing stare before finally obliging him with an answer. 'I was standing at one of the windows in my room when I caught sight of a flicker of light, bright when countered by the black night.'

This declaration both startled and concerned him. 'Where?'

'Moving through the garden towards the treeline,' she said, with a gesture to the pathway unfolding in front of her. 'I thought perhaps whoever—or whatever—it is, was making for the cottage.'

Indeed, he had followed her down the trail, and they were nearing the little building faster than he'd like. If it was someone up to no good—and why wouldn't they be, given the hour?—the last thing he wanted was to risk her safety.

'You ought to return to the house.'

'Gallant, to be sure, but I'm not the one who runs from my own shadow.'

His impulse was to deny her claim, but he settled for narrowing his eyes.

'If either of us is poised to confront some unknown entity,' she drawled through a disarming smile, 'I can't help but feel I'm the better choice of the two of us.'

'I'm not sure I could name a single person who wouldn't startle when set upon unexpectedly. All the same, you're a guest in my home, and I would never forgive myself should harm befall you.'

Silence descended, cradled in the slim distance between

them. The moon was pinned to the darkness somewhere high above the tree canopy, leaving him to wonder if the quick crease between her brows was just a trick of the shadows.

At length, she said, 'How very right of you.' For Miss Boyton, the few syllables appeared sufficient to do away with his concerns, and she continued forward. He once more hurried to meet her.

The cottage came into view, but no glow emanated from within. Undeterred, and in tacit agreement, they moved towards the little gate. It was closed, and Saint was sure if someone had opened it on their way inside, they would have heard the shrill wail of the hinge. Still, he felt they ought to be certain. He lifted a hand, imploring Miss Boyton remain where she stood, then stretched one leg over the fence, followed by the other—something her long, heavy garments prohibited her from doing unless she wished to hike them up to her waist. The thought stiffened his every muscle.

He moved towards one of the windows and, exercising a great deal of caution, looked in. The small lounge was as desolate inside as it had appeared from out. He waited, in the unlikely event someone had entered but had snuffed the lamp. After a minute passed with no indication of movement, he returned to Miss Boyton with a slow raise of his shoulder. Her mouth pressed into a straight line.

When he was again on the same side of the fence as she, he began to retrace their steps to the house, before quickly realising there was only one set of footfalls—his own. He looked behind himself to find her standing, tapping her toes impatiently, and motioning down the walk that would take them to the beach. He gave a firm shake of his head and nodded in the direction of Sylvancliffe.

Miss Boyton's full lips split into a devious little grin, and she backed down the path, disappearing slowly into the trees, as if she herself were a phantom.

Saint cursed under his breath and stomped towards her, to her evident delight. Once he was within arm's reach, he surprised them both by taking her hand and holding it tightly in his own. She appeared nonplussed but didn't wrest herself away from him. They advanced further into the woodland between the house and the beach, past encroaching branches and under the quiet composition of nocturnal creatures rustling through the underbrush. The night hummed with life, but his world narrowed to just the two of them.

His musings were interrupted by a firm squeeze to his hand. The unexpected strength of her grip pinched his fingers. She halted, forcing him to do the same. His eyes followed hers, soon landing on the object which had transfixed her interest.

A light bobbed ahead. The person holding the lantern was weaving through the tree trunks, making it appear as if the flame were snuffed and rekindled with each step.

'Beach?' Miss Boyton mouthed, and Saint nodded.

They slowed their steps, and when they came to the edge of the trees, which stood tall and proud on a little knoll that rolled into the sandy shore, they stopped completely. A feminine silhouette appeared in the small window of the boathouse, set some distance from the water's edge. Saint looked to Miss Boyton and felt irrationally pleased when she shrugged, answering his silent question: who was out there?

The whistling night wind tugged at Miss Boyton's hair, and wild strands crept up around her chin and cheeks. She gathered the tangles of loose curls and held them bunched in the curve of her neck. Saint watched, mesmerised, his hand aching to touch her, to trace a finger along her jaw, graze the corner of her lips with his own.

Her gasp struck him like a riding crop. He whipped his head towards the boathouse. A second silhouette had appeared. The two were embracing, ardently.

'We certainly cannot leave now,' she whispered.

Saint found himself divided, having no desire to insert himself in what was unfolding and knowing a scandal occurring on his property could taint him and his sisters. That thought gave way to another. The profile hadn't looked like Ellena, and he didn't truly believe she would do such a thing, mischievous as she could be. Still, once the idea took root in his mind, it was impossible to dislodge. With a resigned sigh, he tugged Miss Boyton a little further from the edge where they stood, enough that they could not be seen from the shore but were able to maintain their view. He sat, pulling her down with him, so they were side by side against the trunk of a birch tree. Her cloak pooled around her, and her dressing gown caught up around her knees, revealing silk stockings muddied at her ankles and a pair of filthy shoes better suited to a ballroom.

'Your least favourite pair of kid slippers, I hope.'

'What was I to do? Spend valuable minutes lacing up my boots and perhaps lose the light? I'll choose intrigue over practicality always, thank you very much.' She adjusted her layers of clothing to make herself more comfortable.

Neither said anything further for a long interval.

'Tell me a secret.'

His gaze flicked between the boathouse and her. 'Beg your pardon?'

'Everyone has at least one. The two people in there, I suspect, have several.'

'What makes you deserving to know mine?'

'Who will I tell? I've no friends.' Her reply was glib, but a quiver of emotion rippled under his breastbone.

'You have many, as you well know.'

'Acquaintances, yes, but not a single friend I would confide in, with the exception of Vivienne; but I promise not to tell her. Go on. A secret confessed loses its power. You may whisper it, if you'd like.' She cupped her hand around her ear for added effect.

Saint stared down into her open, earnest expression, considering his answer. Every corner of Sylvancliffe was shrouded in darkness and death. Each creak echoing in the empty halls signified the groan of disappointment, each gust of wind slipping along the glass panes, the sigh of a dying man. Behind every door was his father's ghost, a reminder of how quickly life could change—how quickly his *did* change. He'd spent twenty years living in his memories. With one simple sentence, Miss Boyton had made the impossible act of laying aside his burdens seem as effortless as breathing.

A quiet but seismic shift happened within him.

'This place has terrified me since I was in leading strings and has never stopped.'

He heard the quick draw of her breath, noticed how she picked at the skin framing her nail.

'I—If I'd any inclination, I would never have startled you. You ought to have locked me in the cellar.'

Saint flashed a wry grin, despite himself. 'And ruin your fun? What kind of host would that make me? Besides, you couldn't have known. The last trip I took with my father was to Sylvancliffe. He died here. His expectations…' He sighed. 'It often felt like he wished I were a man of twenty-something years and not a boy of nine. On our last day together, we went for a ride in the morning. He complimented my seat and seemed pleased when I jumped a fence. Afterwards, we went out on the boat and just drifted down the coast. It was peaceful, easy. He smiled at me, genuine, happy. The smile it seemed he so often reserved for my sisters. That night, he took to his bed and never again left it. But his spirit didn't go easily.'

She put a hand on his forearm where it rested in his lap. He stared at her slender fingers, wrapped round him in silent solicitude, and fought the urge to cover them with his own.

'For more than a sennight he drifted in and out of consciousness—sometimes speaking of regrets and disappointments, his own or mine, I've never been certain. His skin lost all colour, and his gaze always seemed to be looking beyond what was in front of him. The physician came. A nurse was hired, too. But my mother was hysterical, seeing him in such a state, and was banned from his room for her health and that of the twins, who had not yet entered the world. And my sisters—the eldest was in Ireland with her husband, the other two were hundreds of miles away on a tour of the Lake District.

'I didn't want him to think—' Saint's voice cracked '—to think he was alone, that the family he had done so much for had abandoned him. I would sneak in, mop his brow with a damp cloth, soothe him in the midst of a terror only he could see, promise him I'd look after the family as well as he had. Sometimes it felt as if he were breathing in all the life left around him, hoarding it for himself, including my own.' The slow wheeze when his father took in a breath, and the deep rattle between his ribs when he exhaled—the sound of a spirit looking for escape—still haunted Saint.

He could feel tender concern rolling off Miss Boyton and worried that if he turned to her, he would break before he finished.

'So often, more times than I could ever begin to count, I've wondered what my life would have been like if he hadn't become my father at an age when most men were bouncing grandchildren on their knees. I question again and again what I did wrong, how much time I wasted without knowing, what I could have done to get more moments like the one we had on the boat. When I consider the future, I am plagued by doubt and worry, fearful of repeating the same mistakes with my own family because I know no other way.'

His words were swallowed by the night, little bits of grief eaten up by the prowling shadows as hungry to consume his pain as he was to be rid of it.

'That poor little boy, too young to understand disappointing ourselves or others, making mistakes, failing from time to time—those are just varied ways we know we're human. If ever he wished you a man full grown, no doubt it was because the awareness of his own mortality had settled upon him.'

He blinked and gasped for air to fill his suddenly sore throat and lungs. In his periphery, Miss Boyton pressed the tips of her fingers to her eyes—entirely unaware her insight had caused him acute mental disarray—and he caught the rasp of a quiet sniffle.

With the pad of his thumb, he brushed away a tear before dragging his hand back. 'Come now, it's not so bad as that.' He pulled a handkerchief from his coat pocket and passed it to her.

'No,' she agreed in a watery voice, dabbing at her wet cheeks. 'For all that is awful, you will forever have a cherished remembrance of your time with him at this house.' Her thumb traced his initials, stitched in the corner of his handkerchief.

'Valentine Matthias Ainsley. Valentine means strong, healthy. Matthias, gift from God.'

'A heavy burden for a child,' she observed, a note of understanding in her voice, as she continued to rub small circles over the embroidered letters in the linen. 'When we are full young, often only the most formative moments take root in our minds, and memory is a powerful thing, the way it can reach back and grab only what it wants. Undoubtedly, there are other happy instances in your conscience waiting to be rediscovered.'

His body tensed, contracting around a feeling he wasn't yet ready to name. Needing to distract himself, he said, 'Your turn. And don't pretend you have no secrets—you just admitted to it.'

'I did nothing of the sort.'

'You said everyone has at least one.'

The intermission after he spoke was a long one. Miss Boyton picked at the edge of his handkerchief without seeming to realise it. When a single orange leaf dropped into her lap, she startled, almost imperceptibly.

Eventually one corner of her mouth lilted upwards. 'When I was a child, I wanted to go to Astley's school and grow up to perform on my horse. Such a dream was impossible to follow, of course, but I taught myself how to juggle.'

His brows rose with interest, but he said, with a slight bump of his shoulder into hers, 'I give you something that has tormented me my whole life, and you give me juggling?'

'Perhaps I have no other secrets to choose from.' She replied with a light laugh, but there was an undercurrent of bitterness in her words that made him doubt her statement.

'Tomorrow, you will have to prove it to my satisfaction.'

'Or what?'

He had leaned in, or maybe she had. The warmth of her arm rolled down his own and filled him with needy heat. He was captivated by her mouth, the way her lips remained parted after she issued her challenge, the way her tongue ran over them before retreating once more into a space he wished his own could explore.

'Or I claim a pledge of my choosing.'

If he tipped his head, only a little more, he'd know whether she tasted of vanilla or melted chocolate or apples and cinnamon.

An owl hooted from a branch somewhere above. Miss Boyton didn't jump, but he heard her harsh inhale and felt a rift in the spell around them. She yawned behind her hand but didn't scoot away. He fought the urge to wrap his arm around her and forced his gaze from her face. Shoulder to shoulder, they watched the boathouse, the only sound between them that of the small, soft waves pulling the sand back out to sea.

13

A chill was seeping into Anabel's bones. On her cheeks lingered delicate, clinging moisture. She shivered and fumbled behind her for the counterpane, thinking the bed felt much harder than she remembered and cursing herself for not stoking the fire before she went to sleep.

Rather than sinking into silk and soft down, her hand landed with a crunch. She wrapped her fingers around whatever had made the noise, squinted one eye open, and discovered she was holding a clump of leaves and loamy earth.

'What on earth?' Her voice was hoarse with sleep, and her vision hadn't yet adjusted to the faint light of morning. She looked up. High above her, grey sky was scattered between the treetops. Her heavy eyelids dropped only to snap open a second later. 'Trees!'

Beside her, a deep groan of displeasure.

A rush of memory from the night before made her head pound. She dropped the foliage and stretched a hand across her forehead to squeeze her temples. The rhythmic throbbing intensified with her growing awareness of the situation. She and St Germain were entwined like the roots of the birch—his arm under her, her leg threaded between his. Fragments of bare skin absorbed the memory and imprinted it on muscle and bone.

She put a hand on his chest. She could feel the latent power contained beneath his coat and wondered what his naked flesh would feel like under her palm, her lips, her body. Beads of sweat prickled in her hairline and all down the dip of her spine. She pushed herself halfway up.

Eyes still closed, St Germain reached out to pull her back down to him. His knuckles grazed her breast when he wrapped his hand around her arm. The unexpected touch caused a twinge of wanting at the juncture of her legs.

She couldn't afford to tarry over the feeling and shook him, unable to stop the torrent of 'Get up, get up, get up,' tripping breathless from her mouth, one syllable chasing after the other.

'Since when do you only speak in multiples, imp?'

'Since we fell asleep outside—together—my lord.'

St Germain shot up, knocking her off her balance. She landed with a thump on her rear.

'Can you perhaps refrain from making this worse?' She ground out the words, adding a glare for effect. 'How did you let this happen?'

He cast a quick look around. 'This is a *we* problem, wouldn't you agree?'

'I'll agree to anything, so long as you tell me how we're to fix this.'

A flash of humour crossed his face. 'Anything?'

Anabel blinked. It was impossible to mistake the provocative tone of his voice, despite every instinct within her railing at such a conclusion. On a confused growl, she thrust her hand out in an ineffectual attempt to topple him.

He made a gesture of supplication. 'Very well, very well.' Dipping a hand into his pocket, he checked his watch. 'It's only half five, which will make it much easier to smuggle you back.'

'Just me?'

'You're going to make me say it?'

She huffed. 'Because you're a man? Because you've no virtue to compromise?'

St Germain answered by standing and pulling her up with him. He rubbed a hand over his angular jaw and up to his cheek. Anabel was momentarily distracted by the sight of fine blond whiskers smattering his face and the scratching noise they made when his hand glided across them. Her fingers twitched with curiosity and want.

'The terrace door in the library will have remained unlocked.'

She cast one last glance towards the boathouse, standing dark and empty under the few stars still clinging to the dawning sky, before they began to wend their way through the trees. Another problem presented itself at the edge of the wood, where it met the formal garden. Once she stepped out from the cover of dewy trunks and wet leaves, she would be visible from any of the windows on that side of the house.

St Germain faced her, and she flinched when his fingers skimmed her cheekbone. His indifference had always prevented Anabel from searching for meaning in his touches.

'You've got a little sand. Close your eyes.'

Her eyelids fluttered, her mind turning over new possibilities with a mix of longing and disbelief. She waited for the brush of warm skin, or perhaps soft linen. Instead, she felt the heat of his hands as his palms cradled her face. The blood in her veins surged like a frantic tide, and her whole body tightened with anticipation.

A mild gust of air tickled her skin. Not wind. St Germain blowing the sand away. Her mind grabbed at a sliver from her past, tucked away for safekeeping. His breath was a cool contrast to the hot swirl of desire and uncertainty within her.

The soft current ceased, but his hands remained. He grazed a thumb over her burning cheek and along the ridge of her jaw, then edged his fingers into the hair at the nape of her neck, sending a shiver from her scalp down her spine to the tips of her toes.

A faint, rough noise slipped from him, and Anabel's cheeks grew suddenly cold. Her lashes lifted, and the world came into view once more. He had taken a small step back but brushed a leaf from her cloak.

'There's nothing so odd about an early morning walk, and your slippers are caked in enough mud you may pass them off as boots.'

She found it impossible to advance towards the house and away from his lilting smile and careful ministrations.

'Go on,' he said.

Anabel remained fixed to the ground where she stood.

'I suppose I could carry you back, although that will likely give rise to the kind of talk we're trying to avoid.'

Finally she forced one foot forward.

'Miss Boyton.' St Germain captured her hand as she moved past him. 'I've never questioned your honour, nor would I ever allow anyone else to.'

Her nod was slow, heavy, like his words where they settled in her chest. If they failed to come through unscathed, he was willing to marry her to protect her reputation. The offer was one any honourable gentleman would make. Anabel accepted it as such and dismissed it with equal swiftness. She would flee the country before adding to his burdens.

She retrieved her hand from his and wandered towards the house, adopting the casual stroll of someone who had not woken with twigs in her hair and who had not begun to doubt truths she'd considered self-evident.

Without looking back, she knew St Germain's intense gaze followed her, waiting to see if an early-to-rise groundskeeper spotted her, or worse, a guest. When she passed the hedges bordering the gravel path between the garden and the house, she turned and made her way up the wide, shallow stairs of the terrace.

Anabel peeped through the library window but saw no maid within. Before slipping through the door, she allowed herself one quick glimpse over her shoulder. St Germain was too deep in the trees to be seen.

She closed the door with care and tiptoed across the room, peering down one side of the corridor and then the other and listening for the sounds of the servants going about their morning work. Everything was quiet. At the entrance to her room, she fumbled with the handle and bumped into the door before it was open. Finally inside, she shut out everything that had happened with a resolute click and slumped against the wood.

'My apologies, miss. If I'd known you were up already, I would've presented myself sooner,' said Harriet, coming in through the servants' entrance to the room.

Anabel pushed away from the door. ''Tis quite all right. I was only out for a walk.'

Harriet, having been Anabel's maid for many years, and well versed in Anabel's usual habits, gave her employer a side eye and stared very hard and very pointedly at the young miss's ruined slippers, peeking out from under her stained dressing gown and muddied cloak.

'Such strange noises I hear sometimes,' Anabel said by way of explanation, her voice pitching higher than normal. She cleared her throat and tried again. 'Something woke me, perhaps an owl or a magpie knocking on the window looking for something else to make off with. I thought a short stroll through the garden might relax me enough to give over to sleep once more, and boots are so cumbersome, you know, particularly when one has not yet brushed away the final tendrils of fog curled tight round the mind. If I'd stumbled into the garden barefoot, I'd have been only half surprised. Speaking of...Do ring for a pot of coffee, Harriet.'

The maid set down the pitcher of water she was holding and came closer, eyes squinted in silent study of her mistress. Without a word, she extended an arm and plucked something from Anabel's hair, the long loose curls caught and snarled in large knots down her back. Pinched between the maid's fingers was half of a veined and stiff red leaf.

'The autumn winds are nothing to be trifled with.' Anabel was very proud of herself for saying so with dignity to match the king's.

'Nor are you. You're filthy. Let's get you out of those poor mud-stained things before this fine room is covered in—Is that sand? Heavens, child.'

Not so many minutes later, a maid came in bearing a tray with a silver coffee-pot and one cup upon it. Shortly thereafter, several others carried up hot water from the kitchen for a bath. Anabel let the bustle of activity distract her. However, when her room was quiet once more, except for the sound of Harriet working the comb through the tangles in her hair, the thoughts she wished to ignore pushed in.

She catalogued each moment spent in St Germain's company since she'd arrived, wondering if she'd misinterpreted every glance, every gesture. The dull ache of unrequited love in her chest longed to find suggestions of admiration and affection in their exchanges, but the knowledge of her own failings cautioned her against putting too much credit in such an improbable notion. She stifled a sudden sob.

'Are you all right, Miss Ana? Did I pull too hard?'

Anabel murmured in confusion. She'd forgotten about her maid. 'No. Not at all. I'm quite well.'

A short stretch of quiet greeted her statement.

'If that is what you'd have me believe.'

Anabel's face felt wet. From the bath water or tears, she couldn't tell and didn't know it much mattered. She cupped her hands, splashed her face, and willed her mind in another direction.

'Harriet, have you heard much about the other guests below stairs? Possibly another lady's maid or a valet has been keeping odd hours?'

'Oh, lord, child. What are you getting at?'

She lifted her foot out of the tub to see if her toes looked like raisins yet. 'What happened to Lady Cecilia isn't the only secret this house is keeping.'

14

Saint stood at the edge of his thoughts, grappling with the tumult of emotions surging through him as he watched Anabel go. He worked his jaw and convinced himself the promise of an offer had everything to do with decency and honour and not those moments between sleep and wake when he'd been conscious of unexpected contentment, of the most restful slumber he'd had since arriving, of the lithe warm body curled into him.

There had been a brief, wild rip in time after she'd woken him when he'd hoped for an unexpected twist of fate—a witness to catch them in a compromising position and force his future upon him. Even as he thought so, stealing away her choice in a husband would only sink him further into the turmoil in which he was mired. He wasn't even certain she wished to be married. Her closest friend had not. Saint's brows gathered, and he sifted through the fringes of his mind, where she'd existed for so long. She'd been out for several seasons, and Saint couldn't recall her ever showing even a vague appearance of interest in any respectable gentleman. Maybe the *ton* as a whole was as much of a slow-top as he was.

He'd spent years in her company—or at least in her orbit—without ever thinking how much he'd like to see her dress on his floor and her in his bed, without ever feeling he'd like to see more of her everywhere and at all times. It was becoming too easy to slip her into a future that terrified him. *She* terrified him. Trapped in his desire for her was the reminder he would, one day soon, need a wife, have children, expose himself further to his father's censure from beyond the grave. There would be more people to care for, to protect, to disappoint. *But not her. Never her.* Saint was accustomed to hearing his father's voice in his head, yet that thought stirred in his own conscience, unbidden.

He tipped his face skywards. The sun wouldn't rise for another hour. When it did, it would be buried behind stout grey clouds. From the branches overhead drifted the soothing autumn song of a robin. He tried to track the bird. It took him several minutes to discern the small brown-and-orange body, easily mistaken for a leaf at a distance. An idea began to take shape in his mind. He studied the robin a moment before dashing off to the house.

Wilde answered the bell nearly as soon as Saint had pulled it, once in his room.

'We're hunting this morning.'

The valet's face remained expressionless, but his 'my lord' held a hint of question.

Organising even an informal hunting party without notice was unusual, chaotic, and done with only one aim: to settle himself, without being tempted to drift to Miss Boyton's side at every opportunity.

'We'll leave at eight. Tell cook to set out a light repast in the breakfast parlour in an hour, and send a message to the gamekeeper.' Saint stripped to his shirtsleeves. 'Have a footman bring water. I'll shave myself. And send up a pot of coffee.'

Wilde acknowledged his orders and slipped from the room.

Saint skipped breakfast, and after the valet returned to help him dress, went to see the gamekeeper himself to ensure all was in order. No one had hunted on the estate since his father was alive, although he knew pheasants were plenty and the gamekeeper had continued to keep hunting dogs.

'What are you about, Saint?' asked Freddy, strolling up with the last bite of a honey cake in his hand. 'Damn near killed my valet when he came in to rouse me. Thought he must be an intruder, early as it was. If you wanted to hunt, don't see why you couldn't have said so last night.'

'Made no difference to me,' said Sir Marcus. 'I was already awake when my valet came in. A quiet noise intruded on my dream, a whisper of fabric or shushed footsteps. By the time I'd rubbed the night from my eyes, only silence remained. I suppose nothing was there to begin with?' The end of his sentence tipped up with uncertainty.

Saint bobbled the glove in his hand, and the article of

leather landed on the ground in front of his boot. He was quick to retrieve it, and when he stood, the gamekeeper nodded at him. He mounted his horse and said to the gathered group, 'Let us be on our way. We should arrive just as the pheasants begin their day.'

The gamekeeper took the lead, the men falling in step behind him.

'In all the years we've been friends,' began Glassbrook, riding up alongside Saint, 'I've never seen you hunt.'

'Never hosted a house party either, for that matter.' Saint could tell his response didn't assuage the curiosity lurking beneath his friend's statement.

'A rather large commitment—raising the birds, keeping dogs, maintaining the guns—all for a day of shooting. A rough and ready one, at that.'

Saint slipped the man a narrow look. 'Pheasants have been raised at Sylvancliffe for decades.'

'Including the ones you've been absent.'

'The gamekeeper sees that the birds are distributed to local families. My grandfather was a generous man, or so I've been told. My father did the same. Regardless of my presence here, I sleep better at night knowing tenants have food on their tables. Hopefully the next owner will feel the same.'

'It's a pity you're selling such a fabled manor.'

'You and my sister are of one mind, Glassbrook,' Freddy said from just behind the pair. The small group left behind the house for the unfurling countryside in easy strides. 'Quite a bit the two of you have in common, thinking on it.'

'Our dry wit? Enviable bone structure? Pre-eminent powers of observation?'

Saint scoffed.

Glassbrook glanced at him. 'You would disagree? If I were the lady's brother, I'd consider your pithy noise an insult.'

'Not at all. I question your assessment of yourself, not of Miss Boyton. She's everything charming and amiable.' The words felt awkward in his mouth and sounded hollow to his ear. Miss Boyton was both those things, but she contained magnitudes more Saint couldn't put words to.

'Undeniably,' replied Glassbrook mildly. 'We had the most agreeable exchange during our stroll yesterday. The more time I spend in her company, the deeper becomes my appreciation of her person.'

Roberts laughed. 'Careful, Glassbrook. You might end up a betrothed man before we see a single pheasant.'

A quick burning sensation tore through Saint's chest. He only realised he'd groaned at the pain when the other men all turned to stare at him.

'Are you quite well?' questioned Freddy.

Saint put a hand to his breastbone where an acute sting had settled, noticing as he did so the tingling in his limbs. 'Quite. Spasm in the neck. Slept rather awkwardly.' He moved his fingers to the correct spot for effect.

Glassbrook looked on, a hint of incredulity in his languid stare. 'Miss Boyton isn't rushing towards the altar, nor am I. Although I confess, I'll be pleased to see more of her in town next season. We've only ever exchanged greetings at a dinner here and ball there. This house party has revealed to me the amusing company of which I've long been deprived.'

'Hear, hear. Let us hope the birds are as agreeable,' said Sir Marcus, dashing off to close some of the distance that had grown between the men and the gamekeeper.

'Indeed.' Saint urged his horse forward, despite the wave of discontent that washed over him and made him yearn to turn back to the house.

15

The entire time Anabel sat in front of the fire in her room waiting for her hair to dry, she practised her most neutral expression, determined to meet St Germain with equanimity, dignity, and not the faintest implication she was analysing every interaction, weighing even the unspoken words against the inconceivable prospect that something she'd been taught from childhood was beyond her reach had any real chance of coming to pass.

At the door of the breakfast parlour, she set a steadying hand upon her churning stomach and pushed in. Irritation brewed like a tempest within her. St Germain wasn't at the table. None of the gentlemen were. Only Franny was present.

'The men have gone hunting,' she said. 'I'd be a little put out, if not for the fact it means Saint has unbent, at least a very little.'

Anabel couldn't sort through her emotions quickly enough to reply.

'Why my children feel the need to write separate letters when they live under the same roof—the expense of it alone—not that they have enough sense yet to consider such a thing.' Franny leaned her head back, her chin angled heavenward, and released an audible exhale. 'I've not yet had a chance to review the menu, and I suppose now it must change if we're to have pheasant. Do you mind?'

Anabel stilled at the sideboard where she was filling her plate. The request was perfectly reasonable. Every lady of her station had been reared to run a large house.

'Not at all.'

It was the only answer she could give, unless she claimed sudden illness and fled the room. She let the piece of toast she'd skewered drop back into the chafing-dish, her appetite diminished. Willing her hands to stop trembling, she walked slowly to the table and set her plate down next to Franny, who slipped the menu towards Anabel with an appreciative glance before returning to her letter.

The sound of the paper sliding along the polished wood caused Anabel's muscles to tense. The fibres holding her body together quivered with panic. Her alarm made everything worse. There were several short words she could identify: soup, jelly, mint. The rest were a jumble, backward and upside down.

Her vision constricted to a fine point, like a spot of ink on a sheet of blank paper, and her ribs smarted from the strength of her heart striking forcefully into them. The column of her neck grew hot, and her eyes burned from the misery of such a situation. She tried to take a breath without drawing attention to herself and missed the entrance of Ellena and Hero, failing to realise they had come into the breakfast parlour until their plates landed on the table with a faint thud.

'Don't tell me you have tasked our guest with a chore, Franny. Honestly, you could have just waited till I came down. Hand it over, if you'd like.'

Anabel looked at Ellena's outstretched hand. Her mind was slugging through the sentence, unable to grasp the reprieve she'd been bestowed.

'You speak as if we haven't known Anabel an age,' Franny replied, standing to retrieve the menu and take it to her younger sister. 'Or as though determining what we are to eat is as equally taxing as washing the linens. Hero, with the men out of the house and the day a bit drab, I had the sunroom turned into a makeshift art studio and am hoping you will lead us through a simple watercolour painting.'

Hero agreed with alacrity, but the roar of panic had yet to subside in Anabel's ears, and she could not make out her friend's actual reply or the conversation which followed. True relief came only when the ladies finished their meal and removed to the other room—everyone except Lady Hester, who had missed breakfast and whose maid appeared in the doorway just long enough to say her mistress had slept fitfully and would not join them.

Anabel glanced up from the row of paintbrushes she'd been inspecting with idle interest. Disconcerted by St

Germain's absence from the table and by Franny's request, she'd all but forgotten her plan to discover who was in the boathouse.

When she'd pressed Harriet for information that morning, the lady's maid had shared much to amuse but nothing of import. Lady Marrow hadn't spoken to her brother in months after the man said the dress she wore to some ball was made for a girl in her first season; Sir Marcus was jealous of Mr Glassbrook's skill with a cravat and had been trying to outdo the latter's knots since arriving; Lady Hester, despite being the daughter of a duke, was in the habit of remaking her dresses and passing them off as new; and every day, a housemaid found some possession of Hero's left behind in a place it did not belong.

Casting a look around, Anabel swiftly dismissed her companions as suspects. Hero hadn't a naughty bone in her body, and Ellena very much admired St Germain. Anabel doubted the girl would risk losing her brother's respect by engaging in a secret tryst, and under his roof no less. Lady Hester seemed the natural choice—a young lady in good health might choose to remain in her bed for the duration of the morning if she'd been out of it for a considerable part of the night. Her being the daughter of a duke, however, gave Anabel pause. The higher the rank, the greater the scandal.

'Take one of the fuller brushes, and swirl the bristles through the blue on your palette like so.' Hero demonstrated the instruction from her place in the centre of a small half-circle. 'Then, with long strokes, cover the rest of the white space on your paper.'

Anabel's paintbrush was limp in her hand. She couldn't find a care for the colours muddying in front of her. Her eyes and attention kept drifting to the windows and the expanse of green and gold unfolding beyond.

Eventually, a tea tray was wheeled in, Lady Marrow strolling in behind. Franny inquired after Lady Hester with true concern.

Lady Marrow began her reply with an affected sniff. 'Already her spirits appear to be making a rapid recovery. She had the nerve to tell me all my fidgeting about with my salts would only drive her to distraction and keep her abed for an even greater duration. "I've not caught a cold nor do I knock on death's door—I'm merely in need of additional rest. Every spirit can benefit from a period of calm from time to time," she said to me. As if being concerned for one's kin is the greatest sin.'

'Come, soothe your nerves with a cup of tea.' Franny took her friend's hand and guided her to a chaise a little removed from where the ladies were painting.

'I suspect I'll age another nineteen years before I understand how my sister counts such a watering pot among her intimates,' Ellena murmured to Anabel and Hero. 'By the bye, I was rather disappointed Sir Marcus's handkerchief had been found. I'd concocted an entire narrative where Lady Cecilia's lover previously stayed in that room, and her ghost was taking his things as a way of communicating.'

Hero shuddered.

Anabel was opening her mouth to respond when a movement out of the corner of her eye attracted her notice. She whipped her head towards the windows just in time to catch an edge of red fabric disappearing around a stony corner of the house. Her pulse quickened.

'Excuse me.' She placed her teacup on an end table. 'I'll only be a moment.'

Ignoring the curious looks, Anabel walked calmly from the room, lengthening her stride once she was in the corridor. She went through the library and down the terrace steps, pausing to scan the garden. The figure had vanished. A quiet suspicion whispered to Anabel that if she were to retreat upstairs, she would find Lady Hester's room vacant.

Despite her desire to dash into the woods on the merest inkling of an intuition, Anabel turned back to the house. She couldn't very well run amok when a soppy sheet of paper and a group of ladies sat waiting for her in the sunroom.

At the top of the stone stairs, she stopped short. A slice of sun cutting through the growing clouds caught on something shiny. She drew near and crouched down. There on the ground was Lady Hester's gold locket. Anabel dropped the necklace into her open palm and ran her thumb over the cold metal, knowing she was going to peer inside even while lecturing herself against the impropriety of doing so. Very likely, nothing more exciting than miniatures of the duke and duchess would be found within. She bit her lip, paused in silent apology to the lady, and opened the locket to discover a tuft of dark hair.

'Miss?'

Anabel sprang up at the sound of the housekeeper's voice, nearly gagging on her own surprised gasp. Her hand curled around the piece of jewellery, and she tucked her fist into the folds of her skirt.

'Mrs Crane! The unsettled weather is as capricious as the Patronesses of Almack's. This sliver of sun veritably called my name, and alas, even as I say so, the clouds eat it up once more. How I love the earthy, mineral aroma of the outdoors after a good rain. You may find me out here once more when the storm passes through, risking my health for an invigorating inhale of damp grass. 'Tis exactly how the colour green should smell, do you not agree?' She brushed past the bemused housekeeper, her countenance a façade of placidity. At the door, she glanced back. 'By the bye, when you come upon Harriet, tell her I'll wear the ruby silk for dinner, not the violet.'

Anabel hoped the task, simple as it may be, would distract from her own odd behaviour. In the hall, she dropped the locket into her stays and returned to the sunroom. It was another half-hour before they sat down at their works in progress, and she spent every minute with her gaze fixed on the outdoors.

'Select a smaller brush, one that's thin-tipped, like so.' Hero held up an example. 'Swirl it in the darker green on your palette. Now, dapple along the branches of your tree. Go slowly at first. The motion will help you create a full, leafy effect.'

Progress was gradual, but eventually the scene came together—the hills in the background, a narrow river and lush foliage in the foreground. On the tip of her brush, a dab of yellow to add flowers. Anabel was considering her placement when the men strolled in through the open door.

Franny sprang into action and made for the bell-pull, flicking a pointed look her brother's direction. 'We weren't expecting you until dinner.'

'You may place the blame upon the inconstant weather. Rain chased us back.'

In a show of support for St Germain's pronouncement, droplets began to patter against the windows.

Anabel forced her focus back to her painting. A hint of something rich and woody with a sweet finish filled her nose, and she knew he had come near. Her mouth went dry, and her hand with the brush jabbed at the canvas in short, jerky movements.

'If you use your liner brush instead, you'll achieve more definition in your botanicals.'

The sentence slipped over her in a voice languorous and velvety, not the warm, full-bodied baritone she expected. She glanced back to see Mr Glassbrook smiling down at her, a darkly playful glint in his look.

Uncertain what he was about, Anabel said, 'I fear I'm too heavy-handed for the delicacy of watercolours.'

'Allow me.' He picked up another brush and held it out to her. When Anabel took it, he folded his own hand around hers.

The gesture came as a shock, but she made no effort to retreat.

'Like so.' He guided her hand first to the paint and then to the sturdy paper.

At the edge of her vision, she noticed St Germain move towards his younger sister.

Mr Glassbrook bent his head near her ear and, sounding gleeful, whispered, 'I relish being a pawn in your game. Almost as much as I relish holding court before a full gallery.'

'A game implies there is a prize to be won. And, we may put this on record for your files if you like: it is you who instigated this moment, not I.'

Ignoring her statement, he leant closer to her than was proper. 'Is he looking?'

'How should I know when you block my view?'

Mr Glassbrook adjusted his position, angling for a look, and took the paintbrush in their entwined hands with him.

'Oh, goodness.' Anabel laughed. 'You're making my painting worse!'

'An easy fix.' He blotted the streak of colour with the little piece of cloth on her palette. 'If only the same could be said of other matters. Shall I regale you with tales from the hunt?'

'I've never cared much for chasing down defenceless animals.'

'Then I won't say a word of St Germain, or the pheasants. Least interesting part of my morning, despite the handsome plumage, strutting gait, and riveting behaviour.'

She refrained from seeking clarification as to whether he referred to the man or the birds.

'I had the pleasure of once more being the object of your brother's matchmaking scheme.'

Anabel swallowed a snort, which resulted in her choking on a cough.

Mr Glassbrook's chuckle was smooth against the ragged noise she made.

'Just so. It seems we're both adored and envied for our whimsy, dashing good looks, and keen perception. In fairness to Freddy, he only said we have many commonalities —I took the liberty of describing what those were.'

'What a fine line I walk in your presence, Mr Glassbrook, teetering between humour and humiliation.'

'It's a gift,' he remarked, with a dramatic bow and satisfied quirk of his lips. 'I made certain to mention neither of us were rushing toward matrimony. You may put your mind at ease on that score. However, I may have mentioned that the prospect of seeing you in town fills me with pleasure. True, of course. We would never suit, you and I, though we are kindred spirits, both a touch out of place in our own skin. I confess, however, I haven't quite resolved why you feel so.'

Anabel pushed back her shoulders and shifted in her seat.

'In the meantime, we wait for my own matchmaking stratagems to bear fruit.'

She shook her head repeatedly. The chatter in the room burrowed in her ears and a sudden dizzying sensation had her reaching for the arm of her chair to help steady herself.

'You mean well, but please, I—' She snipped her sentence as though she'd cut off her tongue with a pair of scissors. For a brief, reckless moment she'd thought of confiding in him and begging him to put an end to his efforts. Already she suspected her time at Sylvancliffe would haunt the rest of her days. 'I'm not even certain I wish to saddle myself with such baggage as a husband.'

Mr Glassbrook surveyed her from under a raised brow. 'Not the most charming sobriquet, although I doubt he'll mind, so long as it's your lips from which the word falls.'

Anabel made no reply. She was too busy considering whether Lady Cecilia's time in the house had simply driven the poor woman mad.

16

'Not to put anyone in a panic,' announced Lady Hester, descending the grand staircase the following morning to join the gathered company bound for Blackthorn Court, 'but my gold locket appears to have grown a pair of legs and walked away from the chest of drawers in my bedchamber.'

Anabel's hands stilled on the buttons of her pelisse. The only correct course open to her was to confess to being in possession of the missing item. Curiosity got the better of her.

'Do you recall the last time you wore it?'

'I leave it on always, even when I sleep. I fear I've grown so used to its feel, I can't say with any certainty when it may have fallen off.'

Hero frowned. 'I remember Anabel complimented the locket while we played whist two nights ago. Yesterday, Lady Hester, you remained abed for a time. Did you happen to take the air?' The lady's lashes flashed up, revealing a guarded, narrow-eyed gaze. Hero appeared not to notice and continued speaking. 'The fresh air is always restorative, and if so, we'll know better where to search.'

'She did not, poor dear,' Lady Marrow interrupted, fretting about as though the missing object might reappear on top of an end table or around someone else's neck. 'Franny, do say you will have all the rooms thoroughly searched, guests and staff alike.'

With a gentle touch, Lady Hester stilled her aunt's fluttering hands. 'Quite unnecessary. I wouldn't feel the least comfortable making such a request of our hostess. No one under this roof has given me any reason to distrust them, and searching people's private spaces won't endear us to a staff who appear both competent and capable—a difficult combination to find these days. If Franny might simply make mention of it to those who have eyes in the house's nooks and crannies. It has been my experience in life that things show up when they're meant to, even when it seems you'll never see them again.' Her speech balanced dignity with complacency, but the corners of her mouth were turned down and her fingers rubbed the bare skin of her chest.

Guilt gripped Anabel's conscience.

'Franny,' called Sir Marcus, joining the fray while still fiddling with his cravat, 'I'm beginning to think you've had a stern talk with the weather, as one might with a child misbehaving. However did you manage such a fine day in the middle of October?'

'Make the most of it. Grimm says his knees haven't

stopped aching since we arrived, which means the temperate hours are anything but guaranteed.'

'Then let us make haste.' St Germain entered then to announce the carriages were ready and led the party outside to a line of waiting vehicles.

Mr Glassbrook offered his arm to Anabel. 'Indulge me with your company for the length of the journey?'

She extended her hand in acquiescence, only for it to be captured by another.

St Germain's hold was firm, and she wondered if he could feel how her pulse throbbed rapidly in her palm.

'I'm afraid Miss Boyton has already agreed to ride with me.'

Her mind encouraged her to find some excuse, but her legs worked against the effort, following where he led with no concern for her heart, caught between the two.

St Germain assisted her into the curricle without allowing his eyes to come too near her bemused expression. As a result, Anabel imagined his gaze falling on other parts of her body and recalled with vivid clarity the graze of his knuckles over the swell of her breast only the morning prior. Her nipples hardened against the cotton of her chemise, the tickle of sensitivity almost more than she could withstand, and a heavy heat settled between her legs. The mere act of contemplating whether he showed some little interest in her unbound the part of herself she'd formerly considered to be under her firm control.

The open carriage dipped under his weight when he took his place beside her and encouraged the horses forward.

They hadn't exchanged more than two words the whole of yesterday, excepting their conversation in the morning. After an unremarkable dinner monopolised by Roberts and Sir Marcus sharing details of the hunt, about which no one but themselves cared, and an indifferent period of time spent in the drawing room staring into the fire, Anabel passed several sluggish hours in the belly of night arguing against herself. Her initial examination of events suggested she had been the one evading him to avoid any remaining awkwardness resulting from their night on the beach. But then, after further contemplation, she arrived at the incontrovertible decision he was the one set against her company, for reasons known only to himself, but which Anabel attributed to something like regret or relief.

His manoeuvre had upended her conclusions, hard won at the expense of restful sleep and nearly all her equanimity.

She regarded him with a pettish set to her countenance. 'My apologies.'

'Whatever for?'

'My faulty memory. You'll forgive me for not recalling a conversation I'm certain we've never had.'

St Germain made an awkward noise, somewhere between a grunt and a cough. 'Glassbrook drives like a lunatic.'

'You're saving me at the expense of your own sister, whom he took up in my stead? How gratifying.'

'Is it? I am pleased to hear you say so. I'd not been certain my compliments held any weight with you.'

Their exchange tread with delicate steps along the near imperceptible line between quarrelling and coquetry.

'Beg pardon. I'd no measure how serious you were in their issue. Should the opportunity arise, I'll be sure to accept your next compliment with the very right amount of gratitude.' Anabel yanked each finger of her glove till the whole came off, feeling a little frantic for the damp air to cool her. 'That's not a solicitation, by the bye.'

For the first time, he glanced away from the road to look at her. His unguarded expression caused her stomach to swoop.

'Shame. If it were, I'd mention the extensive study I'm making of your eyes—the way a ring of fog wraps round a golden autumn leaf—or tell you how each time you smile at me, my head spins in such a way I'm sure I've been enchanted. I suppose I'll have to pocket such a disclosure for the future.'

Anabel put her bare hand to the valley of her ribs.

The possibility of his being in possession of a single tender feeling for her was so new, and in such startling contrast to her lifetime shaped by criticism, the astonishment she felt hearing the object of her unrequited affection speak in such a manner was so staggering as to exist beyond expression.

To her great relief, he said nothing further.

The curricle carried them through woodland Anabel hadn't yet seen. Orange and yellow leaves blanketed the thick green moss hugging the ground around the tree trunks and lay scattered into the lane. Beautiful but brittle, the leaves gave a satisfying crunch when the curricle rolled over them. The air was crisp with the distant promise of winter and fragrant with the earthy scent of wet foliage, with a hint of smoke rising from a faraway chimney.

Anabel tipped her head back and allowed herself to slip into the safety of darkness. The weak sun stippled her skin through the long branches overhead and burst in bright flashes against her eyelids. With no expectation of regaining her composure, she remained in such an attitude until she knew herself capable of, at the very least, engaging in unexceptionable conversation.

Her eyes flitted open to find St Germain studying her.

She spoke without overthinking her comment or considering why the sentiment was at the forefront of her mind. 'I'm sorry this place brings back unhappy memories for you.'

An indiscernible emotion brushed over his face. 'And I'm sorry it has been a disappointment for you.'

'What?' The word wavered with an uncertain trill of mirth.

'As far as I can tell, you've yet to come across a trapdoor, solve Lady Cecilia's disappearance, or make friends with our resident ghost, the one who has no doubt made off with Lady Hester's necklace.'

'No,' she said through an airy laugh, feeling herself once again on familiar and steady footing. 'Although, I've a confession to make.'

St Germain looked briefly from the lane to her.

'I may—or may not—but very likely, most certainly, am in possession of a gold locket which does not belong to me.'

'Miss Boyton!'

She shrank back into the seat when he cried out, his tone somewhere between shock and censure, although there were identical grins upon both their faces.

'It was very wrong of me not to say something to her, particularly this morning, when she made its disappearance broadly known.'

'Yes, you sound quite cut up.'

The corners of her lips twitched, and a soft heat dawned in her chest.

'You see, the thing is, she was wearing it two nights ago, and yesterday she remained in her room until dinner, or so she claims. If the locket was around her neck before bed, and she kept to her chamber the following morning—'

'Then the locket, in all likelihood, would be in her room.'

'I found it yesterday. Outside.'

'Ah.'

Anabel rewarded him with a broad smile. 'Exactly.'

'You think it was she we saw in the boathouse?'

'Without doubt. Her maid said she'd not slept well—not at all, conceivably—and while in the sunroom yesterday I caught the vague shape of someone wandering outside. Lady Hester searching for her locket, I think. The colour of the cloak also matches that of the person I saw weaving through the trees when I came in through the conservatory the other day.'

'You saw an unknown figure on the grounds and kept such information to yourself?'

She lifted a shoulder. 'There was a gentleman, too. This being a house party, the oddity was in their furtive manner, not in there being people strolling about.'

He pried his focus from his horses long enough to raise an indulgent brow at her, and she counselled herself to temper the contentment overtaking her senses.

'I don't need to ask if you looked inside the locket, do I?'

'A lock of very dark hair. Not Freddy's or yours. Too rich in colour to belong to Roberts, not that he would be so bold as to risk his mama's wrath with something as exciting as a clandestine affair.'

St Germain snorted. The sound was so foreign to Anabel, she momentarily forgot what she was speaking about before recovering her place in the conversation.

'My guess is Sir Marcus,' she said. 'Mr Glassbrook also may be a match, but for all his outrageous behaviour, he strikes me as someone careful of avoiding exposure of any kind.'

He stared at her such an extended duration without speaking, she wondered if she needed to remind him to watch the road. 'More than once, I've considered if you and Glassbrook—'

'Oh, for mercy's sake. Has Freddy been in your ear? Do not answer, and do not finish that sentence. Should I ever meet a lady I wish to punish for eternity with a most provoking husband, I will put her in the way of Mr Glassbrook.'

St Germain seemed to sit up a little straighter in his seat. 'It gives me great pleasure to hear you say so.'

Anabel worked her mind and mouth for a response. 'That is—I—' She broke off her sentence with a loud cry and jerked back to dodge a bird swooping inches from her nose. 'Goodness,' she panted, hand to her chest.

The silence in which the word landed surprised her. She turned to St Germain. His shoulders bobbed with suppressed laughter. Anabel watched him a moment, a feverish kind of giggle welling up inside her. When the sound finally burst forth, it was impossible to contain, and she laughed till her side pinched with a stitch, wiping a tear from her eye just as the ruins came into view.

17

Saint brought the curricle to a stop near where the footmen were setting out a light repast of cheese, fruit, meats, and sweet treats, and knew it was not blood thrumming through his veins but the musical chime of Miss Boyton's laugh. He went round to help her down, but instead of taking the hand she offered, he grasped her waist, startling a gasp out of her.

She lightly took hold of his shoulders as he swung her around. He let her body slip down his own slowly, his touch lingering too long, drifting too close to the curve of her breast. The motion stirred a half-formed memory. He felt her ribcage expand and contract with rapid breaths under the warmth of his palms. Miss Boyton watched him with intense curiosity, her vivid gaze never wavering from his own. He wondered what she could read in his expression, if she could see his admiration and desire for her, if her yearning matched his own. Miss Boyton proved generous with both time and feeling but not her private thoughts, which were of the most interest to him.

Her hands slipped to his chest, recalling him to the moment, and curled around the lapels of his coat. Saint tipped his mouth towards hers, and he noticed the keen way she studied his lips. He should say something, but there wasn't enough space between them for words. He pried himself away just as several more carriages pulled off the small country lane.

'I'm glad for so fine a day,' said Hero, as Freddy helped her down. 'There's something about ruins I always find unsettling, and I don't think I could bear coming here when the skies are perfectly dreary and filled to bursting.'

Saint scanned the horizon to the east. The few meandering clouds had gone, and the sky shone a soft, clear blue, but in the distance, signs of a brewing storm threatened to blanket the day in grey and soak the county in rain by dinner.

Lady Marrow brushed her skirts. Next to her, Franny adjusted her shawl. 'Perhaps they're unsettling because they're haunted. I imagine most are.'

'You're surely not serious,' replied Saint.

'Why ever would you think I'm not? I said as much some evenings ago. You've heard the story of the headless horseman, I'm sure of it.'

'You'll need to be more specific. There are so many headless horsemen in this part of the country.'

Franny tsked. 'The one who haunts these ruins, naturally. The story used to come up at every party Father hosted at Sylvancliffe. Of course, you were rather young then. I suppose you don't remember.'

His discussion with Franny had garnered the interest of the other guests, and several begged to hear the story while they settled themselves on the sheets spread over the ground for their picnic. Saint offered Miss Boyton a plate, which she accepted after a brief thoughtful pause, and seated himself near her side.

Franny looked his way, giving Saint a chance to turn the conversation if he so wished. His lips were compressed in a firm line, but he neither protested nor brought forth a more palatable topic.

'I'll tell the tale,' Franny announced to the group, 'but only if you're certain.' When a chorus of *yeses* came back, she began. 'Many years ago, this was a grand manor called Blackthorn Court. It was home to a fierce and feared nobleman and his family. During a violent, months-long battle, Blackthorn came under siege. The lord was beheaded defending his property and protecting his wife and daughters from a fate far worse than death.'

Hero gasped, and Ellena shivered. Lady Marrow looked as if she might swoon and grasped for her salts. Miss Boyton leaned in. Saint dropped his head to hide the appreciative curve of his mouth.

'As the final blow was struck, his spirit lingered in the air—a restless guardian forever bound to the walls he vowed to defend with his life. His wife, hysterical with grief, threw herself on the sharp blade of a nearby sword. What became of his daughters is less certain. Those who have no wish to comprehend the full horror of the children's loss say the enemy general treated them with compassion and sent them north to live with a relative. More likely, and widely accepted, is that they were taken captive and forced into a life we can only pray was short.'

Sir Marcus grunted. 'Heavens.'

'The story goes that the lord's head was never recovered.'

'Of course it does,' muttered Saint, attempting to focus on what was ridiculous about the story and not the horrible truth of it.

Miss Boyton surprised him by replying in a low, dulcet tone edged in mild amusement. 'A cavalier response from someone startled by his own shadow.'

He shot her a mock glare but warmed under her playful teasing.

'Some,' Franny continued, 'suspected it rolled into the stream and was carried downriver. Others said the opposing army fed it to their beasts. His spirit, restless and driven by vengeance, still roams the grounds astride his great black horse. On foggy nights, the headless horseman can be seen galloping through the surrounding fields, following a spectral light illuminating his path. The chilling neigh of a dead horse and the sounds of hoofbeats herald his approach. Those who hear him coming flee to their homes and lock their doors. When the heavens open, it's not the pitter patter of rain people who live near hear, but the wail of his widow and the sobs of his darling daughters.'

Profound quiet settled around them. Even the birdsong that had greeted their arrival died as the starlings and sparrows moved on to seek shelter from the coming storm. Oppressive stillness, heavy with unease, suffocated any conversation. Several people looked behind themselves where the ruins crumbled into the wild grass and hungry soil. Time and brutal squalls had altered the landscape. Half-buried pieces of flint rose from the ground like gravestones scattered up a hill. At the top, the remnants of a lookout.

The awful tale pressed on the most tender parts of Saint's greatest fears. He wondered how long the family had watched and waited, how many times the father had regretted every choice that put his family in peril, what his final thoughts had been, knowing he'd failed his wife and children. No doubt the truth fractured with every generation repeating the story, but he felt the same weight of responsibility paralysing him every time he thought about stepping towards his future. He brought a discreet hand up to rub his chest and blinked in surprise when a bony elbow knocked his.

Miss Boyton sent him a faint condolatory frown and fixed upon him a gaze filled with quiet concern and understanding. He entwined his fingers behind his back to keep from reaching for her, perceiving as he did so that the pain he'd been attempting to alleviate had vanished.

'Well.' Franny clapped her hands together in front of her chest. 'Shall we explore? Perhaps we'll be lucky and find a bone protruding from the ground.'

'Lord, Franny.' Saint pinched the bridge of his nose.

People stood and began to mill about. Some went

cautiously towards the ruins, and others traipsed to a little coppice of orange-flecked maples guarding a small stream.

'There's a lovely little prospect behind the watchtower, if I remember correctly.' Franny spoke to no one in particular, her attention given over to inspecting a slice of apple held between her fingers.

Miss Boyton rose. 'Sounds promising. Hero, would you care to walk with me?'

A hint of hesitation flashed across Miss Glassbrook's countenance. 'I'd thought to sketch an interesting grouping of flowers I saw as we settled, but I daresay they will keep for another day.'

'There is not the least need for you to sacrifice your pleasure for my own. I am perfectly capable of walking without assistance.'

'Allow me.' Saint presented his arm in invitation, feeling himself desperate for her company. 'I've heard startling reports of wild and reckless birds swooping without a care for charming bonnets or fine faces at risk of grave injury.' That wasn't true at all, of course, but the gleam in her eye told him she appreciated his remark. A dangerous sense of satisfaction bloomed within him.

'Perhaps it is you who wishes for my escort,' she said, when they were a little separated from the others. 'The grass may still be wet in some places, and you no doubt wish me to break your fall.'

'I've known your family—your parents, brothers, sisters, *you*—for more of my life than not, but this tormenting creature who appeared at Sylvancliffe is rather a mystery to me.'

'Teasing.' Miss Boyton grinned. 'Not tormenting.'

'Do you take nothing seriously, not even yourself?' The question was gently put, although asked with real interest.

'I've no wish to be taken seriously, only to be taken as I am.'

He stared a moment, speechless by her declaration. 'Who are you, Miss Boyton? I cannot puzzle out the whole of you, although I'd very much like to.'

She laughed, but it wasn't at all like the happy, pleasing sound from earlier. 'My own family could not make such a claim. They seem to forget about me half the time, what with a gaggle of brothers and sisters, many of whom are having their own families. It's easy to go on unnoticed, which I suppose must be the better alternative to receiving attention for reasons of dishonour or disrepute. You cannot understand, because you are impossible to overlook, to ignore.'

Heat crept up Saint's neck and into his cheeks, and an inexplicable sadness filled his chest, a softer shade of grief. She was all he saw, and each day his eagerness to be near her, to discover more of her, increased.

'You don't give yourself enough credit, Miss Boyton.'

Her brows scrunched together. 'Beg pardon?'

'If you think you have escaped everyone's notice. Nothing would astonish me more than to learn I am the only one who perceives a woman with the remarkable ability to make the people she's speaking to feel heard, not just listened to with polite but feigned attentiveness. A woman with a benevolent spirit, delightfully overactive imagination, and a twinkle of mischief lurking in her canny, observant eyes. In being true to yourself, you encourage others to do the same.' The last bit startled him as much as the whole of his speech seemed to surprise her. A strange emotion skipped across her face that he couldn't decipher—incredulity, or perhaps uncertainty.

She looked poised to speak, but tripped on her next step. A gasp ruffled the air around them.

He reached out to catch her with his free arm and wrenched her back. Her slender frame slammed into his. The softness of her breasts gave when held to the solid plane of his chest, and he hardened instantly. She dropped her stare to the seam of their bodies. When her gaze came up, her look was examining, and her lips somehow closer to his own. Her perfect lips, the colour of pink honeysuckle in the summer, with a gentle crescent at the top.

'Are you all right?' His voice was hoarse with desire.

Miss Boyton nodded, and her fingers compressed around the mound of his bicep where they'd settled.

Saint dipped his head and let himself drift nearer.

Her mouth parted. He trailed his hands up her back and curled his fingers in the fine hairs at the base of her neck, warm from the gentle autumn sun.

The anticipation in the hitch of her breath turned his skin to gooseflesh and made him tremble.

'Beg pardon! My apologies. I—I—no matter.' Miss Glassbrook spun in an awkward circle, several of her sketching pencils falling from the clutch of items in her arms.

He flung Miss Boyton from him with such force, she would have tumbled to the ground had he not caught her hand in his own—a hand which she immediately snatched back and used to smooth her skirts before rushing forward to help Miss Glassbrook retrieve her things.

'Hero, have you come to draw the view? It's lovely indeed.'

'Yes—no.'

Saint knelt to pick up a pencil. A fat, wet drop landed cold upon his hot cheek.

Miss Glassbrook's wide-eyed gaze jumped between them. 'Franny wished me to collect you both before the rain begins in earnest.'

'Of course.' Miss Boyton gave a jerky nod and rose to stand, the movement stiff and a little uncoordinated. 'Of course, we—I—certainly have no wish to keep anyone lingering in foul weather. How awful to be the cause of a cold, should one of the ladies—or men—catch one. Have you all your pencils?' Miss Boyton turned quickly around herself, captivated by the ground beneath her feet.

'Yes. I thank you. Both of you.'

Saint offered his assistance to Miss Glassbrook where she crouched, which the young lady accepted but dispensed with as soon as she had righted herself. Once on her feet, she took several steps back, the three of them forming an uncomfortable silent triangle.

Miss Glassbrook looked skyward, but Saint hadn't a care for the weather. He watched Miss Boyton, desiring only to know what she was thinking, if her heart raced as quickly as his, and if she suffered the same disappointment or harboured a similar hope. The closed expression she presented gave nothing away.

'Let us return to the carriages.' Miss Boyton bolstered her declaration by linking an arm through Miss Glassbrook's and turning them downhill. 'Did you manage to finish your study of the flowers before the weather turned?'

Saint allowed the ladies to gain a little distance, for their benefit as much as his own. He dropped his head, feeling himself on the edge of a swoon, and his chest burned like he'd held a breath too long. The shape of his life had shifted entirely, taking on the unmistakable outline of the woman walking down the hill.

18

Anabel traipsed down the hill at Hero's side, but she was struggling to outrun the fire crackling under her skin. Never in her life had she experienced such dizzying minutes as those spent in St Germain's embrace. The gentle tease of his fingers in her hair, the glow of pleasure lighting his whole countenance, the growing ache he excited at her very core. Her treasonous body still throbbed with want. In the vein of her neck, she felt her jagged pulse, disappointment and disbelief fighting in each beat. She hardly believed the last quarter hour was anything more than a fever dream.

'Anabel, if I'd known—I cannot express how profoundly sorry I am for interrupting.' Hero's delicate features twisted with anguish.

'You did no such thing.' It was a monumental feat for her to keep from darting a look over her shoulder. A wry laugh erupted at her side.

'I'm an innocent but not so naïve as that. If I'd a man like St Germain wrapped round me, I'd murder the person who interrupted and rely on my brother to exonerate my crime of passion.'

Anabel swiped at several raindrops as they landed on her lashes.

'I'm very happy for you,' Hero went on, 'and Antony will be pleased his efforts were successful.'

'Oh, no. No.' Denying any understanding between her and St Germain sent a streak of pink through Anabel's cheeks. 'I don't mean I make a habit of letting men…' The uncertainty which halted her sentence was nothing compared to her general confusion. No longer could she doubt his interest in her, but the origin of his attraction and reason for it appeared to Anabel as even a greater mystery than the disappearance of Lady Cecilia.

'Of course not. Only, he isn't known for trifling with young ladies, so I assumed…I've put my foot in it again, haven't I?' Hero thwacked herself in her forehead with the soddened sketch-pad in her arms.

'Peagoose.' Anabel infused the term with as much levity as she could muster and debated with herself over what to say next. She hadn't even confided her feelings for him to her dearest friend. A wistful twinge of yearning for Vivienne surged through her. 'St Germain has known me more years than not and has never before shown such pointed interest. Who can say with certainty, besides the man himself, what he was about? Swept up in the atmosphere, as likely as not.'

'Is that lie for your benefit, or mine? People change.'

'In days?'

'In a moment, if the impetus is strong enough.'

Clarity settled upon Anabel. Her stomach clenched around the fruit and cheese she'd eaten earlier, and she swallowed convulsively to overcome the rising bile in her throat.

A little way down the hill, Franny waved them onward towards the carriage, where the rest of the ladies were hiding from the rain. 'Come quickly, girls. You will not melt in the rain, but not all of us look charming when sodden.'

By the time the wet wheels rolled to a stop in front of Sylvancliffe, Anabel's thoughts had splintered a dozen different directions, each one a painful thread pulling her apart.

St Germain had stolen from her the safety of wonder and denial. Until that afternoon, she'd understood herself to be living a prosaic, unexceptional life, comfortable, if not satisfied, in the knowledge she would never attach a man like him, much less the gentleman himself. The truth was much worse. She had been wearing his indifference like armour, protecting herself from ever even having to contemplate a refusal of the future she most wished for.

With only a parting word to Franny, she dashed upstairs for the quiet refuge of her room and hid herself, fully dressed, under the counterpane on the bed. Soon afterward, Pip arrived to investigate, the light pressure of her paws tracing a path towards the tips of Anabel's fingers, which were clutching the hem of the fabric. Anabel let the kitten lick her for several seconds until the door opened, and she folded the blanket down just enough to see. Pip twittered and flicked her tail before jumping from the bed in dismay.

'Tea for you, Miss Ana. Heard the weather got clever with the party.' Harriet set the tray on a table before scouting the room for her mistress. 'Never say you caught a cold. Not like you at all.'

She approached the bed, and Anabel revealed a little more of her person in the hope of convincing her maid she was, physically at all events, well enough.

'Not a cold, mayhap a crisis of a more personal nature.'

'You're too young and too flush in the pocket for such a thing.'

She met Harriet's indecorous comment with a fleeting half-smile but continued to stare up at the canopy of the bed, making a list in her mind of both the advantages and dangers of throwing herself down the stone steps in the dubious hope she might restore her memory to any point prior to her arrival at Sylvancliffe. She'd heard of such a thing happening to people who fell off horses or had the bad luck of crashing their carriages.

Her short reply began with a weary sigh. 'Be that as it may…'

From the corner of her eye, she saw Harriet return to the tray and pour out a measure of tea. She pushed herself up to sitting. When she took hold of the saucer, the delicate china cup upon it rattled.

'Don't fret the shadows, Miss Ana. Wait for the thing to appear.'

Anabel mulled over this advice while the tea grew cold. Several hours later, after completing her toilette, she descended for dinner, by which time Harriet's counsel had permeated her agitation enough that she presented the perfect picture of complaisance. She also had the good fortune to be seated a great enough distance from St Germain to prevent conversation between them.

Her fragile even temperament faltered, however, at the musicale afterwards, when he sat in the open chair next to hers. It had taken years for Anabel to dull the stab of wanting every time he drew near, and in days, her body's awareness of him had grown into an irrepressible force, spiralling through her like she'd swallowed a storm.

'That dress is most becoming on you, Miss Boyton.'

'Thank you.' Her chest grew tight and breath difficult to come by. 'Look, Miss Glassbrook takes her place at the harp. She's rather talented, is she not?'

St Germain's stare bored into her.

Anabel tapped her slippered foot on the floor, the tender sound barely rising into the closed air between them. 'The harp looks deceptively simple, but it takes real skill to pluck the strings as she does.'

He made a noncommittal humming sound but said nothing more. The few bites of dinner she had managed to swallow stirred about her insides in an uncomfortable way. She was on the verge of excusing herself when he spoke again.

'I believe you still owe me a performance. Tell me what

you best like to juggle, and I will send for the items at once.'

Anabel could hear his smile, hated how the amusement in his voice swept her to him as she was trying to pull herself out to sea. She blinked compulsively, trying to scold back her senses and cursing him for not having the decency to ignore her.

'Perhaps you have other talents secreted away: expert whistler, animal mimicry, limerick composure.'

A ripple of applause erupted around them, and she couldn't be sorry for the interruption.

Franny rose from her seat. 'What a lovely performance, Hero. Who might we have the pleasure of listening to next? Ellena? I won't put anyone out, and we may entertain ourselves very well some other way if the other ladies would prefer to maintain an air of mystery.'

Who are you, Miss Boyton? The phrase entered her mind and played over and over, like one finger hitting the same sharp key. By design, Anabel gave the impression her character lacked substance, and her dependence on charm and chatter was now of such lengthy duration as to overcome by superior force the one or two qualities she possessed worthy of personal pride. St Germain's observations ripped open a wound buried with time and long forgotten.

She jumped from her chair, suffering under the vague sensation of someone pulling the meat from her bones.

'Ah, Anabel. Yes, wonderful.'

Anabel jerked her head to look at Franny. Her hostess was smiling; the other guests staring.

'Can I send a footman to retrieve your sheet music, dear?'

The realisation of her mistake happened too late for her to pursue another course. She had not yet added exhibiting on the pianoforte to her growing list of things she would rather do than resume her place next to St Germain but found herself shaking her head and approaching the instrument.

'I thank you, but I didn't bring any music with me,' she said, taking her seat at the keys.

She noted the widening of Franny's eyes for only a moment before the lady nodded and moved away.

Having as many brothers and sisters as she did, some of her earliest memories were of listening to the musicales they put on at Woodruff Abbey. Two of her elder sisters were exquisite on the pianoforte, and another had the voice of a skylark, just like her mama. Even Freddy played, although not ever outside the family home, which was a shame, as far as Anabel was concerned. Not that she performed very often, either.

She trailed her fingers over the cool ivory keys, reverence in her slow caress. She couldn't read sheet music. The notes all looked the same to her, crossed through, too. But unlike sorting through words, when Anabel played a note, she knew what should come next—what *could*—and had learnt to play by ear. Some days, whole stretches of time were lost to thinking up new arrangements.

Before she began, she spared a momentary glance at the grouping of familiar faces. Freddy looked on with a mix of mild astonishment and amusement. Franny fidgeted with a fan in her lap. Mr Glassbrook widened his eyes and slipped them in St Germain's direction. That gentleman had leaned forward, elbows resting on his knees.

Drawing a protracted breath, Anabel shut out the room and let her fingers guide the way. Several measures in, she began to sing. It had been an age, and she was a little rough around the edges as she experimented with the texture of her voice. Her heart skipped when her vision cleared at the end of the song. Sometime between start and finish, she'd forgotten where she was.

She stood and dipped her head at the applause, waving off Franny's effusions with a sheepish smile.

The music had settled her. When she returned to her place next to St Germain, she felt able to tease him once more in her usual way.

'Juggling, playing the pianoforte, and lurking in the shadows waiting to startle skittish men. Those are the only three talents I boast,' she whispered, smoothing out her dress as she dropped down next to him. 'Ought I learn to whistle, or are those sufficient?'

Her question was flippant, and in return, she expected a similar reply. But St Germain probed her with his vivid brown eyes, and when he opened his mouth, his words sent a tickle of awareness up her spine. 'You are not sufficient, Miss Boyton. You are magnificent.'

19

The following morning, while the house was still quiet, Saint slipped out. Fog lingered in the trees of the wood and spilled onto the sand of the beach, stretching out over the water like a cat on the prowl. He cut through the heavy mist and made for the boathouse, a flicker of a smile pulling at the corners of his lips with the memory of waking next to Miss Boyton.

Inside the aging structure rested the old rowboat. Like everything else on the estate, it had been maintained, despite its disuse. With several grunts, Saint lugged the wooden thing to the shoreline.

Clear water lapped at the white paint. He removed his gloves and crouched down, floating his hand about the fine sand and letting the cold sea lap at his exposed skin. A breeze skittered through the trees behind him, the rattle of dry leaves singing a refrain with the shush of water pushing and pulling. A chill ran down his neck and arms.

When he stood, he didn't make any effort to ease the boat into the water. Instead, he climbed in and simply sat on one of the two benches. Part of him wondered—expected even—the spectre of his late father to appear across from him. He pinched his eyelids tight. A scene played out in the dark. His father smiling at him, ruffling his hair. *Valentine, my boy.* Saint could hear the words of praise in his father's voice, grown gruff with age. The man held tight to the phrase, reserving it only for the moments he was best pleased with his son, few and fleeting. But Saint had heard them twice that final trip—once on the boat, and again the last time his father had opened his eyes.

He wondered what his father would make of Miss Boyton, and on his next breath realised it mattered not. Taking her up in his curricle so that Glassbrook couldn't had been an action he'd attributed to an unusual fit of pique. But as he watched her tramp down the knoll, chattering kindly to put Miss Glassbrook at ease, affection and esteem unfurled in his chest in such a combination—and so swiftly— he was compelled to denominate the broader feeling under which both fell and that had left him gasping for air: *love.* The most terrifying version of his future had become the one that didn't begin and end with her.

'What an unusual method you've adopted.'

Saint whipped his head around. Ellena was coming towards him, her thick cloak billowing around her. Clutched in her gloved hands, a steaming mug.

'Did you bring a cup of hot chocolate to the beach?' he asked, momentarily distracted.

She shrugged. 'It's cold out. Shall we? Well, by *we* I mean I'll sit and savour my chocolate while you row. Here, hold.' She held out the cup for him to take, then gathered the fabric around her legs and climbed in. Once seated, she reclaimed her drink.

Saint stepped out onto the sand and urged the boat forward. It bobbed into the water with a gentle splash, sending ripples cascading into the endless expanse. When he climbed back in, the boat rocked slightly, and he waited for the movement to cease before using the oars to cut a delicate line through the undulating surface.

'How is it you find me out here?' he asked.

'I saw you from my window. I see *everything* from my window.'

Saint checked himself, refusing to fall prey to his sister's baited statement. She smirked into her mug. When it became clear he wasn't going to reply, she returned a similar question.

'Why are you out here?'

'I couldn't sleep.' He'd tossed and turned all night. Twice he'd been sure he'd heard footsteps passing by his door, but when he'd taken the time to look, the hall had been empty. The remainder of his restive night had been spent in furious debate over the strength of Miss Boyton's feelings for him—sturdy regard for his own discernment had prevented him from believing her indifferent—and whether she was in expectation of receiving the offer she deserved after they were caught out by Miss Glassbrook.

'You're too hard on yourself, Saint.'

He watched the oar slice through the water. 'You

haven't the slightest clue what kept me awake. Why don't you ever call me Valentine?'

'No one else does.'

Her answer was simple and expected. For a time, his elder sisters had alternated between using his name and his title. But as he grew up and grew into the role, the use of his name had seemed to fade away with his youth. By the time Ellena and Edward were old enough for the schoolroom, Valentine had gone from his sisters' vocabulary altogether. He missed hearing his given name.

'Go on, then. Tell me I'm wrong,' she said, pivoting between conversations.

He gave a short, hollow chuckle.

'Before you approached, I was thinking about our father. How vivid his presence remains despite each year we go on without him. How I've let phantoms prevent me from seeing what's real.'

Saint had kept them parallel to the shore. He watched the treeline grow sparse as trunks and roots and bark and branches prepared to give way to open fields.

'I know you hate this place,' her face twisted with a small frown, 'and so you won't appreciate my saying so, but you have seemed more yourself this past sennight than you have for months. Perhaps it's not Papa's censure you feel here, but his guidance.'

'What a credit to me you've become.' He winked at his sister, who rolled her eyes. He would give due consideration to Ellena's words but was certain a roguish young lady deserved the greater portion of acknowledgement.

'Father never expected a perfect son. I don't think he would have liked it much, anyhow.'

His gaze snapped to hers. 'Have you been speaking to his ghost, then? I knew Sylvancliffe was haunted. I had no notion, however, you were able to communicate with spirits.'

'I've heard the story of you holding up the—what was it, ace of hearts?—however many years ago. For Hazelhurst to shoot, at a great distance. I could never determine if I thought you brave or foolish. Foolish it is.'

Saint set his mouth in a firm line.

'I haven't been talking to his ghost,' she added wistfully. 'Although I would if I could.'

He felt a sharp pang of sorrow for the specific kind of emptiness his sister would always bear.

'I've a packet of letters exchanged between him and Mama,' Ellena said. 'They were in Catherine's possession for quite some time. She thought I might like to have them and included them in the last parcel she sent from Belgium.'

Saint wondered how the missives found their way into his eldest sister's possession and why she hadn't offered them to him.

'You are welcome to read them. In fact you should do so, by the sounds of things. While he doted on the girls, you were his long-awaited heir. You *existing* was a point of pride for him. His commitment to teaching you everything he could before he was gone never wavered, nor did his belief in you. Papa was more stubborn than all the rest of us combined. He wouldn't have left this world had he not been sure of the hands holding us all together.'

A lump in Saint's throat made it hard for him to swallow. He looked skywards, followed the path of a seabird gliding with still wings until it faded against the horizon.

'You're not a monolith, Saint, and you have no need to be. Papa let himself be loved. He hosted parties because he understood the value of connection. Do you know why he married Mama? Because after the death of his first wife he'd felt like the *petals of his heart had drawn closed.* Then they met and everything changed, according to the poetry he wrote her.' Ellena grinned.

His arms locked mid-row, his mind jolted by the discovery his father was, it appeared, astoundingly romantic. He recalled Miss Boyton sitting by his side at the beach, speaking of the way memory was capable of only grabbing at what it wished.

'Speaking of ghosts, I've organised something for the party.'

His sister unfolded the whole of her scheme, hardly taking a breath between words. Although a shoot of unease sprang up within him, he had no wish to forbid something which brought her such evident enjoyment. Upon their return to the house a short time later, they went directly to the breakfast parlour, where she shared her plan with those gathered.

'A séance? Gracious, child! You are a step away from paganism,' cried Lady Marrow, frantically searching for her smelling salts and likely suffering regret for choosing that particular morning to break her fast outside her rooms.

Lady Hester, immune to the outbursts of her aunt, asked, 'Is this a jest?'

'Not at all. It feels particularly fitting with the apparent theme of this house party. Missing people. Missing things.'

Saint curled his fingers over the back of an empty chair and cast a quelling look at his youngest sister. 'No one from *this* house party is missing. I would thank you for not making such a suggestion.'

'And my handkerchief was found,' noted Sir Marcus.

'Very true, although I've been unable to find a little figurine I left sitting on my sketch pad.' Miss Glassbrook sent a rueful glance across the table to her brother. 'Lady Hester, perhaps you will receive intelligence on the location of your locket.'

Saint coughed.

Ellena raised a brow as she passed him on her way to fill a plate. 'It's only done in fun. No one need participate if they have no wish to. Lady Marrow, you may take a tea tray in your room if you choose. Alone, while a spiritualist works to purge the house of—'

'Ellena.' Saint's stern tone put a period to his sister's sentence, and she held the rest of her statement behind her pinched lips, although her cheeks glowed with restrained amusement.

'Doesn't everyone wonder what happened to Lady Cecilia?' she asked.

Lady Marrow shook her head. ''Tis not the way to go

about it, lighting candles and claiming to speak to the dead.'

'Then you think she's dead?'

Saint interrupted before his younger sister could provoke poor Lady Marrow further. 'Who is conducting this experience, and how did you happen upon them?'

'There's a very fine spiritualist in the village. Or so says the local newspaper. I spoke with her the other day.'

'Did she provide you with any proof of—of her abilities?' asked Franny.

'She did not, and I did not ask for any. Instead, I went on my way and called at several of the shops, mentioning my good fortune in meeting such an interesting woman as Mrs Hale. She appears to be well respected in her parish.' Ellena selected a seat at the table. 'I should mention Mrs Hale did not use the word séance and makes no claims to speak with the dead,' she clarified. 'Rather, she sees herself as a conduit for spirits and the like, to communicate with the living. She uses a deck of cards. Oh, and she will be here after dinner, at half nine.'

Two lines of dismay appeared between Franny's brow.

'A protest, Franny?' Saint's question lilted with surprise. 'Only yesterday you regaled us with the story of the headless horseman.'

'At Blackthorn Court. Not inviting them into my home.'

Ellena tore apart a bread roll. 'It's not your home.'

'The point remains the same, you quarrelsome child,' huffed Franny.

Saint pressed the bridge of his nose with his thumb and forefinger. 'Goodness, you two.'

'Indeed! Enough chatter about your séance, Ellena.'

'Séance?' repeated Miss Boyton, just then entering the room with her brother.

'Tonight. It is to be a day of uncommon experiences, it would seem.' Franny set down her knife and fork. 'I have something planned for after breakfast I'm certain none of us at this table have done before or are apt to do again.'

20

Anabel was ready to engage in any activity which might distract her from the unrelenting mayhem of her mind. Every thought when she was awake, and her dreams when she finally fell asleep, were haunted by the man standing behind one of the last open chairs around the breakfast table. She'd spent a fitful night shifting between the sheets till she was so tangled among the linen, she felt like a marionette doll caught in her strings.

St Germain pressed his sister. 'Well? What have you planned for us now, Franny?'

A swell of excited guesses rang out, one on top of the other.

Anabel approached the table, upon her plate, one slice of buttered toast and a single piece of bacon. St Germain pulled back the seat behind which he was standing. Her newfound awareness that she was the object of his attention cast every gesture in a new light. What she had once interpreted as politeness had become gallantry, what was civility transformed into solicitousness. She sat, with a rare shy glance for the man as he pushed in the chair. He moved to another part of the room once she was settled, and she could no longer see him without making her effort to do so apparent.

Franny smiled over her tea. 'It will be an experience for us all, I daresay, except for myself, as I will be one of the judges, as well as Lady Marrow and Mrs Bates, our cook.'

'Judges of what?' asked St Germain.

'Oh! It's the most delightful scheme. I can't begin to tell you how pleased I was when I hit upon it at yesterday's picnic. *Such* a novelty.'

'We will never know, Franny dear, if you don't get on with it.'

Anabel heard St Germain's tolerant smile though he remained beyond her field of vision. Her little grin broadened into a yawn she concealed behind her cup of coffee.

'Very well,' Franny replied, not the least ruffled by her brother's impatience. 'We'll begin by picking apples in the orchard, and then…' She surveyed the company, savouring all the eager eyes on her. 'We'll go to the kitchen and have a pie-baking contest.'

A chorus of surprise swelled in the room, concealing Anabel's gasp when a nip on her toe through the satin of her slipper startled her.

She tore off a small piece of bacon. With a covert glance around the table, she dropped her hand. A rough kitten tongue lapped at the fingers holding the meat, and she was forced to hold her laugh in her throat. Several times when she'd retired for the night, she'd found Pip curled up on her pillows with a terribly lifelike toy bird clutched between her tiny paws.

Ellena stared at her sister. 'The *kitchen*?'

'The kitchen!' repeated Franny, the words vibrating with excitement.

'Capital. Capital! Can't even boil water myself.'

Franny turned to look at Roberts, whose attention had been consumed by his breakfast until then. 'Exactly so! Not at all the thing, going below stairs.'

'I find it thrilling,' chimed Mr Glassbrook, with a flourish. 'How often are we given permission to do something we've been reared to think so wrong? So beneath us? How positively *common*. I couldn't love the idea more.'

Anabel appreciated the undercurrent of sarcasm in his tone, which managed to straddle a line between contempt and delight which she had not known previously to exist.

'Everyone will have half an hour to change, and then we'll meet on the veranda, where you will choose your partners.'

Anabel and the others finished their breakfast with great haste. Less than an hour later, all but one person was present outside. The group turned as one to watch the slow arrival of their host.

'How good of you to join us finally, Saint.' Franny levelled a brief look of displeasure at her brother. 'Now that we're all here, select your person and pick your basket.'

In an instant, Freddy was at Anabel's side. 'Shall we?'

'What? No. We spend more than ample time in one another's company.'

'Ana,' he whispered. 'How do you think pies are made? There will be a recipe.'

The blood drained from her face, and alarm tingled in her veins.

'Frederick, you cannot partner your own sister.' Mr Glassbrook approached the pair. 'Not when my own is desperate for a reprieve and there are so few gentlemen to choose from.'

Hero sighed with false disappointment. 'You know I hate it when you make me agree with you, Antony.'

'Pray, permit me,' interrupted Franny. 'Glassbrook, you go with Ellena. Freddy, you and Hero go on. Anabel, that leaves you with Saint. Lady Hester and Sir Marcus are already paired.'

Anabel could not prevent her sweeping gaze from appraising the secret couple before landing upon St Germain. She detected an almost imperceptible twitch at the corner of his lip. He walked away to collect a basket. On his return, he said, in a very handsome way, 'Shall we?'

She nodded, ignoring the concerned parting glance from her brother. The party set out for the apple orchard, set an easy distance from the main house and down a path Anabel hadn't yet explored. Between them, the basket that St Germain held and silence with hard edges.

They both spoke at once.

'I—'

'Yesterday—'

His warm, open expression was irresistible and devastating in its power to make her forget who she was in favour of who she wished she could be.

'You go ahead, Miss Boyton.'

Anabel protested. 'The thought has already flitted away, landing on a branch out of my periphery.' It was true. She'd not the slightest idea where her sentence had wished to go. She spoke only because she couldn't bear the quiet nestled between their two bodies.

St Germain shifted the basket from one hand to the other and back again. 'Yesterday, I—I—'

Anabel studied his profile, the way he licked his lips before he continued. His back was as straight and stiff as the trunk of a maple tree.

'I was disappointed to be interrupted by Miss Glassbrook but not sorry.' He stopped just at the beginning of the orchard and looked down into her face. His eyes appeared to be searching her countenance for something, but his own mien told her nothing.

The other teams had already scampered ahead, their faint laughter nothing more than sound soon drowned out by the heavy flow of blood to her ears. She was desperate for him to say more and equally fretful he would.

'If you are decided against marriage, or marriage to me, one word from you will ensure my silence on the subject.'

The air shuddered in her lungs as though someone were tightening a belt around her chest, each rapid beat of her heart pulsing in three syllables: *unworthy, unworthy, unworthy*. She clutched her throat in a futile effort to calm the rising tide of disquiet. An uncontrollable lightness detached her mind from her body, and she swayed, at risk of collapse should he say anything more on the subject.

'Miss Boyton?' St Germain released the basket from his grip to steady her by the arms. 'You did not anticipate this thread of conversation.'

She shook her head. 'Not in the least.' Her sight began to return, although observing the crease of concern between his brows and worry in his eyes made her wish it hadn't.

'Come. For the present, let us set our minds to the task at hand and consider how we may best the other teams.'

Marriage. Anabel ought to put paid to the very notion before he could rightfully ask, but her tongue caught between her teeth, and she closed her eyes to the hot swell of tears. She followed St Germain deeper into the orchard. He drifted several trees away from her, his posture heavy and his expression cloudy as the sky.

She paused beside a low-hanging branch heavy with fruit. The weight of St Germain's disappointment bowed her shoulders. She plucked an apple, studying the splatter of red in its pale green skin. Her stare slid back to him. With minimal deliberation, she lifted her arm and threw the apple. It thudded into his back, and she watched on with silly satisfaction.

'What—?' He whirled around, very likely guessing the answer to the question stuck in his mouth.

Keeping her eyes fixed on him, she reached above her head, her lips trembling to hold back a smile, and palmed the first piece of fruit she touched. She twisted it free and threw that one, too. Harder this time, which in fairness wasn't *that* hard, and watched it hiss past his left side. A tame wind ruffled his cropped curls and carried away an emotion on his face too quick to catch.

Anabel raised her arm again. St Germain darted toward her, and she dipped between two trees with a shriek.

'Smart of you to bring the basket closer,' she called out. 'I might not miss my target by such wide margins.'

He came through to the row in which she'd disappeared and dropped the basket at his feet. Instinct sent Anabel two steps back. St Germain was wrapped around her in an instant. She squinted into the silvery light of the sun, muted behind a veil of clouds, her pulse pounding. His tongue skimmed his parted lips. Her fingers dug into the snug fabric of his coat where it clung to his sides, trying to reach the skin beneath. Scepticism whether her acceptance of a future without him could withstand his kiss floated in the back of her mind, but a lifetime of want conquered her reasoning and his marked attraction to her filled her with recklessness. She tipped up her chin and waited for the soft fullness of his lips to claim hers.

'To the house!' Franny came through the orchard, herding the neat pairs of guests like a mother duck shepherding her ducklings.

He let his arms fall, and she lingered longer than she ought before stepping back. St Germain retrieved the basket. Wordlessly, Anabel dropped in an apple. They collected a dozen more as they exited the orchard. Somewhere over her shoulder, the melodic hum of a bee. Under her feet, the rustling of grass as they moved forwards.

In the kitchen, each team lined up beside one of two

long wooden workbenches, which had laid out upon it bowls, mixing spoons, flour, sugar, spices, two aprons, and a recipe. Anabel's breath backed up in her lungs. In the orchard, she'd forgotten all about the written element of their adventure.

She averted her eyes, fixing her scrutiny instead on Lady Hester, then bent her head towards St Germain and whispered, 'Do you think Lady Hester and Sir Marcus have some secret agreement existing between them or are merely entertaining themselves with a dalliance?'

'I probably shouldn't say so, having heard this bit of information at my club, but her father will only accept an earl or better—and it very much depends on the earl.'

'The intrigue deepens. Whichever it may be, neither gives anything away in company. I've been monstrously hopeful of catching some slip.'

St Germain observed the pair. 'For my part, I appreciate their discretion. I'd prefer to avoid being in the unenviable position of hushing up a scandal, if such a thing can be helped.'

Anabel pouted, and he nicked her chin, the same way he had at Miss Kent's picnic many months past. This time, however, his open, appreciative gleam raked over her, with the same effect as if it had been his hands exploring the whole of her body. She transferred her weight from one foot to the other and wiped her dampening palms on the fabric of her dress.

'Mrs Bates, as a fellow judge, will not be assisting in the bake.' Franny earned everyone's attention with her statement. Nervous glances and worried murmurs went round the room. 'However, because none of us have ever set foot in the kitchens, each team will have a maid to help them.'

The assembled company looked towards a neat little line of kitchen maids standing in fresh uniforms.

'Mind you,' stressed Franny, 'they are not to make the pie for you. Merely answer questions, make suggestions, and hopefully ensure when it comes out of the oven your pie is edible.'

Franny ushered a young woman named Julia to where Anabel and St Germain stood. 'You two may begin. Do try to make something toothsome.'

She surveyed the items on their workstation and forced a dry swallow. With a quiver in her limbs, she picked up an apron and studied the folded fabric.

'May I, miss?' The maid asked, before taking the garment and tying it around Anabel's waist.

'Thank you, Julia. Apple pie is one of my favourites. I'm very much looking forward to preparing this treat myself, and I appreciate your help.'

The kitchen maid pinked and stumbled through a few words before finding her footing and directing them to start by peeling the apples.

Anabel released a hopeful breath. With Julia's assistance, she might be spared referring to the recipe at all. She picked up an apple and stared, a little stupidly, at the knife on the counter, wondering exactly how one began peeling an apple.

'Well done, my lord.'

The maid's praise startled her. She glanced over to discover St Germain had already cut an apple into quarters and was using one of the small knives provided to strip off the skin with the deft movements of someone who knew how the work was done. Her brows pinched together in curiosity and appraisal.

Attempting to imitate him, she held the knife in one hand, put her other on her chest a brief moment to settle the unexpected fluttering within, and then tried to cut the apple. It rolled out from under the knife's sharp blade. She grabbed the piece of fruit from the edge of the wood countertop and tried again with similar results, the quiet but unmistakable sound of male laughter rising from St Germain's side of the workbench.

'You'll need to hold the apple steady, miss.'

'Like this.'

Her spirit lurched from her body when he stepped behind her, his chest floating against her back. He set her hand back on top of the apple and curled her fingers under themselves, so her knuckles rested lightly on the skin.

'Now you won't chop off your own fingers, assuming you like them well enough.'

She cast him a dubious look over her shoulder, forgetting their nearness. St Germain's lips skimmed her temple, and she shivered under his tenderness.

Julia coughed.

Anabel fixed her attention once more on the apple. St Germain placed his other hand on top of hers where it gripped the knife.

'We'll go slowly but firmly, or the apple will bobble.' He pressed down, and her hand moved under the pressure of his.

She heard the satisfying crunch as the skin and flesh of the fruit gave way.

'Well.' She wondered if he detected her breathlessness.

He retreated from her, and she ignored the slight tremble of her knees, the prickle of heat slipping from her belly to between her legs, the way her body called him back.

'If you feel comfortable with the task, you can cut the apples into quarters, and I'll peel them.'

With a nod of agreement, she began to work earnestly, chopping the fruit the way he'd shown her. He was much quicker, peeling and slicing at a pace almost too fast for her to keep up with. After she'd quartered all of them, she saved a piece and decided to try stripping off its skin. If he could do it, so could she. She brought the knife to the edge of the peel and began to work the blade between the skin and the apple's crisp insides.

'I don't see what's so hard about—Ow!' The knife dropped with a clatter onto the wood, and she brought her thumb to her mouth.

St Germain whipped his head up to face her. 'Let me see.' He set his own knife down and pried her hand from her face, his careful, concerned touch having a dizzying effect on her.

A spot of blood pooled on the pad of her thumb, and Anabel couldn't suppress a whimper.

'Lady Marrow always carries smelling salts.' His voice was dry, but not mocking. A teasing glint in his eyes accompanied the words and such evident affection she had to look away.

The maid had bustled off when Anabel cut herself and returned holding several strips of clean linen and an unmarked brown bottle.

'Mrs Bates uses this tincture to help prevent infection,' said Julia.

St Germain released her to remove the stopper. She longed for his warmth as soon as it had been withdrawn.

'Hold still.' He poured a bit of the liquid over her finger, catching the excess on a strip of fabric he held underneath.

She hissed at the sting. He set the bottle down, took her hand in his once more, and blew on her thrumming wound. A spray of gooseflesh cascaded down her body.

'Better?'

'*Mine*,' her heart demanded, with a frolicking beat.

'Miss Boyton?'

She nodded, knowing if she tried to speak, not a word would come out. Youthful folly had caused her to fall in love on so slight a temptation as kindness, but time had deepened her regard into an impenetrable binding, impossible to separate from the framework holding her body together. With each touch and glance and word of tender regard, a relentless, unyielding energy stirred under her breast, as though her latent love recognised its own origin. The strength of it, growing too immense to remain contained by her skin, had begun to devour her whole.

21

What the hell was he thinking, blowing on her cut? Saint was still holding Miss Boyton's hand, his thumb tracing circles on her palm with a care only for her comfort and not a single thought spared for the company surrounding them. The twist of pain on her face unbound the last remaining strings holding his pieces together.

'You know how to prepare apples for pie.' A hint of agitation threaded through Miss Boyton's voice and her colour was a little high. She reclaimed her hand, pressing a bit of linen to the small wound. 'How?'

'My sister was wrong.'

'Would you prefer to savour that statement or may I inquire further?'

He smiled. 'One of my favourite people at Belmont was our old cook, Mrs Hartwhile. Beginning at five, or maybe six, whenever my tutor released me from my studies, and then eventually on school breaks, I'd visit her in the kitchen. She would teach me how to cook some simple things—a few pies, kidney soup, artichokes with an oil and vinegar sauce. They're my favourite vegetable.'

Her brows lifted, and she examined him as if to determine the veracity of his story. He hoped his revelation was a pleasing one and watched her countenance for any sign of judgement or disapproval.

The beginnings of a grin tipped the corners of her mouth. 'Sylvancliffe's very own chef.'

He let out the air trapped in his chest, then dropped his head and gave it a little shake. 'It's a very good thing my father is too dead to hear you say so. Mrs Hartwhile was safe from his reprimands, but if he caught wind of my spending time in the kitchen, he would send for me. He felt there were better things for a young boy to be doing than learning how to make an apple pie.'

The sun came in sideways through the high window and caught her eyes. He could see with unspoiled clarity each enthralling ring of colour—grey, green, amber, like an autumn evening through which he could wander forever.

'Perhaps your father would have adjusted his ideas had he known your time in the kitchen might one day win you a competition. By the bye, did you hesitate to join us on the terrace because you felt guilty for your advantage? Or pity because you already knew your guests were doomed to fail?'

'Reluctance. I worried repeating a happy memory from home might somehow diminish the original. I suppose now I've revealed my secret, I can't very well let us lose.'

He chuckled and removed the strip of linen she held to her thumb before reaching for a clean one. The bleeding had stopped. He tied the fresh cloth snug around her finger. 'Julia, are there any ripe figs that Cook won't miss?'

'I believe so, my lord. If you will give me a moment.' The maid scampered off through a door at the opposite end of the kitchen.

'Figs?'

'A secret ingredient. Their sweetness is an excellent complement to the tartness of the Bramley apples. Of course, they will have to be stemmed and chopped, and 'tis better to let them stew, but we will make do.'

She sucked in the bottom corner of her lip.

'If you'd like, I'll chop the figs—if there are any—and direct you through making the pastry.'

Julia reappeared then, setting a small basket on their table filled with a dozen or so figs, for which they both thanked her.

Saint placed one of the bowls that had been sitting on the counter in front of Miss Boyton and instructed her to add the flour. He tried to ignore how much he enjoyed being in possession of her rapt attention and the way a loose piece of hair tumbled along her neck, accentuating her graceful lines.

'Now, this is the most crucial thing of all, Miss Boyton: don't overwork the butter. The colder the butter, the better the crust of the pie.'

She nodded, more to herself than to him. 'Cold butter. Very well.'

Saint diced the figs and guided her through cutting the

butter into small cubes and incorporating it into the flour, smothering a grin when he noticed how diligently she attempted to keep her warm fingers from resting too long on the fastidious ingredient.

He scooped up the figs using the edge of his knife and added them to the apples. When he opened the jars of spices, Miss Boyton paused to watch.

'Sugar, cinnamon, vanilla, a pinch of salt. Mrs Hartwhile sometimes added a splash of port. How is your dough?'

Miss Boyton tipped the bowl for him to see.

'Very good. The second most important thing when making a pie is using just enough water in the flour to bind the ingredients, without making the mixture too wet.'

With her tongue peeking out between her lips, she reached for the glass of water.

He turned to stir their filling, losing countless minutes to his absolute joy in sharing a cherished experience with the person who had so quickly become his favourite.

'Does this look as it should? Mayhap I used too much water. I poured in small increments, but how quickly the dough progressed from dry to moist.' She frowned and swiped the edge of her wrist over her face.

It wasn't the dough he noticed, but the streak of flour across her cheek.

'You have a little something, right here.' He brought his finger within a hairsbreadth of her skin.

Miss Boyton repeated the same sweeping motion but only succeeded in smearing the flour further. He chuckled.

'Don't just laugh,' she pleaded through a giggle of her own. 'Help!'

Saint ran his thumb across the blaze of powder, brushing infinitesimal flecks off as he went and pretending not to savour the moment, not think about how easy it would be to lower his lips to hers.

'You're making it worse, aren't you?'

'Why would you think so?' He wasn't, not really. He had managed to remove some of the white but had also sent some specks to her brows and hairline.

'Oh, I don't know why I would think such a thing.' She spoke in an airy kind of way, fluttering her hand about him. 'Because you hold me responsible for ruining your favourite coat? Because you gave me your life's torment and I gave you juggling? Because my mischievous influence is beginning to take hold?' She punctuated her statements by dragging a flour-covered finger down the bridge of his nose to the peak of his lips.

The playful gesture startled him. He stood still as an old tree, with roots so deep, the centre of the earth knew not where they ended. Humour suffused her countenance, but something warm and lambent, too.

Her merriment faltered when his silence persisted. Seeing her expression dim brought Saint back into his body, and he reacted in the most unexpected way. He scooped up a handful of flour, brought his open palm to his mouth, and blew, sending the fine powder snowing down on her.

Her gasp and subsequent cry of, 'Beast,' turned all eyes in the kitchen in their direction. For one moment, everything ceased—the clanging sounds of people at work, idle chatter, Saint's heartbeat—and then, with a merry, tinkling laugh, Ellena tossed a fistful of flour at Glassbrook.

Chaos erupted. Teams turned on one another, everyone flinging flour at everyone else, until a pale haze filled the air. Saint had a stitch in his side from laughing so hard. He and Miss Boyton had dropped behind the large workspace to hide. The falling flour gave the kitchen an ethereal, otherworldly glow, and he felt weightless, suspended in a perfect fragment of time. She beamed at him, and all the stars realigned in the space of a single breath.

'I don't suppose any pies will get made today. It's unfortunate all this will go to waste.'

'It won't.' Whatever was necessary to spare her disappointment would be done. 'Everything in here is salvageable, even if a thousand grams of flour managed to float into someone's bowl.'

He stood and helped her to her feet. It seemed to him she kept hold of his hand a moment longer than necessary. People began to disperse, desirous of bathing before dinner. Clouds of flour trailed in their wake. Saint would add extra to the servants' pay for the considerable mess.

They walked out of the kitchen together, following the others upstairs.

'I'm nervous.' Miss Boyton spoke so quietly, he almost didn't hear her.

'About what?' he whispered back. The ghost of a smile touched her lips. Happiness almost too great to be contained rippled through him.

'I've never baked a single thing. What if our pie tastes terrible?'

'Impossible. You will have to trust me.'

A shadow of feeling touched her face but slipped away before he could identify it.

They came to a stop at the entrance to her room. She twisted the knob and eased opened the door.

'Miss Boyton.'

She faced him. Some of the flour had fallen from her dress as they walked, but a thin layer clung to her skin and her hair was white as a ghost's. He wished to ask the question he had not got to in the orchard. Their position in the hall, and his own uncertainty he had broached the subject too soon, prevented him.

With his fingertip, he traced a tiny heart in the dusting of flour between her collarbone and the rise of her breast. He heard the breath snag in her throat.

'Of all the days I've spent in a kitchen, none has given me as much pleasure as today.'

A flash of pink appeared under the fine specks scattered across her cheeks. She dipped her head in acknowledgement and stepped inside, closing the door behind her.

22

Anabel stood in her room, a sifting of flour still smattered across her skin, and stared out over the tops of the changing trees. Dry leaves caught in the corners of the wind. A small brown bird stood solitary on an outstretched bough.

In some other life, St Germain had declared himself in the apple orchard, and she had shattered with exquisite bliss, but their time in the kitchen had further proved the impossibility of her ever being a wife worthy of his station or regard. She had managed to avoid reading the recipe, but only because he had been there to guide her through each step. He would forever be leading her, and before many months had passed, his life would grow to resemble a drudge. How soon after they wed before he wearied of her incompetence and total dependency on him, before he regretted offering his name to a woman who would struggle to sign her own in the church register?

She blew out a breath that fogged the window. At the same time, Harriet bustled in, a line of maids behind her carrying water to fill the bath. After they were gone, Anabel walked to the tub and waited for help undressing.

'What's this?' Harriet squinted at something just under Anabel's chin.

'Flour.' The word slanted up at the end, almost like a question, Anabel failing to comprehend how her maid could mistake it.

Harriet snorted. 'Yes, I see that. In the flour.'

She went to look in the mirror. St Germain's heart stared back.

ANABEL'S LIMBS were heavy as she descended for dinner, the last to enter the drawing room. From the corner of her vision, she saw St Germain watching her. She greeted Freddy, who was hovering near the door in conversation with Roberts, and Hero, who complimented her dress, and then made her way to Lady Hester, who was sitting beside her aunt.

'Beg pardon for the interruption, Lady Marrow.' She smiled and reached out a hand. 'Your charming niece promised me a few minutes of her time.'

Lady Hester blinked several times in confusion, but set her fingers on Anabel's open palm.

She separated them from the rest of the company, pulling the young woman to one of the windows and angling their backs to the room, before retrieving the gold locket from her pocket. 'Yours, I believe. I apologise for not putting your mind at ease sooner.'

Covering her heart with one hand and taking the necklace in the other, Lady Hester exclaimed, 'Wherever did you find it?'

'The terrace. While we were painting.' Anabel paused. 'Something had caught my eye.'

'I see.' The other woman's shoulders stiffened, and she cleared her throat. 'How odd for the locket to make its way out there.'

'Indeed.'

Under a guarded gaze, Lady Hester said slowly, 'The terrace is not visible from the sunroom.'

'No. It was the tail of your red cloak I saw.' She watched Lady Hester's chest swell with a gasp and was exceedingly impressed with her ability to swallow the sound.

'Do you know?'

'Suspect, more like.'

After a short period of hesitation, Lady Hester said, 'My father won't countenance a match with Sir Marcus. A better title is more important to him than a better man. We're eloping from here in a few days' time.'

Anabel choked, attempting to smother the noise before drawing attention.

Lady Hester watched on with a wry grin. 'I want for nothing as a duke's daughter, except true friendships and true love. We've planned our flight as best we could to lessen the scandal—and truly, 'tis not so bad; he's a baronet, not a blacksmith. What's more beside, our plight and subsequent flight can only be aided by the renown of the house.'

Anabel's mind was blank with shock, and she grappled for a reply, considering what she would most wish to hear if she had been the one to disclose such a thing. 'Your affairs are your own. Your confidence is not misplaced.'

Surveying the guests before settling a sober look on her, Lady Hester replied thoughtfully, 'No, I don't think it is. You may tell St Germain. Penance for keeping you both under the stars and not in your beds.'

Her mouth dropped open. With a parting wink, Lady Hester brushed past her just as Grimm appeared to announce dinner.

The levity of the flour fight carried through the first half of the meal until Ellena reminded everyone she had hired the spiritualist. The house as a whole held in a breath, worried Mrs Hale might reveal the secrets long trapped in the walls.

Sir Marcus grew restless and fidgety. Twice, he dropped his fork. Anabel dabbed her lips to smother her laugh. From his place at the head of the table, St Germain caught her eye and raised an inquiring brow. All she could do was give a subtle nod.

Lady Hester went on with her customary composure; Lady Marrow drank more wine than was typical; Mr Glassbrook studied each individual, parsing out more intelligence than would please anyone. Under the table, Anabel began to pick at the skin of her finger. The macabre delight she'd felt when first hearing of the séance had departed once she'd realised her own secrets risked disclosure.

The door opened, and a stream of footmen came in, carrying carefully balanced cake stands.

'Instead of our usual dessert course, I thought we'd sample the pies,' said Franny. 'Although there is a cake with plum compote for anyone who's had their fill of apples today.'

Anabel took a thin slice from each pie, as well as the cake. Nearly everyone else did the same, except Freddy, who didn't care for plum, and St Germain, who declined despite Lady Marrow's fervent claims the dessert was a triumph of flavour and one of the finest treats she'd ever sampled.

The bits of fig in the pie she'd made with him gave theirs away. A sudden swell of apprehension gripped her, and her fork hovered above the slice. She pierced one of the others instead. It was good, although a touch sweet for her palate.

'Reserving the best for last?'

St Germain's rich voice sunk right down to the pit of her belly.

'*Nervous*,' she articulated without a sound, an echo of her earlier confession.

'*Trust me.*'

A shiver tripped up her back.

She worked the edge of her fork through the tip of the slice and brought the bite to her mouth. He watched on with a softened expression. Anabel's eyes fluttered closed, and she couldn't hold back the little groan of pleasure when the tart apple and sweet fig medley hit her tongue.

Gradually, her vision focused once more. St Germain watched her still, his stare vivid and hungry. Her pulse skittered.

'I hate to say it, because it's not the pie Miss Glassbrook and I made, but this one with the figs is divine.' Freddy ate the last bite on his plate and filled it with another slice.

'Lady Marrow and I agree,' said Franny. 'No doubt Cook will as well—that is, if Freddy manages to save the woman any.'

He had the grace to look sheepish.

'And the winners are…' Franny left space for the answer.

'That honour belongs to Miss Boyton and me.'

Anabel smiled wide, a gentle heat spreading through her chest.

The guests very diplomatically congratulated them on their success, while Franny motioned to one of the footmen.

'A little something for the winners.' She opened a small box and withdrew two white squares. 'Handkerchiefs. One for each. When held side by side they complete the image of a maple in the autumn. Quite clever, I thought.' Franny passed one to St Germain and the other down to Anabel.

She fingered the fine threads of the embroidery, one half of a whole.

Franny stood. 'Grimm, tell the others that after Mrs Bates has taken however much she'd like, they may finish off the pies. We are for the drawing room to await Mrs Hale.'

Hero came alongside Anabel and linked arms as everyone withdrew. 'My nerves are in an even worse state than Lady Marrow's.'

'Then you may sit near me. It's not the dead I fear.'

Mr Glassbrook appeared at her other side. 'Is it too soon to offer my congratulations?'

Anabel glared. 'Not if you're speaking of the pie contest.'

'Certainly,' he drawled.

They funnelled into the drawing room, where a large round table had been propped up, surrounded by chairs. The great wooden thing was impossible to ignore, but everyone seemed to move about with practised care, particularly Lady Marrow.

The quarter-hour before the spiritualist's arrival stretched on, conversation becoming stilted the more people drifted in and out of their own thoughts. The weight of expectation descended, casting a pall over the room that Grimm's entry only seemed to worsen.

'Mrs Hale.'

A tall, thin woman, nearly the same height as St Germain, entered, on hushed, unhurried steps, a footman carrying a large closed basket coming in behind her.

'The impending storm is an ominous promise breathed to life,' Mrs Hale said. 'Do you still wish to call forth the spirits?'

Each guest looked at Ellena with a mixture of caution and curiosity.

'Yes.' She was firm in her response.

Mrs Hale nodded once and moved to the table, without being told to do so. With the flick of a finger, she commanded the footman to drop the basket. One by one, she pulled out half a dozen thick, short candles and arranged them to her liking.

'A taper.'

Anabel was mesmerised by the woman's clipped tone, her command of a strange room and the people in it. Freddy retrieved a slim candle, careful to guard the swaying lambent flame. Mrs Hale lit the others, giving life to blazes that hissed and popped and glowed with preternatural brightness.

'Extinguish the rest and sit.'

A footman with a snuffer moved to the chandelier in the middle of the room.

St Germain pulled out a chair directly across from the woman. 'Miss Boyton?'

She sat, sandwiched between him and Hero. With interest but no enthusiasm, the rest of the party chose seats.

Weighty raindrops began to pelt the windows, lethargic and loud. The room descended into near darkness just as the heavens tore open. Mrs Hale glanced into the black night beyond and waved an open palm, as if to say, 'I asked them.' She placed something on the table, rectangular and wrapped in silk, and was the last to settle.

With reverent motions, she pulled back the fabric and picked up a deck of cards. She shuffled. Once. Twice. Seven times. Then laid out three. 'A reckoning has begun.

Do you feel the fissure in your bones? Your being? The answer is yours. I've no need of it. What we say to ourselves always grows louder than what is said to us, often burying truth under pretence.'

Little beads of sweat gathered in the shallow dip of Anabel's spine.

'What of Lady Cecilia?' blurted Ellena.

Without glancing up, Mrs Hale replied, 'She will speak if and when she wishes to,' and flipped two additional cards, humming low while she studied the images. 'Do you know what happens when we eat our feelings'—the inquiry wasn't punctuated with a question mark but a piercing, omniscient stare that seeped like rot through Anabel's bones—'they sow doubt in our bellies—of ourselves, our abilities, our worthiness. Only when what has been constructed has been demolished can something new be built. Look forward. Future is another word for choice.'

She swept the cards off the table.

Over the ringing in her ears, Anabel could hardly hear the crisp snap of the deck being split, nor the rustling of the cards being folded in on one another before Mrs Hale set out three more. The woman murmured to herself, cleared the table, shuffled, and laid down another three. 'Lady Cecilia does not desire to be found.'

The room sucked in a collective breath. The candles on the table sputtered.

'She's alive, then?' The question rushed from Ellena's mouth.

'Lord,' Lady Marrow muttered under her breath, holding tightly to the cross round her neck.

'Her truth hides in the spaces light barely reaches, between fractures of wood and stone and beneath a canopy of leaves.' Mrs Hale flipped two more cards. 'She will say no more.'

In one swift movement, she swept away the deck. She shuffled again, but instead of three cards, she set out ten—six in the shape of a cross and four stacked in a vertical line next to it. She fixed her keen, uncompromising gaze on St Germain.

'We come to the real reason the spirits have guided me here.'

In the grate, the low burning fire flared with a sibilant rustle and flames licked the surround. Several guests gasped. Lady Marrow clutched her salts. Hero jumped in her seat. Under the table, Anabel gave her friend's forearm a reassuring squeeze.

Mrs Hale passed a hand over the cards face up on the table. 'Cups, cups, cups. Cards of emotion, connection, the hidden realm of your mind.' She tapped several in quick succession. 'Here, here, here—present, problem, past: guilt, burden, loss. 'Tis easier to go on in fear than sit still in sadness.'

St Germain stiffened, taut as a drawn bowstring. His palms scraped over his thighs. In her lap, her own itched with yearning to touch him.

'This,'—the woman stabbed a fingertip at the centre of a card with a skeleton and scythe—'transformation. The old ways, the thoughts that age with you, no longer serve the purpose—but you've already begun to figure that out, haven't you?' Her slight smile unnerved Anabel. 'Compassion, forgiveness, are always yours to give, to yourself as well as others, have you the courage to make the offer.'

Anabel's nose twitched at the sudden rush of scent surrounding her. She licked her lips and breathed deep, tasting tobacco and brandy on the back of her tongue. No one else seemed to notice the change in the air around them. She stole a look at St Germain and could discern the rapid rise and fall of his chest, the shimmer of moisture in the corner of his eye.

She let her hand drop into the narrow space between their chairs. Almost immediately, the back of his own skimmed hers, his warm skin running along the ridges of her knuckles.

Mrs Hale cleared the table, shuffled again. She laid out new cards, her mouth moved.

For Anabel, everything faded when St Germain's little finger clasped around her own.

Another half-hour passed. Mrs Hale cleared, shuffled, dictated into the strained silence of the room. Then without warning, she pushed back her seat.

'The angels have imparted their final words for tonight.' She flicked her finger for the footman, snuffed the candles with a swift, graceful wave, and disappeared before Anabel's sight had adjusted to the darkness.

The atmosphere in the drawing room could not recover in her absence, and in quiet agreement, everyone retired for the night, with only a few hushed observations between them, and a stout sigh of relief from Lady Marrow.

23

An eerie stillness hung about Saint's bedroom. He could not sleep with Mrs Hale's declaration ringing loud in his mind and his nose still snagged upon his father's scent, a full-bodied mix of tobacco and brandy.

'I miss you.' He set the words free in the dark, hoping his father would hear them, wherever his spirit tarried.

Beyond the windows, angry clouds gathered, swelling low and threatening above Sylvancliffe. A thunderclap rattled the silver candle-holder on his table. He had opened the curtains before moving to his bed, preferring to watch the storm rather than simply feel it shake his bones, but the relentless black, pushing hard at the glass, smothered him as though someone held a pillow to his face.

When a streak of lightning cut the night sky in two, a long shadow cut across his room. Saint's body went rigid. A trick of his agitated mind, surely? Still, he called out into the obscurity beyond the close glow of his candle.

'Hello?'

The question was met with silence. Saint counted the seconds and drew in a quivering breath.

He lay there, hands folded over his abdomen, attempting to focus on anything else—the soft feel of the bedclothes skimming his warm skin, the chill in the air as winter drew closer, the way his stomach grumbled. He'd been so distracted by Miss Boyton, he'd refused both tea and cake.

Just when his heart had resumed its normal rhythm, a creak, loud and tortured, echoed from just beyond his door.

'Enough.'

With a sturdy clearing of his throat, he righted himself and climbed out of his bed, picking up the banyan robe slung around one of the posts. If he couldn't sleep, he would eat.

'If you wish to kill me, do it now, or you'll have to follow me to the kitchen.'

His statement was met with a low groan—the sound of someone shifting their weight on the old floorboards, or maybe it was only the house bolstering itself against the tempest raging around it.

Saint picked up the candle and made his way on quiet steps down to the kitchen, hoping to find a bowl of fruit or some bread out on a counter. He swung his eyes from one side of the room to the other, disappointed. There were pots and pans hanging from one of the walls and a roasting screen in front of the range, but nothing for him to eat. He grinned at the wooden countertop where he and Miss Boyton had made pie and set the candle down.

Then he heard it, between the crack of lightning and the growl of thunder, a rustling coming from the other side of the closed larder door. Cold, cruel beads of sweat formed in an instant at his hairline, and he felt his veins constrict with fear. He picked up a rolling pin and tiptoed across the room. Holding his makeshift weapon ready to strike, he shoved the door open with one firm push.

Miss Boyton yelped and collided with the shelves behind her, causing containers of salt and sugar to shake and topple from great heights above her head. She dropped the plate of cake she'd been holding and threw her arms up to shield herself. At the same time, Saint reached out to pull her from harm's way.

Her palms splayed across his chest, rising and falling with his erratic breaths. He watched her fingers twine in the thin edges of his robe, could feel how they clenched and the material pulled tighter over the flesh underneath it.

A shout of thunder rent the charged air around them, and she drew him closer. Or maybe it was he who held her tighter. He was certainly the one who would have held on longer.

Her slow outpouring of breath was cool on the sliver of exposed skin just below his throat, where his heart beat hard beneath his flesh. Slipping along his neck, the give of fabric as her scared grip slackened. Their eyes met. He felt her relax into him and loosened his embrace but didn't let her go.

'Had I been a burglar, were you going to turn me into a pie?' Not waiting for an answer, she added with a slight downturn of her lips, 'You made me drop my cake.'

'You were lurking—in the dead of night, mind you—in a pantry. How was I to know a criminal wasn't hiding behind the door?'

'Because what burglars want is cake and bread and butter.'

Saint smiled down at her. 'What about what I want?'

Her thin nightclothes did little to conceal the roundness of her breasts or the way her nipples hardened under his ardent gaze. She ran her hands up his arms to his shoulders and gripped him with rigid restraint. He clenched his fingers where they rested in the dip of her waist and watched her tongue trace the petals of her mouth. Need stretched him out in every direction.

'Anabel.' Her name was his guiding instinct.

With a shallow exhale, her lashes fluttered shut, as if the weight of a dream had settled upon her. Saint studied the way the fine brown hairs fanned out on her cheek until she opened her eyes, slow and deliberate. Her firm grip eased, and she filled her lungs with a measured breath. Saint relaxed his grasp, making it easy for her to slip away.

She stooped to clean up the broken plate and smashed cake. Coming to his knees to help, he reached for the same jagged piece of porcelain as she did. His fingers lingered over hers. He began to feel he'd only ever be content when touching some part of her. Anabel pulled back slowly with a quick clearing of her throat. She found a cleaning cloth and began to wipe up the crumbs and the little shards of plate that were too small to pick up barehanded.

'Let me.' He gestured for the cloth.

'I'm perfectly capable.'

'Of worsening the mess,' he teased in a low, caressing voice.

Her gaze sparked. 'It's your fault there's a mess at all. As you will.' She stood, dropping the cloth from between her thumb and forefinger as she did so.

The storm had settled overhead. A deep rumble of thunder rattled through his chest down do the tips of his toes. She padded around the room, taking something from one shelf and moving it to another.

'What are you doing?'

'Getting another piece of cake. You may have frightened the hunger out of yourself, but I remain as famished as when I came down.'

A bang of lightning lit up the whole space, and she jumped. He wished for flash after flash, the light allowing him to see her more clearly.

'You were saying?'

He delighted when she made a dramatic show of rolling her eyes. Then she took her fresh plate of cake and stepped around him, standing at the marble-topped table in the centre of the pantry used to keep the space cool. He deposited the rubbish into a bin and lingered near the doorway rather nonsensically, watching her savour the bite in her mouth and transfixed by the way her tongue peeked out to lick a crumb off her lip. She released a great, gusty sigh and pushed the plate in his direction.

'It's all that's left, and I couldn't find the cheese.'

Saint wandered to her side and stared at the fork resting there on the white porcelain. The fork only a moment ago she'd been holding. The fork her lips had wrapped round and caressed as she slid delicate sponge and bits of plum behind her inviting lips. He picked up the utensil, warm from her soft grip, and used the side to cut into the generous slice. She was studying him, and when he brought the bite to his mouth, he held her gaze. He could see the muscles in her throat work as she swallowed.

'You've got a little something,' she said, waving a finger near the corner of her own mouth.

Using his index finger, he wiped the bit of plum compote he could feel tickling the rim of his lip and, without breaking their stare, licked it off.

'Is it gone?'

'Yes.'

He appreciated the hitch in her breath as she responded.

'Your turn.' The fork bit into the cake again, but Saint held it out this time, daring her to take the bite he was offering.

Anabel glanced from the small morsel to his face. The edge of her mouth tipped up in the whisper of a cheeky smile, and she leaned forward, watching him as every slow second ticked by.

His lungs constricted, the breath streaming out of his chest to make room for his heart to expand. She swallowed and wet her lips. A speck of plum eluded her, settling in the dip of her cupid's bow. Saint set down the fork and dragged his finger through the compote and down her lip, resting it at the seam of her mouth. Using her teeth and the tip of her tongue, she cleaned his finger of the fruit.

'We have spent years attending the same parties, the same musicales, circulating in the same ballrooms and drawing rooms and dining rooms. How blind I have been.' He let the confession slip into the darkness.

Lightning cracked. The bright outburst lasting just long enough for him to catch the glitter of unshed tears in her eyes.

He took a step and tripped over a sack of potatoes on the ground. His feet skidded out from under him, grappling to find purchase on the tiled floor. He landed with a hard thud on the tip of his tailbone. The pain caused his breath to seize in his lungs. His head dropped back against the floor, and he closed his eyes. A swish of soft fabric brushed along the skin of his wrist and hand, resting limply on his stomach. When he looked up, Anabel was bent above him, concern tensing her pretty features.

'Have you died, then?' Her words quaked.

'Doesn't appear so. I hope that's not disappointing,' he said, attempting to tease away her worry.

'You are the one fearful of ghosts, not me. If you came back to haunt me, I hardly think things would be much different than they stand at present.'

Her curious statement distracted him from his discomfort for several seconds while he tried to parse out her meaning. She straightened and dropped a hand to help him up. He reached across and tugged her down to him, catching her to his chest. A bark of thunder smothered her gasp, but he felt her heart where it pounded in time with his own. She softened into him, leaving no room for the frisson running between their bodies, for the shine of lightning, for waiting.

A stray strand of hair tickled his jaw. He tucked it back behind her ear, his fingers grazing the regal line of her neck. Beneath his fingertips, her skin turned to gooseflesh. With the pad of his thumb, he explored the gentle rise of her cheekbone, the sharp angle of her jaw, the outline of her perfect mouth.

Inches separated them. Her breath shook. Saint lifted his head from the floor, just long enough to brush her lips with his. His fingers skimmed the base of her throat, her collarbone. The air in his lungs caught at the back of his throat, and he waited. Waited. His body strained, the pain of anticipation almost unbearable. A tentative hand cradled the side of his face, and Anabel dragged her thumb over his bottom lip. Pleasure shuddered through him. Her fingers snaked around his neck and curled into his hair. Her head dipped. Her mouth hovered above his for the infinite, endless stretch of a heartbeat.

Then she pressed her lips to his with a touch so soft, tender, exquisite, he was overcome by light-headedness, his consciousness ebbing with desire and disbelief. In her kiss, the taste of plum and pining, sweet and a little spicy. He moved slow, with reverence in every caress, and let his fingers trail down her back, carve into the curve of her waist. His tongue glanced along the seal of her mouth, and her quiet moan echoed through him. He was ready to spend nearly as soon as he hardened against her lower abdomen.

As he gently adjusted her, the subtle shift of her body brushing his length made his thighs quiver. The soft gasp that broke their connection told him the swell of his cock had found that sensitive bud of pleasure beneath the layers of fabric separating them. She made a hesitant circle with her hips. Sweat gathered on his brow, his body straining to prevent release.

'Tell me how that feels.'

Her answer was ragged, unsteady. 'Like I cannot think of anything else at all.'

'Then you need not.'

She responded by rubbing herself along his stiffness, the motion uncertain and probing and creating sublime friction that threatened to undo him. Before long, her trembling breath tickled the rim of his ear, and her pace worked into something deliberate and determined. As soon as her body tensed and her soft gasps peaked, he came, wet heat soaking into his nightshirt and spreading up his belly.

Her forehead dropped to his. Their breaths mingled in quick bursts, laboured and intense.

'Marry me, Anabel.'

The tip of her nose brushed his when she shook her head. 'You only say so because—because.'

'I say so because the very notion of living a life without you grows ever more inconceivable with each new day spent in your company.'

The pause between his words and hers was pronounced.

'We would never suit.'

Saint's heart stopped. 'I'm forced to disagree.'

'Please.' Her voice wavered, and her face dropped to the crook of his neck.

A sudden pain began to throb inside his skull and reason eluded him. 'Do I fail to make you happy? You are not indifferent to me, but do you feel—is it because your wishes and affections can never match my own?' An affirmative answer would shatter him so completely as to render him beyond hope of repair.

'Say no more. Please, I beg of you.'

Saint heard the distress in her tone and smoothed small circles over her back. Something warm and wet touched his collarbone. He blinked in confusion.

'I should return to my room.' She pushed herself away from him and back onto her knees, swiping at the moisture on her cheeks and patting her face.

He nodded, concern overtaking every impulse except the one to soothe her. He lifted himself onto his forearms.

'Have I—? Was I wrong to—? I thought—' Her reaction to his proposal was so unexpected, the endings to his questions remained a mystery, even to him.

'No.' Her shoulders caved with a heavy exhale. 'Your voice calls to me, and I will answer it always. Even if I am not the light you are drawn to but the darkness hiding behind it.'

She rocked herself up, and with a wan, tearful glance at his face, hurried away.

Saint watched her go, bewildered and troubled on her behalf.

He bent a knee to push himself off the ground and was overcome by faintness. His body listed like a sinking ship, and he laid back down, resting one hand at the ridge of his ribs and the other on the cool floor beneath him. He attempted a full inhale, struggling through the effort, and slid the hand at his midsection to rub the muscle over his heart, where a little spot of pain was growing bigger.

A thread of concern grew, and he wondered if he'd done real damage to himself when he fell. Once more, he tried to sit up and was forestalled by a stabbing sensation in his abdomen so severe, he rolled to his side and curled his legs to his chest.

'Good god.' Agony forced out the exclamation, despite no one being near to hear them. He groaned into the silence of the pantry.

Several minutes passed, but when the sharp pain failed to ebb, Saint forced himself inch by slow inch along the floor to the base of the table. With one hand stacked on top of the other on a sturdy leg, he hoisted himself up to his knees, wheezed out a strained breath, and then pulled his body to a standing position, leaning almost all his weight on the tabletop. Using the sleeve of his robe, he wiped the droplets of sweat dappling his forehead.

'Now,' he said, compelling himself upright. 'One step at a time, old boy.'

He wobbled as he took an uneven stride, bracing himself against the wall. Another burst of agony in his stomach doubled him over, and he grasped for the door-frame to keep himself from pitching forward, back to the floor.

In this tortured way, he arrived at the stairs, the idea of mounting them almost more than he could bear. He knew if he stopped moving, he wouldn't go a foot further and sank to his knees. On all fours, he crawled to the landing, where he was sorely tempted to roll onto his back and die right there on the spot. Surely such acute pain could only be caused by someone's soul being torn from their earthly form. Every breath was hard won. His whole body shivered like a scrawny branch in a bad storm, and the torment in his gut was worse than anything he'd ever before experienced.

One more flight of stairs stood between him and his rooms. He thought of ringing a bell, but if he were dying, he'd prefer to do so alone, rather than leave that lasting image singed into the mind of whichever servant answered his call. By the time he'd ascended the final few steps, he was ready to retch—and did, into a large decorative vase that sat in a place of prominence in an alcove. It had been a gift from King George III to Saint's father, after he'd hosted the monarch for a visit. With a hand on the wall, Saint dragged his failing body down the corridor to the door of his room.

Clutching his stomach, he staggered to his bed and collapsed.

24

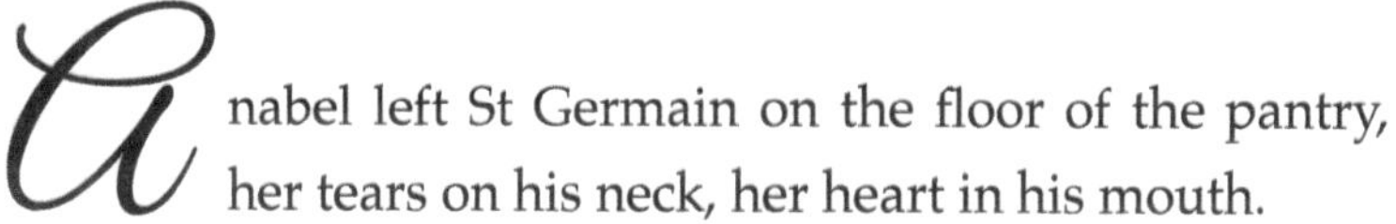

Anabel left St Germain on the floor of the pantry, her tears on his neck, her heart in his mouth.

In the kitchen, at the deepest point of night, she had been able to imagine herself someone else, someone who could give him everything but her hand. To reflect overlong on the dizzying sensations his body coaxed from her own, or to contemplate what she'd done with any significant examination, was impossible when guilt and despair ate her up with each step she took away from him. Once in the confines of her room, she grabbed a pillow, held it tight over her face, and screamed. The noise curdled with anger and pain and frustration.

Her heart had often asked of her, *What am I to you that you must break me again and again?* But never before had it cause to ask, *How will you find peace within when you have broken his?*

She dropped the pillow onto the bed and ran to the

small cabinet tucked into a discreet corner, flinging open the top and heaving into the clean chamber pot. Every spasm of her stomach sent acrid torrents of cake and bile up her throat. Sweat and tears soaked her face. She swiped at the moisture in violent lashes and groped around for something to wipe her mouth. Her hand landed on the handkerchief given to her by Franny.

Still half-bent over the porcelain bowl, she covered her ears with her hands to block out the dejection in his voice. Her eyes were jammed closed, so tightly, the muscles of her face convulsed. The darkness was worse. She raked her fingers along her skull and clawed her hair, tearing at the hurt and confusion on his face until the violence of her keening pitched her forward once more.

When the biliousness ceded, she slumped to the ground, overcome by bone-deep exhaustion, and leaned her full weight against the cabinet. It was a long time before she found the strength to move, the first signs of dawn watching her from the window.

Finally, she heaved herself onto the bed, covered her face with a pillow, and determined to weep till she had enough tears to wash away every haunting memory of her time at Sylvancliffe.

'My salts,' Lady Marrow wailed. 'Where are my salts?'

On her way to the breakfast parlour, Anabel had heard a commotion in the morning room and paused in the doorway, but her weary mind struggled to take in the scene unfolding before her.

Lady Marrow was prone on a reclining couch, a little maid airing her with a fan while another ran off, presumably in search of the cried-for salts. Two footmen were loitering, appearing uncertain whether they should remain or tend to their duties. Mrs Crane was muttering to herself, trying to force a glass of something reddish-brown down the woman's throat. Franny held her friend's hand, murmuring in soothing accents.

Perched on the edge of a chair, Hero ran a handkerchief through her fingers. Her brother stood at her side, hand on her shoulder, countenance drawn with concern. Roberts had had the sense to turn and look out of a window, as if nothing out of the ordinary at all were unfolding around him.

'What—?' was all Anabel managed to get out, throwing her befuddled gaze wildly around the room.

Ellena, poised at the back of the couch, answered her incomplete question. 'It seems my brother—'

'Poisoned!' Lady Marrow barked out through another bout of tears. 'So young, so handsome he is, too.'

Anabel's heart ceased its relentless beating in her chest. The room began to disintegrate at the borders of her vision, the people within becoming shapeless blots of colour and sound.

'He's not dead,' Franny stated calmly.

Tentative relief surged through her, the force buckling her legs. She held herself upright with sheer determination and set a trembling hand on the back of a nearby chair.

'And not poisoned,' added Ellena, in an undervoice.

'He was! He was!' protested the afflicted lady. 'Whatever else could it be? You brought this upon him, wretched child, inviting that spiritualist into this house.'

Anabel, more confused than when she entered the room, traded a glance with Ellena.

'Dead!'

The maid, waving a vial of smelling-salts under Lady Marrow's nose, jumped at the outburst.

'Saint is not dead,' said Ellena over the woman's sobs. 'Although we're presently uncertain about the precise nature and cause of his ailment.'

Lady Marrow hiccupped. 'Very well. *Dying*. Are you satisfied? And a man of such excellent character, such countenance. His whole life still before him! He hasn't even known the joys of marriage or children or—or Cook's cake.'

Anabel coloured.

'Franny, Franny! My dear, sweet friend. Whatever will you do without him? Who will keep your family together?'

Ellena cleared her throat loudly. 'Well, Edward—our *other* brother—is still very much alive, despite his best efforts.' *As is Saint*, she mouthed to Anabel.

'Edward. Poo. He's no more than a youth. A cub. Who will teach him a thing with Saint dead and gone? And his papa, too, living as a memory so many years now.' Reflecting on the plight of Edward appeared too much for Lady Marrow's weakened sensibilities and she withered into the couch.

'Let us return you to your bedchamber, Kitty, dear,

where you'll be more comfortable.' Franny sent a meaningful glance to Ellena and signalled to a footman. The young man pried Lady Marrow from the couch and assisted her from the room. In their wake followed Franny, Ellena, Mrs Crane, and the little maid, skipping to keep up.

The silence was quick to become burdensome. None of those who remained were certain what to do next. A movement out of the corner of Anabel's eye spooked her.

'May I interest you both in a walk. Miss Boyton? Hero?' Mr Glassbrook had come within arm's reach. 'The rain has stopped, and I know my sister finds fresh air curative.'

Hero nodded, looking like a fox first cornered then set free.

'You go ahead,' Anabel said. 'An indulgent cup of coffee will set me to rights after so much excitement.' She added a smile, or something she hoped resembled one. Her cheek twitched with the effort.

'Are you certain?' Mr Glassbrook pressed, with touching solicitude.

Her chin trembled, but she nodded and watched them go. Roberts had also absented himself from the room, although she'd no notion when. She remained where she stood, worrying the tips of her fingers and the skin around her nails before fiddling with the ribbon on her dress. She tried to swallow her unease, jagged and painful in her throat. Somewhere between Lady Marrow's swooning and Ellena's strained tolerance was the truth of the situation. The unknown was going to pull at her until she snapped like a worn bootlace.

Forcing her arms to her sides and lifting her chin, she

walked out of the parlour, turning towards the breakfast room with determined steps. Passing the stairs, she paused. When her gaze skated upwards in the direction of the private chambers, she scolded herself. There were things even she wouldn't dare do. Pushing into a gentleman's room, in the middle of the morning and in a house full of people, topped such a list. She could, however, just stroll down the corridor. The man himself may be coming down to breakfast at that very moment, proving the whole thing nothing more than a silly misunderstanding.

Yes. She nodded along with the thought. Perfectly rational. Sparing a peek over one shoulder, then the other, she drifted upstairs. Drifted for the first few steps, at any rate. Then she took them two at a time, slowing only at the landing. The hall was empty—no St Germain, no physician or valet or maid carrying a tray of rags and tonics. There was not a muffled peep to be heard from behind his door where she stalled, unsure what to do next. Returning downstairs for breakfast without the slightest bit of information on his current state was impossible. Yet she couldn't bring her hand up to knock, the last vestiges of her ingrained propriety holding tight.

Something rippled the skirt of her dress. She stifled a shriek but jumped out of her skin, knocking into the glass and gold table against the wall. The vase on top of it tumbled just beyond her reach and landed with a clumsy thud on the ground. She was spared the mortification of watching the irreplaceable piece shatter into a million pieces by the edge of the runner. A heavy breath of relief pushed through her lips, and she placed the vase back on the table. Pip darted down the hall—Anabel seeing only a scramble of black from her periphery as the kitten ran away from the commotion she'd caused.

'Come in and spare my furniture.'

She glanced around, considering for a moment whether the walls had come to life.

'Anabel?'

Her gaze fixated on the door and her heart churned in her chest at St Germain's easy use of her given name. She reached for the knob with a sweaty hand and opened the door just wide enough to accommodate her head.

The drapes were open, letting in stifled sunlight that reflected in a small brilliant burst upon the glass of a gilt brass skeleton clock near the window. On the walls, gorgeous paper in a deep blue the same colour as his counterpane. She was at once struck by the elegance and masculinity of the room. *His* room.

St Germain was lounging against a wall of pillows and wearing a silk brocade robe, different from the night before. The fabric covered him with a lazy drape, revealing a dusting of light hair. His bare skin beckoned her, the hard valley between his chest muscles stirred a phantom sensation in her fingers, as if she'd known the joy of touching him in every life she'd lived before. She swallowed, her mouth unusually wet, and forced her eyes up. He looked well, if a little paler than normal, and regarded her with unabashed mirth.

'How did you know it was me?'

He arched a brow. 'You were the last person to see me, Anabel, and in the kitchen no less. I presume you wish to confirm whether I am, in fact, near death. Did not you inquire last night, as well? What did you put in the cake? Arsenic? Nightshade?'

She gasped, her whole body knocked back by shock. She flung the door open wide and stomped into the room in a whirl of fury.

'How *dare* you accuse me of something so heinous? To suggest I'd do such a thing to *anyone*, much less someone I —someone I—' She cut herself off just in time to foil the word *love* from completing the sentence but floundered to recover.

His lip twitched. 'Someone you…what, Anabel?'

'You keep saying my name.'

'I like how it feels in my mouth.'

A flush stole up her neck, but there was a mulish set to her jaw, and she reminded herself he'd just accused her of attempting to murder him.

'Consider this a spot of retribution.' His mouth lifted in a gentle lilt that sent a current of heat swirling in her belly. 'I know very well you didn't poison me. Fact is, I don't think I've been poisoned at all.'

'You've sent Lady Marrow into hysterics for amusement?'

St Germain chuckled. 'Kitty Marrow can send herself into hysterics with no help from me. Shortly after you departed, I became quite ill. It was rather a struggle to make it to my room, the details of which I will spare you.'

Anabel's heart clenched with remorse. 'I shouldn't have left you there.'

'I think, perhaps, this time it was I who scared you.'

His handsome face wore an expression that managed to be both teasing and concerned. 'Wilde called for the physician early this morning. While I was being examined, he went to the kitchen. For as far back as I can recall, I've had a severe reaction to anything containing ginger.'

'The cake?'

'The cake. Cook confirmed she'd mixed a small amount with the plum, thinking to compliment the sweetness. A bit of an experiment. Layered in with her remorse was disappointment, too, that the flavour didn't come through.'

Anabel had somehow drifted so near the bedside, she could chart the expanse of his exposed collarbones, lose herself in the hollow where they met. She didn't, but her whole body strained with resistance. 'You poisoned yourself, then.'

'In so many words.'

He looked up at her, his gaze gentle and compelling.

'Anabel.'

She watched his hand slide to the edge of the bed, her heart skittering and frantic, like a bird trapped in her chest. He lifted a finger, tracing the space between each of her own. Her skin tightened, every fine hair on her body rising to his touch.

'Help me understand what happened last night. Will you tell me what I did wrong and grant me the chance to fix my error?'

She dropped and wagged her head. 'You've done nothing.'

'I must have, for you to flee from me in such a manner —after such a moment.'

Heat overspread her cheeks, and her core tightened. 'You asked me to trust you, and now I'm requesting the same.'

His thumb swept back and forth over the back of her hand. 'That was pie, Anabel. This is forever.'

The tears came where speech refused. She couldn't make St Germain understand without exposing herself, but her love prevented her from ever asking him to share in her disgrace, or to keep her secret, or to risk his own standing by taking an inept wife with a mind both backward and slow. He was a man of rank and fortune, and the whispers of her moral failings, her lack of intelligence, and her want of refinement would be ruthless. Mr Allen was still being punished by the *ton* and he had merely selected the wrong colour waistcoat. Anabel understood the implications of her impairment, and so would St Germain, the moment she spoke of her failings aloud, even if he hoped to deceive himself into thinking otherwise.

She stared at the hand covering her own unable to imagine anything worse in the world than watching his affection for her transform into scorn and resentment.

'I cannot be the wife you wish for, the wife of which you are most deserving.'

'Have I no say in the matter?'

'If things were different—If *I* were different—'

'No. You are perfect because I love you.'

The rhythm of the day faltered, each second folding in on itself, and Anabel went so still, she could feel the earth turning beneath her. In startling contrast to the blankness of her mind came the awareness she'd lived above twenty years and never before heard those words spoken to her, for her.

She had spent a lifetime devouring the biting reprimands of her mother, her sisters, herself, cannibalising her emotions and self-regard and mistaking the effort for survival. St Germain had endeavoured to reassure her, but he had unwittingly begun to unravel the tapestry of her body and being, revealing an intricate pattern of shame and self-loathing. She swallowed down the sick at the back of her tongue.

'I have not been a man of my word.' A mournful smile twisted his mouth.

Her brows tugged in confusion.

'In the orchard I told you that if you were set against me, I would remain silent on the subject. I did not, and my penance is living with the pain I have caused you. Please forgive me, and accept my assurances that I will forbear to broach the matter in future.'

He removed his hand from hers. The finality of the subtle gesture dwarfed all other feeling and sliced her open from top to tip. Her body had years of practice wrapping around a secret, a sentiment. The instinct was all that kept her organs from spilling across the rug when she left his room.

25

'Something more, my lord?' Wilde set out a razor, soap, and the basin with hot water for shaving.

'No. Thank you.' Saint preferred to complete the task himself, and his valet disappeared into the dressing room, taking Saint's discarded robe with him.

He picked up the soap, working it into a rich, creamy lather between his palms. The air filled with the scent of wet fallen leaves and freshly dug earth. On every inhale, a suggestion of sweetness hit the back of his throat. He spread the fragrant foam over his face and neck before wiping his hands and taking up the razor, the blade so sharp he wouldn't notice a cut till blood trickled down his skin. With careful precision, he guided the edge down from the top of his cheek in slow, even strokes, glad to have something to concentrate on beyond his exchange with Anabel.

Saint had not been able to resist teasing her, although

he hadn't meant to provoke her into nearly admitting the truth of her feelings for him. The word '*love*' had been about to slip from her mouth—he was certain—and she'd caught it between her teeth, which made both her refusal and her distress all the more baffling. She spoke of herself as though she were the hoydenish daughter of a fishmonger, and not a lady deserving of a man twice his worth.

He dressed after his shave and went through the house guided by restless agitation and with no real purpose. Honour and probity forbade him from pressing her further but could not prevent him from considering if the whole of every day for the remainder of his life would be spent wondering from what she was guarding herself and if anything he could have said or done would have resulted in her accepting him.

In discovering his love for her, Saint had entered eternity. The feeling stretched on with no beginning or end and would remain untouched by the passage of time. He was left bewildered, uncertain how to reconcile the unfathomable depth of his emotions with the constraints of the world around him or alter the nature of his connection with Miss Boyton, which must be done for her benefit and comfort. Treating her with polite indifference would be impossible, but he might endeavour to follow her lead.

He was checking his appearance against the polished mirror in his room before dinner when a chill shook his spine. In the hall, the faint scratching he'd heard nights prior. The sound grew louder. His exhale was both unsteady and resolved. He approached his closed door with determination and yanked it open.

Pip recoiled under the table along the wall, her nails skidding on the stone floor. Held tight between her sharp teeth was a long stick, dragging on the ground next to her paws. She peered at him with open resentment before continuing her journey, the cumbersome nature of her plaything causing her to walk with an awkward gait. The eerie sounds of life in the middle of the night, the monsters under his bed and in his wardrobe, could fit in the palm of his hand. He was betrayed into a hollow, ironic chuckle.

In the dining room, Anabel selected a place far enough to prohibit their speaking to one another, and when she was absent from the table the following morning, Saint held every expectation that Freddy, coming into the breakfast parlour with Glassbrook, would announce their early departure. Instead, the two men were in the middle of some ridiculous debate over the results of a past boxing match. Glassbrook would emerge the victor, but Freddy's ready laughter when his every point met rebuttal riled Saint. He watched his friend pile a plate with eggs and bacon through narrowed eyes.

'Saint can settle this for us,' Freddy asserted, coming to the table.

'You hope for strength in numbers,' replied Glassbrook. 'His agreement, which I don't believe you able to secure, wouldn't make your argument any more valid. I would, instead, be forced to contemplate his lack of discernment in addition to yours.'

Glassbrook bestowed an easy smile on him, in the clear expectation Saint would join the exchange, but the gentleman's mouth turned down in response to whatever he saw on Saint's countenance.

'Now then, Freddy, have you an interest in billiards after breakfast?'

With masterful skill, Glassbrook controlled the conversation, protecting Saint from the burden of participation till he rose and excused himself.

As he passed through the empty hall on his way to the library, he heard the melodic timbre of feminine voices in the drawing room. He walked on his toes to avoid being heard.

'Saint!'

He grimaced at Ellena's call and set his features before retracing a step. Within the drawing room, in addition to his sister who was sitting across the backgammon board from Anabel, were Franny and Lady Hester, the former with a book and the latter with embroidery in her lap.

'Do join us.'

Saint was obliged to smile at his sister. 'I thank you, no. I'm for the library.'

'But you are needed here. Hero promised me a lesson in watercolour, and I'm already late in meeting her. Take my place, so Anabel need not hunt about for some other entertainment.'

Anabel protested this arrangement at the same time he agreed. There was a short length of comfortless silence during which Ellena observed first one and then the other with the same capacity for spectacle as a bloodhound had for prey. She rose, and with a good deal of amusement in her countenance, departed, leaving the chair opposite Anabel empty.

'May I?'

'You may.'

Saint watched her reset the pieces on inlayed points of ebony and zebrawood, the risk of contact preventing him from reaching out to assist. He waited to retrieve the dice till she'd placed them on the centre bar. In unison, they each rolled a single die. The first move was hers: three, one. Saint cast about in his mind for something to say.

'The weather is quite wet today.' He tossed the dice and took his turn.

She maintained her survey of the board. 'Indeed.'

In the leather cup she was holding, the dice clacked together before scattering across the polished wood. Doubles.

'That's a fine roll.'

'Yes, quite lucky.'

'Indeed.' Saint cleared his throat.

Back and forth they went, neither advancing a topic of conversation beyond what had already been introduced. Halfway through, Franny approached. Hovering near Saint's chair, she observed their play for a minute without speaking before venturing to say, 'How unlike you, Saint, to maintain the advantage.'

Although a capable player, he'd gained notoriety among his family for his recurrent losses.

'My opponent has not been as ruthless as her rolls have allowed.' He'd begun to suspect Anabel was trying to throw the game, despite the opposition from her dice, and dared a glance at her from under his brow.

She worked a die between her thumb and forefinger before dropping it to join the other in her cup. 'I'm hardly so magnanimous.'

'The truly charitable rarely think of themselves in such a light. You are more generous with the feelings of others than you are with your own.'

His sister replied, 'It's a game, Saint,' with slight mockery, before moving off.

He and Anabel relapsed into silence until he removed his last pieces from the board, five of her own remaining.

She pushed back her chair, complimented him on a fine victory, and brushed past him with what appeared to be—incongruous with the unhappy turn of their last exchange but not unwelcome—the ghost of a wink.

26

Anabel had not known how to sit across from St Germain and maintain the pretence that neither his heart nor hers had been touched by something scarce and absolute. Nor could she refrain from questioning what he had found in her worthy of his esteem and wondering if there were some other realm in which she might discover of herself the same qualities.

She leaned back against the closed door of her room and rubbed her temples, where a bud of pain had begun to radiate after that unbearable quarter-hour of bland and stiff conversation between them. She *had* meant to lose the game, as a little consolation for the misery she'd inflicted upon him—and the poor man couldn't get a decent throw if he'd weighted the dice—but the wink she'd tossed him upon her exit was unintended and had begun before she could prevent it, a relic of their past ease.

Hardly a day had passed since he'd withdrawn his

attentions at her request, and already she longed to recover some normality in their interactions, although such a thing was impossible, and her wishing otherwise increased the throbbing in her head. He'd called her generous with the feelings of others, but Anabel knew herself to be the most selfish creature in the world where he was concerned, adding another bitter flavour to the contempt she'd come to recognise as her own.

Doubtful of finding any occupation great enough to distract her from the vastness of her grief or the smallness of herself, she pushed away from the door and went to open one of the windows, revelling in the burst of crisp air sweeping her overheated skin. A robin cast a song of sorrow over the still world. The wind howled to life, twisting dry leaves from their branches. She watched one caught in a gust float and sail and whirl. How unjust for life to go on when she had no notion how.

The weak flames in the grate shuddered in the draught. She closed the window and went to stoke the fire until the blaze revived, lapping at the dried wood and filling her room with a sweet, smoky scent. As she tucked the poker back into the little corner where the mantle met the wall, her attention fixed on a seam in the silk damask wallcovering. Her gaze traced the line up and over and back down: the shape of a door. Excitement surged in her veins. She recalled to mind Mrs Hale's words about Lady Cecilia's truth hidden between fractures of stone and wood and beneath a canopy of leaves. Her fingers trembled a little as she stroked an embossed green-and-gold leaf. One of many.

She put both hands out and pushed. Beneath her palms, the panelling gave a little. With a grunt of effort, she shoved harder. A gap in the wall appeared. Her heart quickened.

Before her was an endless narrow passageway, bathed in darkness and smelling of disuse. She retrieved the candle burning from a nearby table and stepped into the unknown, hesitating a moment when she reached for the handle on the inside to close the panel behind her. She screwed up her lips to one side and pulled the door till the edge met the wall but didn't shut her away completely.

The passage grew cooler the further she moved from the warmth of her room, her footsteps making a shushing noise on the uneven stone floor. At the end of what felt like forever, a twisting staircase appeared. With a brief, uncertain glance behind her, Anabel descended.

The last curve brought her to a small chamber. A plump velvet chair with scroll arms was nestled into the corner, the burgundy fabric remaining vibrant while wrapped in a thick layer of dust. A small desk of cherry wood, and the matching seat, sat smartly near the far wall. On top was a packet of dried flowers that would crumble when touched, a pen and pot of withered ink, and what appeared to be a small leather-bound book.

Anabel picked it up and flipped it over, looking for any clue as to whom the item might rightfully belong. She carefully folded open the cover, excitement increasing the difficulty of the task. Her hope, her expectation of the name, made the words easier to read: *Lady Cecilia Walker*. With a quick flick of her wrist, she flipped through the pages, more than half filled in elegant, close writing. It would take her an age to read.

The candle guttered. Soon total darkness would envelop her. Clutching the journal, she went quickly round to the other side of the desk and yanked the chair out of the way, bumping its arm as she pulled out a slim drawer. Disappointment rolled through her when the little compartment proved empty. With a sigh, she shut it, her eyes drawn to an outline of something concealed by the staircase. She squinted. A set of shelves, very nearly full.

Anabel chided herself for bringing a spent candle and hurried to return the chair to its place, feeling oddly uneasy about disturbing the small room. The stretcher between the two back legs caught on the wall. Bringing with her the last bit of light from the flame, she knelt and saw how the chair was hitched on a little lever. She freed the chair and thrust it aside, but when she worked the handle, her effort was met with resistance. She tried again, pulling so hard on the cold metal the tendons of her hands hurt. Light spilt into the hidden space as a narrow door opened, revealing the empty library.

With a sigh of relief, she stepped out and quickly shut the panel. It closed with a quiescent click. She stepped back. The wall looked like all the rest in the library, the lineation noticeable only if one knew what to look for.

'You may be the only person I know who is more interested in the walls of a library than the books contained within.'

Anabel whipped around at the sound of St Germain's voice, thrusting the journal behind her back.

'What have you there?'

Her heart stirred to a gallop, and she shuffled along the perimeter of the room until a table thwarted her going further. 'Nothing.' Her mouth tried for a smile. 'Have you an interest in playing a second game? I may even let you win again.'

He wore an enigmatic expression, but the way he prowled nearer reminded her of the day they'd played charades. A flush of warmth spread from her centre outward.

'Imp. Let me see your hands.'

His tease tingled in her stomach. Somewhere deeper still, a rough jerk of impulse or emotion.

She compressed her mouth, shook her head, and edged closer to the French doors leading to the terrace. 'You've two of your own. Surely mine are no more interesting.'

'Come now, Miss Boyton.' His tone held a suggestion of his former playfulness, but the formal way he addressed her caused a painful constriction in her chest.

She spun on her heel to flee, but St Germain was faster. She dropped the journal while fumbling with the locked door, and he scooped up the thing before she could.

'Yours?'

'No.'

He flipped open the cover. His brows jumped. 'Shall we read this together?'

'No—I—'Tis your house, rightfully the journal belongs to you.' She didn't recognise the panic forming, although small dark spots danced on the outskirts of her vision and her palms grew sweaty. She tried to back away and stumbled over her feet.

St Germain reached out to steady her, his head tipped to one side. 'You, Miss Boyton, are a mystery-seeking, trick-playing, mischief-making sprite, and I can't in good conscience read this without you. I will even abstain from asking by what means the journal was obtained. Come, we've time to sate the worst of your curiosity before retiring to ready for dinner.' He gestured towards one of the couches in the middle of the room with the hand holding the journal and tucked his other arm behind his back.

Anabel winced and resisted the impulse to press her knuckles to the acute pain in her breast. His forbearance, his kindness, his attention to her wishes further exemplified why he was the best of men. Her days ahead would be absent the expected suffering brought on by her refusal of his offer. Instead, she would hang every sunrise on the knowledge he had once loved her. Though he would never speak the words again, they resonated in her ears like a clarion call.

'Miss Boyton?'

Anabel hesitated on the edge of time, just long enough to see a different future: one where she might prevent his regard from becoming an immutable force, like her own, and where he might clear his heart for someone worthy of his love; one where she exercised the same generosity of spirit towards herself as he had and might remake her person in the image of someone she could come to love. Her chest filled with a steady, uncomplicated breath.

St Germain offered her the journal once she had sat down and took the chair set at a right angle. She casually wondered if he perceived the tremor of her hands when she opened the cover.

The words rippled like the surface of a lake during a hard rain. Resolved, she scraped her dry tongue over her lips.

'After—' Anabel cleared her throat. 'After so many moths—' She began again, the pause between each word stilted and conspicuous. 'Mouths. Months. Many months of un—untic—uncet—uncertainty, the—the thing ex—the most—the most thing—'

Her lungs burned and her eyes stung. Anabel tried to swallow, but the walls of her throat felt like they were stuck together.

'Miss Boyton?'

She forced herself onward, ignoring the tearing sensation of a fissure in her middle. 'Ex—exbroad—extroniary—extronridnary—the most extraordinary thing has happened. My hapnesis—happiness—is not so far tadsin—di—stant—distant. My happiness is not so far distant.'

Determined to find freedom from its dark, pulsing keep, the shame she'd swallowed day after day for so many years finally clawed through the sinew holding her together.

She tossed the journal aside and shoved the heels of her palms to her eyes. The cushion dipped with St Germain's weight.

'Miss Boyton?' Tenderness warmed his voice.

Her empty stomach heaved. 'I'm sorry. I'm sorry. I'm sorry.'

'Your confidences are yours alone to keep, but a sagacious woman once told me a secret confessed loses its power.'

The memory of him leaning back against a birch tree, awash in night and grief, candid and confiding, emerged in the blackness of her mind.

'You may whisper it, if you'd like.'

Anabel's love for him swelled till there was no space left within her in which a secret might hide, and she said in a gutted, shaking voice, 'My whole life, I look at a page and the letters shift and scatter. A book, a letter, a recipe—making sense of the words is like trying to catch the bristles of a dandelion shaken by wind.'

'Though I cannot pretend to understand the depths of your frustration and torment, I am grieved by the burden weighing upon you.'

'Do you not see? I cannot be mistress of some great estate, of any estate. I cannot manage the accounts or review the menus. I cannot make sense of a bill of sale or keep an accurate inventory. I cannot write you letters when you're away or send invitations to our friends to join us for Christmas and Twelfth Night. I cannot read to our children.' Her voice gave out. Her heartbeats landed one on top of the other, and she couldn't get enough air.

He carefully pried her hands from her face, but she kept her eyelids sealed shut. There was a subtle bend at her knuckles she could not undo. When she attempted to straighten her fingers, it felt like trying to unfold an icicle.

'Miss Boyton.'

He sounded so far away, yet that must have been him rubbing slow, soothing circles on her back.

'Miss Boyton, Anabel, can you take a deep breath for me?'

She savoured the sound of his voice wrapping around her name but could not do as he asked.

'Anabel?'

His question was not the same as hers: who would she become when she no longer lived bound by the cruel words of others, believing herself worthy only of existing on the periphery, in dark corners and small spaces?

'Anabel!' The cry was female, the voice dear.

Vivienne's arms enveloped her, but Anabel had become little more than a seedling, buried deep in wet earth and new wisdom, searching for a way to reach the sunlight.

27

Tears clung to the rims of Saint's eyes, his neck taut with the effort of holding back a sob of frustration, desperation. Under her charming smile and teasing manners, his beloved was held together by profound doubt and scarred tissue. A hot coil of anger in his stomach surprised him. He shoved his fingers through his hair and dragged them down his face.

'I should see her to her rooms.' It was all he could think to do, a feeble attempt to increase Anabel's comfort and protect her pain from exposure to others.

Vivienne looked up without releasing her hold. 'Hazel will.'

His jaw clenched. 'No.'

'Yes. I do not lay blame for Anabel's current state at your feet,' she stated, reaching out a hand to press his forearm. 'But she's worked herself near a faint, or something like it, and without knowing her wishes, I must commend her to my husband's care.'

After a tense pause, he issued a terse nod of acquiescence.

'Very well, dear friend. Shall we retire for a spell?' Vivienne motioned for her husband.

Hazelhurst approached, a look of apology on his face, and hoisted Anabel from the couch. She murmured but didn't stir.

Grimm was hovering near the door. 'I'll see her lady's maid is sent up, my lord, with a cool compress and restorative tea.'

Saint inclined his head. Vivienne settled her arm under his, and together they trailed Hazelhurst, climbing the stairs at a cautious pace. He felt the painter in her studying his expression, the downturn of his chin, the sag of his shoulders. She was weighing his worthiness against the priceless value of her friend.

'Which room is hers?' Vivienne went ahead to pull back the bedcovers when he opened Anabel's door.

He lingered on the fringe of her room, devastated by her suffering and angry at his own impotence to soothe her pain. He yearned to be the one holding her, to stand sentinel by her side, to promise himself her steadfast champion always, against anyone and anything contributing to her unhappiness.

Her lady's maid bustled in and dipped a curtsey to Vivienne and Hazelhurst. 'Your Graces. I'm sure it will be a pleasure to see you, once our darling girl has had a rest.'

'Ought I to send for the physician?' Saint inquired,

watching another maid enter, this one gripping a tray laden with cloths and tinctures and tea.

'Not at all necessary,' Harriet said. 'I gather from Grimm it's an emotional affliction, not a physical one. A little quiet, some fresh air when she's ready, and she'll be good as new. Out you go now, if you please.' She shooed the men from the room.

'Come.' Hazelhurst gripped Saint by his elbow. 'I'll carry you too, if I must.'

He backed away, keeping his eyes trained on Anabel till Hazelhurst gave him a little shove through the door and closed it behind him.

'Had I any notion what a mess you'd make of things, Saint, I would have come at the start of the party and not waited on my wife.' Hazelhurst bounded down the stairs, Saint's heavy body struggling to keep up. 'Brandy? Study?'

'Two lefts. Second door.'

He stopped in the library to retrieve Lady Cecelia's journal from the couch where it had been discarded and entered the study from the connecting door. Hazelhurst handed him a glass with a three-finger pouring and dropped into a chair by the fireplace.

Tucked inside the brooding, wood-panelled room, he shut out the rest of the house. He hadn't used the space much. Remnants of his father were everywhere: the careful organisation of the desk, the tobacco smoke trapped in the porous leather of the chairs, the book of poetry on top of a stack of educational texts. He settled a hard look on the slim volume. A fragment of memory loosened in the deep recess of his mind: his father tapping the cover. *'Words are nothing without the meaning we instil in them.'*

There was a sheaf of paper laid between the leaves of two pages, the edge just visible. He swilled some of the liquid in his mouth and savoured the burn as he swallowed, before picking up the book. Sliding out the sheet, he recognised his father's handwriting immediately. In the top right corner, a date from the year preceding the man's death.

I sleep uneasily:
The edge of the sea
The summit
The serene singing of someone
Or something
In the distance who knows
How long forgetting takes.

Let me be to you in death
What was not always possible in life:
The word 'father' easy on your lips
My words easy in your mind.
We may go on
Fundamentals unchanged:
Me, always worried for you
You, always my joy.

But between us,
No despair
No sorrows.

Only the continuous line
From where we met once
To where we will meet again.
When you speak
Your words will still
Rush through me
And I will answer you always
If you but understand
My voice might make no sound.

We have lost nothing
And gained only the trouble
Of being separated by the natural world.

Emotion stung his eyes, blurring the words on the page.

'What have you there?'

Saint could not answer directly. He removed to a chair, placed his glass on the table, and after an interval, managed, 'Recently, I've learned my father enjoyed penning poetry.' If Hazelhurst replied, he did not hear it over the words Anabel had spoken in the pantry, rising unbidden in his mind: *Your voice calls to me, and I will answer it always. Even if I am not the light you are drawn to but the darkness hiding behind it.* He knocked back another mouthful of brandy, hoping to wash down the bile rising.

'I'd no idea there was such suffering buried in the earth of her soul.'

Hazelhurst took a measured sip. 'What is buried in yours?'

Saint waited for the grip of what was familiar to wrap tight around his throat: fear, uncertainty, doubt. Instead, there was only melancholy where misery had once lived within him.

He closed his eyes and dragged in a breath. His lungs filled with the rich, sweet aroma of brandy, the woodiness of tobacco. He could feel his father's words but not hear how they rasped with the nearness of death: *I will not live to see the next full moon. I will not live to leave this place I love; but I have lived for you. You, Valentine, my boy, are magnificent.* Saint had folded over the bed to lay his head on his father's chest and listen to the last beats of his heart, counting down the seconds to their earthly parting.

In his hands, the slight rustle of the paper he still held. The smarting that radiated through him was not pain but the lines engraving his spirit.

He breathed out. 'Courage.'

The pair sat in the echo of the word. Saint folded the poem and slipped it into the inside pocket of his coat for further contemplation in the days, weeks, years to come.

A gentle knock sounded, followed by Vivienne's face tipping around the edge of the door. 'She's resting. I'll send word when she wakes.'

Something like relief settled over him followed quickly by a burst of agitation that thrust him from his chair and sent him pacing from one side of the room to the other.

'I don't understand. Her body lacks a single doltish bone. How is it possible she grew to adulthood illiterate?' He thought with pain of their exchange in the garden when he'd believed himself to be paying her a compliment. 'Surely there's some way, something that can be done.' Whatever he might do to ensure her contentment would be done in a trice, whether she ever took his name or not. Her felicity had become an integral part of his own. 'If she would benefit from a tutor, spectacles, some physician or specialist in England or abroad—Anabel cannot be the sole person with this specific challenge.'

Vivienne approached him and set a stilling hand on his shoulder. 'Very likely not. As you say, Anabel is quite clever, and she can read, more than she gives herself credit for, only not with the fluidity and ease of you and me. Her mind simply sorts the letters differently, but they can be arranged to suit her well enough. Let me show you.' She inspected the room. 'Have you paper and pen in here?'

He went to the desk, retrieved both items from a drawer, and withdrew the chair for her.

Hazelhurst wandered over to stand on the other side of his wife. He brushed his knuckles along the curve of her neck. A ripple of envy travelled through Saint, but a moment later he sternly repressed a quivering lip when Vivienne turned a firm eye on her husband. He began to understand how his friend had arrived at Belmont the month prior.

Vivienne dipped the pen into the ink and began to write. 'Through diligent experimentation, we've discovered several techniques that enhance the clarity of the letters and words, thereby improving overall comprehension.'

Saint stared at her writing: *Dear Anabel*. 'Your letters are not connected.'

'No, and you will notice a touch more space between each. Also, see how the bottom of each letter carries more weight?' She paused and leaned back, allowing him a clear look at the paper. 'Writing this way takes extra time, but I daresay you won't mind in the least. Never cross your lines, and always keep them short.'

She returned to her task, every scratch of pen on paper increasing his curiosity. A minute later, she propped the pen in the inkstand and pushed the paper a little forward for both him and Hazelhurst to see: *My dearest wife, I languish anywhere you are not. Say I can return to your side.*

'A line from one of my husband's own letters when he was last with you, Saint. Although I suspect some falsehood on his part. The two of you together are incapable of *languishing* or anything like it.'

'Lord, Vivienne.' A touch of pink tinged Hazelhurst's cheeks.

Saint couldn't stop his grin. 'Still repulsed by you, then, old chap?'

Hazelhurst glared over his wife's head.

'The additional space between the two lines is as important as that between the letters,' continued Vivienne, immune to their gibing. 'Too much space will have the same effect as too little. The practice is imperfect, but these few adjustments make correspondence manageable.'

'Thank you. I've an errand. You'll excuse me.' Saint left the pair at the desk. In his heart, a tentative shoot of hope.

28

Anabel winced at the pain in her face. Cheek to cheek throbbed, and her nose felt doubled in size. Worse, she couldn't breathe through her mouth. With a little grumble, she pressed the peaks of her knuckles hard to her sinuses.

'You're awake.'

She cracked open an eye. 'Vivi?' She blinked both open. 'Vivienne!' Her friend was sitting in a nearby chair.

Memories of the morning overtook her with toppling force, and she was grateful she was already abed. Her hearty groan rattled the open window. Or perhaps it was a gale, although not a leaf stirred on the tree just outside.

'Tell me the worst of it. Has Harriet already packed my trunks? I don't *really* wish to sail with Aunt Mary—who has any sincere desire to be tossed about any time of day or night?—but going home feels—well, it doesn't so much feel like going home, and I can't stay with you when you're little better than newly wed. I've just a few sisters I like very much at all, and of course Alice still lives at Woodruff—'

Vivienne's mouth curved into an affectionate grin. She leaned forward and caught Anabel's fluttering hand.

'How can you *smile* at such a time?'

'I've missed you.'

Anabel raised her stuffed nose to the air. 'And you will miss me more when I flee the country tonight. Tomorrow. The soonest possible.'

'You can do nothing of the sort until you tell me everything. From the beginning, if you please.'

'I wish I had never come here.' She covered her face with a pillow, which Vivienne promptly removed.

'But here you are. Out with it.'

Anabel's dearest friend had always been the more serious, the more determined of the two of them. If Vivienne wished for the whole dreadful story, there was no chance of Anabel escaping her room until the tale was told.

The narrative was erratic, details jumping about in Anabel's mind as she spoke, making them sometimes difficult to catch in the right order. When a maid came in to replace one tea tray with another, she fell silent and her thoughts drifted to St Germain—where he was, what he was doing, how he felt about her confession and the awful scene she'd enacted during her delivery.

Alone again, Vivienne offered Anabel a cup of tea and said, 'In town last season, I'd suspected you had a *tendre* for him. Why did you never tell me?'

She picked at the thin piece of fabric tied round the

healing cut on her finger. 'The same reason you kept your own secret: to protect myself. You would have said something wise and encouraged me to be brave, but only because you think more of me than anybody else in the world.'

Her friend's stare softened. 'I don't believe that to be true any longer.'

'We've hardly been here a sennight complete. What does he know?'

Vivienne smiled at her peevishness. 'How much time did you require to decide no other man would ever do?'

Anabel recalled the afternoon she'd spent eavesdropping from a tree. 'Hours,' she whispered into the cup held between her palms. His small kindness was all it had taken to stain her child-sized heart with love.

'Exactly so.'

'Well, you need not look so smug about it. Furthermore, it matters not a jot. I remain unfit to be his wife.'

'Your selflessness is admirable,' Vivienne remarked with sincerity. 'As right as you are in your intentions, you are wrong in their execution. His future happiness is at stake as well as your own, and he may feel differently on the subject. One conversation with him before you flee.'

Anabel huffed. 'Very well. Rather traitorous of you, siding with a man.'

'I'm siding with a feeling. There are two paths forward: the one you have always walked, and the one which leads you where you most wish to go. Why live in a hollow heart when you hold heaven in your hands?'

'You make the future sound so simple.'

'Future is another word for choice,' said Vivienne, with a delicate raise of her shoulder.

Every hair on Anabel rose in unison. Those were the exact words of Mrs Hale.

~

'YOU LOOK PEAKED, Ana. Are you quite well?'

Anabel slipped a side-eyed look her brother's direction and stepped ahead of him into the drawing room. 'Very well, thank you, Freddy.'

After revealing her secret, and surpassing even Lady Marrow's hysterics, nothing else remained to occupy her embarrassment or concern, and she had readied for dinner with only a vague sense of nervousness.

'No need to skewer me,' her brother said. 'Daresay everyone is a trifle fatigued after the bustle of activity these last days. With any luck, tomorrow will be full of rain.'

He moved off to greet Hazelhurst, and she immediately searched for St Germain, a curl of disappointment and worry winding through her at his absence.

She started towards Vivienne, who was standing beside Hero near a painting on the far wall, when the odd billowing of the drapes stopped her short. The windows were closed against October's chill. She stepped closer, head cocked. With a deep breath, she grasped the fabric and tossed it aside. Five needle-sharp claws stuck into the satin of her slipper. There was enough material to protect Anabel's skin, but her shoe suffered another fate. Pip tried to pull back her paw, but one claw snagged. Anabel shook her head at the slight ripping sound and bent to assist.

'Naughty thing.' She swiped an indulgent finger up over the kitten's nose and between her ears. Pip butted her hand for more. Anabel complied, until the tiny creature caught sight of something no one else could see and went bounding off.

She stood, shaking out her skirt. When she looked up, her eyes locked with St Germain's as he entered the room, and she found herself experimenting with an unusual sensation: timidity. The corner of his mouth lifted in a half-smile. She inclined her head and floated to Vivienne's side, where she stood in silent contemplation dissecting the significance, or lack thereof, of his greeting, until Grimm announced dinner.

The meal was a formal affair due to the duke and duchess's presence, which relegated Anabel to the centre of the seating arrangements, between Roberts and Lady Marrow. She could not be sorry. They were companions of little demand. She progressed through each course engrossed in nothing but her own musings, which seemed to pass through her mind as little more than draughts of air she could feel but not grasp.

When the desserts were cleared, St Germain said, 'We won't separate tonight. My friend *languishes* anywhere his wife is not, and I would never subject him to such torment so long as prevention lays within my power.'

Hazelhurst sat with the impenetrable expression of hauteur reserved for a duke, but Vivienne bit back a slight grin. She peeped at her husband from across the table in such a way as to tug a wistful sigh from Anabel.

Although dinner had lasted several hours, she felt suspended in time. Things happened around her: the harp was brought in for Hero; a foursome sat down to whist; Mr Glassbrook was convinced to share an anecdote from his favourite trial. Everything blurred together, like her attempt at watercolour. She dropped onto an elegant and finely upholstered sofa, undetermined on the best way to occupy an evening she might possibly not remember even by the time the party retired for the night.

'May I join you?'

She lifted her gaze. St Germain stood before her, appearing thoughtful, a touch hopeful, even. A faint tingling buzzed in her fingertips. Anabel gestured to the space next to her. He sat near enough for close conversation, but more space split their bodies than she had grown used to.

'I went to see Mrs Hale today.'

Her mouth rounded in surprise. The smile he returned was a soft ray of sun filtered through the clouds.

'Her home is unexpectedly charming, done all in pale yellow and blossom pink. I went with several questions of great import, her appearing to me as the kind of woman who might know where I could source the answers, even if she herself was not in possession of them. After a remarkably cordial half-hour, she was kind enough to refer me to the local herbalist, a perspicacious woman with a wrinkle for every year.'

Anabel would listen to him speak endlessly of absolutely nothing for the sheer pleasure of hearing his voice, and in her boundless state, she floated on the low, private tone he employed and failed to predict the direction of his conversation.

'This herbalist, Mrs Thyme—yes, that is her name of record—recommended to me two texts with which we may begin. One by a Cruickshank fellow in which he describes numerous cases of children who struggled to read and noted the disconnect between ability and intellectual potential. The other by Locke, is, if I recall, in the library here. According to Mrs Thyme, however, we may discover that text less helpful, as the emphasis is on broader educational theory.'

Her mind sharpened with immediate effect, her gaze too, searching for meaning in the slight lean of his body, the quick rub of his palm on his breeches, the way he seemed to hold her stare for sustained, unblinking stretches of time.

'She also suggested writing on different coloured paper with different coloured ink, if possible. Her grandson shares the same complaint,' he added, so quietly, she almost didn't hear him. 'There's a physician in London, as well, studying what he calls "reading blindness". I left with his direction. Every effort may prove fruitless'—he dropped his eyes to his lap a swift second—'but I'd like to help, if you'll allow me.'

Anabel closed her mouth once she realised it was hanging open, her mind struggling to make sense of what she was hearing. 'How—how can I accept your help when

I should be seeking your forgiveness? If I'd not misled you—'

'You did nothing of the sort.'

'I should have spoken up before—before.'

'Beg leave to inform you, Miss Boyton, there is nothing you could have done to hinder the flourish of my affections, not once I began to see the woman whom I had long overlooked. My devotion remains without expectation, but I beg the honour of being your friend.'

His statement picked at her raw heart.

'Give the suggestion however much consideration you feel due,' he continued. 'Often, when I find myself in need of time with my own ideas, I slip to the cottage. Most mornings, as it stands, about an hour after sunrise.'

29

Anabel rolled over and squinted, trying to make out the narrow hands on the clock across the dim room. She twisted up her foot in the bed-linen, and an impatient sigh disrupted the quiet in her room. With another hearty breath, she untangled herself, tossed aside her bedcovers, and padded to the windows.

The day stood on the shore of dawn, which was beginning to stretch towards the cloud-mottled sky. Morning mist diffused the green-and-gold landscape below her. The sea rippled beyond the treetops, bits of small white waves playing tricks on her eyes. She cracked the window open and listened to the quiet of morning come alive with the sound of the wind, birds, and the soothing rush of the sea.

She'd spent most of her night awake, her mind swinging wildly from one thought to the next as her concerns and her desires waged war with one another, neither emerging victorious. There was more to be said between them than could be accomplished in the drawing room, but which path she would take to the cottage, Anabel had not yet decided.

Turning back to her room, her gaze wandered, seeking out something to occupy her time, and landed upon the fireplace. With quick steps, she returned to her bed and snatched up her dressing gown, securing it tight about her person. In the rush of time and emotion since she'd found Lady Cecilia's journal, she'd entirely forgotten about the small bookshelf tucked away in the hidden room. She picked up the half-burnt candle on her bedside table and made for the secret door.

Giddy with exhilaration and grateful for a temporary distraction, she nudged the panel. The spoils at the end of the narrow passageway beckoned her. Perhaps there were journals from other guests, love letters stashed away for safekeeping, books that appeared to have all their pages but stowed keepsakes or coded missives.

Moving more quickly now she knew the way forward, it took a mere minute to descend the staircase circling down to the little space where she'd found Lady Cecilia's journal. She set her candle upon the desk and turned toward the shelves placed neatly behind the staircase. There were several trinkets in addition to the books: a snail with a pearl shell and a little gold rider perched upon it; a beautiful bronze letter-opener with the bust of a woman on the handle; and a lacquered wooden box inlaid with mother-of-pearl.

Anabel took the box and several thick books to the desk. She brushed the seat of the chair before settling herself upon it. Her heart raced like a wild horse when she picked up the first book. Letting the anticipation build, she opened the cover slowly.

Her disappointed sigh kicked up a spot of dust on the wood. The book appeared to be a book in earnest. She held it by the spine, gave it a shake. Nothing dropped from the pages. She set the tome aside and picked up each of the others in turn. Book, book, book.

She drummed her fingers, shoved all the books aside, and dragged the wooden box in front of her. Without preamble, she lifted the lid.

Inside, bundles of letters. The script was sturdy and masculine and incredibly hard for her mind to track—Lady Cecilia's lover, perhaps. It would take her an age to read through the missives unless she brought them to Vivienne.

'That's that then.'

She packed up the box, returned the books to the shelves, and made her way to the stairs.

Retracing her steps, she came to the door at her room and frowned. Anabel hadn't remembered closing it. She set the box at her feet and pushed on the handle.

The panel didn't stir. Putting the candle a safe distance from her, she used both hands and yanked harder, bending her legs a little and leaning her whole body backwards. The door didn't so much as flinch from her effort. She grumbled in irritation, picked up her things, and traipsed back to the chamber she had just left.

Her ears strained to catch any sound, but it was impossible to tell if the library was occupied. She darkly suspected the thick stone wall could drown out even the most deafening storm.

After depositing both items on the desk, she crouched down to look for the lever on the wall behind the chair, running her hand over the rough surface where she expected the thing to be. A second later, she hit a piece of metal, dark and grey and camouflaged among the stones. She grasped the handle and worked it up in its slot. Instead of pale light pouring in from the library, Anabel heard a click. She released it, took a breath, and tried again.

Click.

Again.

Click. Click. Click.

She knew nothing of locks and even less about secret lever systems, but she recognised the unmistakable sound of peril. The chamber she was in had no intention of releasing her.

Leaving the box, she picked up the candle and hurried once more toward her own room. Depositing the flame on the ground a little way from her and muttering a series of incoherent words, she pushed and pushed and pushed without success. Balling her hands into fists so tight her bones begged release, she pounded with all her might, calling out as loud as she could. There would be a housemaid coming through soon, and Harriet too. She battered the wall until her shoulders and arms burned. Until her cries scratched her throat raw.

She sunk to the ground, buried her face in her knees, and sobbed. Eventually, she rubbed her eyes and looked at the candle. A quarter of it had burned away. There were maybe two or three hours of light left. The cold of the stone was coming through the layers of fabric under her. She stood and tried the handle again, without much effort. After a few rough swallows to bring moisture back to her throat, she called out to anyone who might be in her room and pounded the door with her sore fists. The wait for response was short and hopeless.

She didn't even trouble to sigh as she plucked the candle from the ground and returned to the small chamber.

Feeling she must try, but without the least expectation of help arriving, she struck the impenetrable wall between her and the library, each hit growing weaker than the last.

If there were a silver lining, it must be that she was spared the wrenching task of confronting her own future. Maybe, with a stroke of good fortune, she might return to haunt St Germain.

On a humourless chuckle, she went to the velvet chair in the corner, curled her legs under herself, and watched the candle burn.

30

Saint paced from one wall of the cottage to the other and back again, the ticking of the clock nagging at him. He'd spent almost an hour in the constant expectation Anabel was about to appear. A deep sense of misgiving settled over him.

He was crossing the lawn on his way back to the house when Franny came running, or as close to running as his sister was capable.

'She's vanished, Saint, vanished!'

Whether it was his sister's shrill cry or the innate knowledge of who *she* was before Franny told him, her pronouncement seeded a pit of terror in his belly.

His pace quickened, and Franny paused her own steps, putting her hands to her thighs and panting to regain her breath.

'Franny!' he called, his voice somewhere between demanding and irritated.

She made a staying gesture, her head bobbing where it hung parallel to the ground. 'Yes.' The word came gasping out between breaths. 'A moment.'

Saint barked his sister's name again. 'Forgive me, but I must request you couch your alarming statement in some context, and, if you can manage, in a pitch which doesn't cause my teeth to grind together.'

'Anabel! Not a sight nor sound from her all of this morning.'

The fine hairs on his arm stood at attention.

''Tis hardly the breakfast hour.' He spoke in a steadying tone, more for his benefit than his sister's. 'Perhaps she's in the library or out for a walk.'

'A walk!' Franny cried, throwing her arms wide into the grey, murky morning. 'Shows what you know.'

'I don't know anything because you haven't told me anything.'

'Harriet went to wake Anabel at the usual hour, but she was absent. Her bed had been slept in, and her maid said there is no note and nothing missing from the room—no luggage or such—and her half-boots are where they ought to be. And besides, the clouds will drench us at any moment. What young lady would risk such a hazard to her person for a little air and exercise?'

Saint felt a flash of heat on his cheeks and ran a hand over his face.

'Several maids checked the halls and primary rooms, but Anabel is nowhere to be found. Nowhere, Saint!'

He continued towards the house, and Franny turned on her heels, scampering to keep up with his purposeful strides. Once inside, he snapped orders at the first footman he saw. Within minutes, every servant on duty had joined him in the drawing room, along with Grimm and Mrs Crane. The commotion had also brought around the guests who'd already come down to the breakfast parlour.

'What's all this?' asked Freddy, lingering in the doorway.

'Your sister is missing.'

Freddy scoffed. 'Wouldn't put it past Ana to be simply conning the lot of us.'

Saint's jaw jutted, but he pushed down the irritation. 'While that remains a possibility, as she is a guest in my home, I'd prefer to put in the effort to determine her whereabouts. The maids will search the house thoroughly from the top down. The footmen will comb the gardens, surrounding woods, and the beach.'

'I'll assist with the search indoors,' offered Miss Glassbrook, worrying the ribbon on her dress. 'And Antony and the other men can help out of doors.'

Franny nodded and lightly grasped Miss Glassbrook's arm. 'You dear girl. A fine idea.'

It appeared nothing more needed to be said. Those in the room dispersed with haste, and Saint found himself standing alone, feeling torn between a wish to shout and a vague desire to throw something. With a growl, he fled the room and dashed up the stairs. He entered Anabel's bedchamber without pause. Inside, he was assailed by a heady, floral scent, and the sight of her brush on the dressing table, her shawl draped over a chair near the fireplace. She had woven herself into the fabric of the room.

A slight, plaintive cry caught his attention. His focus jumped around. Near the fireplace, he spotted Pip. The kitten was sitting and staring at him with her big green eyes. She mewed again, more insistent than he'd ever heard her.

'Quite a wail, dear one.' Saint crouched down to pet her for a moment. 'You know I know you've betrayed me by sleeping in this room so very often.' She opened her tiny mouth and let out a sound twice as big as she. 'Yes, a sentiment upon which we can agree. We'll find her. I promise.'

He rose and looked around the room for some hint where Anabel might have gone, setting a firm boundary at rifling through her belongings. There was no sign of a struggle, no sign she'd packed a valise and run off, no sign of anything out of the ordinary, which was perhaps the most unsettling thing of all. With a frustrated exhale, he walked back into the hall. He jammed a hand through his hair and contemplated what to do next, before taking the backstairs down to the kitchen.

Pip darted after him, her sharp, strident mews bouncing as she bounded down the steps and weaved in and out of his legs.

'Lord, Pip. You cannot have considered who will feed you if you kill me.'

Work in the kitchen came to a standstill when he entered.

'Any news on the young lady?' Mrs Bates asked, her expression crestfallen when Saint shook his head.

A part of him had hoped—what had he hoped for,

exactly? To find Anabel standing there eating a slice of cake, with an air of mischief hanging about her?

He left and went to the breakfast parlour, the library, the music room, the sunroom, and the conservatory, passing the maids and Miss Glassbrook and the other ladies who had joined in the search since it began. In every room, Pip wailed louder than the last.

Saint abandoned the kitten inside and retraced his steps to the cottage. The small space was darker and colder than when he'd left. He went to the boathouse next, impervious to the fat drops of rain pelting him when he crossed the wet sand. Anabel had vanished into the ether like smoke from a chimney. He cupped his hands around his mouth and yelled her name. The only answer came from the swell of the sea nipping at the shore.

By the time he returned to the house he was soaked through, but wretchedness would kill him long before a cold. Not knowing what else to do, he stalked into the study and swiped everything from the desk with a bellowing roar that echoed off the walls. He dropped his hands to the solid surface, fingertips white with pressure, head hanging between his rounded shoulders.

Pip trilled at his feet.

He heaved himself upright, air hissing from his lungs, and scooped her from the ground.

Instead of settling in the crook of his neck, she squirmed and tried to jump. She would have, too, with no regard for how dangerous such a leap would be, if he hadn't dropped down to a knee to set her back on the floor.

'I don't know what you want, biscuit.' Through one of the windows, Saint watched the dark livery of the footmen bobbing in and out of sight. 'I don't know what you want, or where our beloved is, or how I am even to think of anything else when I hardly remember who I was before my love for her existed.'

31

Saint had gone through every room in the house twice, with the exception of the guests' chambers. He had opened every cabinet and cupboard and sideboard, looked behind and under every piece of furniture, as if Anabel might simply be playing a game of which no one else was aware.

The housemaids had turned up no sign of her, and the footmen had returned indoors with bowed heads. Even Freddy seemed to be taking his sister's disappearance more seriously by the time the sun began to sink under the bristling tree-line and everyone had reconvened in the drawing room.

'Perhaps you ought to send a note to London—to the runners,' suggested Franny, patting his arm.

He dragged a hand down his face and sighed. Instead of addressing his sister, he went to Vivienne. 'You were with her most of yesterday. Did she say something—was there anything—?' In a roomful of people he couldn't finish the question.

Vivienne shook her head. 'I'm sorry. She's mischievous to her core, but she wouldn't ever do such a thing as this, worrying the people she cares about most.'

Her voice faltered at the end, and Hazelhurst clutched her to him.

Saint coughed to clear the emotion in his throat. 'Dinner will be served early this evening. Cook thought everyone might be both weary and hungry after the day's efforts.'

He excused himself and advanced his steps in the direction of his room. The corridor was silent. Her door sat wide open, waiting for her to come through.

Pip darted past him into the heart of Anabel's chamber, howling as she went.

'Leave it, Pip.' The tenor of his voice was firm but fatigued. The kitten ignored the command, looked at him from her position near the fireplace, and yowled. She had already trained him well. Saint walked to where she sat, glanced down, and said, 'You may stay here and carry on, but I will not be participating.'

Pip stood on her hind legs, her tiny paws pressing into his shin, and meowed again. Before he could bend to pick her up, she went to the wall and began scratching.

'Beg your pardon. If you wish to destroy the decor, you must first get your own house.'

She ignored him, both paws working furiously at the embossed damask.

His body sagged with weariness, and suddenly even

standing felt like more than he was capable. He dropped into the nearby chair, resting his head back against the shawl draped over it. Reaching around himself, he took the edge of the fine fabric between his fingers. The longer he sat, the less certain he was of ever moving again.

Pip's cries had become as frantic as her pawing. Saint inclined his head a moment and watched her. The image of Anabel in the drawing room running her fingers along the wall and asking him about trapdoors came easily to him. At the edge of his mind, another memory, a canopy of leaves. A new sense of urgency compelled him from his seat.

He went to Pip, knelt, and began to glide his hands over the material hoping, begging, to feel something. There was nothing, no hidden handle or raised edge. The kitten had gone quiet at his side, quiet and expectant.

The sun was nearly set, and darkness had begun to creep into her room. Saint went to retrieve a candle. Careful with the flame, he methodically canvassed the area where Pip remained. Then he saw it. A barely discernible line where the fabric had been cut. Once he knew what to look for, he could see the thread-like seam in the wall outlining a narrow door.

With his breath caught in his lungs, he pressed. The panel wished to shift, and the wood creaked under his effort but did not move. He set the candle on the mantel and then scooted Pip a little out of the way. Aligning his shoulder with the centre of the door, he used his full weight to drive into it. A harsh grinding sound, like something breaking, reverberated as the wall opened before him. The kitten sprang forward into a pitch-black passageway. He called Pip's name, but before chasing after her, he dragged a chair over and propped open the door.

'Anabel?' His voice disappeared into the void. 'Anabel?'

Saint went as fast as he could through the tight stone corridor, minding his steps in the limited visibility. At the end was a stairway, and from somewhere down below, Pip chirped. He quickened his pace, calling Anabel's name again. He descended the last step and came to an abrupt stop. She was in front of him, curled in a tight ball on a large velvet chair. Her head rested in the crook of her arm, her form much too still. An icy fist of terror choked him.

'Anabel?' he repeated, her name a fragile, desperate plea.

He drew closer and set the candle on the desk. In the low light, her skin appeared ruddy and streaked with tears. Agony ripped through his every fibre. He crouched down, and with one gentle finger, led a stray curl back behind her ear.

Her quick gasp startled him. The relieved intake of air into his own body nearly knocked him off his feet.

He whispered her name. When she mumbled, he said it again as gently as he could manage, emotion shaking his voice. 'Anabel.' His fingers wound through her hair, his thumb stroked her flushed cheek.

Time took a breath and held the world in its lungs.

Her eyes blinked open. Even in the near-dark, he could see they were bloodshot and swollen from crying. Confused and uncertain, too.

'Was this your second attempt to kill me?' Saint smiled. It was slight and concerned and, he hoped, reassuring. 'Had I not found you, I think you may well have succeeded.'

Her chin trembled, and she burst into tears.

Saint gathered her from the chair into his arms. He sat back on the floor, holding her to him. She gripped the lapel of his coat and wept with the violence of someone who had no expectation of being recovered. It was the worst thing he'd ever heard. He held her closer, and murmured into her dishevelled hair again and again and again that she was safe.

Pip wedged herself between their two bodies and purred, the sound a steady, comforting hum.

The outpouring of tears gradually lessened, and he was beginning to think she had fallen asleep once more when she confessed into the damp fabric of his chest, 'Despite my pleas and prayers and the divine bargains I made with Providence, I hadn't expected to see you—anyone—again in this life.'

He leaned back a little to look at her and then took her face between his hands. 'Pip was scratching at the wall. I admonished her for spending so much time in your room, but she is the one to whom I owe everything.'

Franny's distant call echoed through the small space.

Saint mustered a deep breath, hating that he had to let go. His eyes dropped to her lips. Her tongue swept over them. Her mouth wasn't his to claim, but she was breathing and full of life, and he might never have her so close to him again, so he indulged in temptation, with the greatest restraint he could, and dropped a fleeting kiss on her forehead.

'Come, let's get you out of here.'

He stood and pulled her up with him. Once they were on their feet, he didn't release her. He held her hand tight in his own, picked up the candle, and followed Pip as she led them back to Anabel's room.

32

Anabel clutched St Germain and didn't let him go, even when Franny and an army of footmen met them in the tight passageway.

'My little lambs!' Franny wailed, sounding more like Lady Marrow than herself.

Anabel was certain if there had been room enough to move, the woman would have squeezed both her and St Germain until their ribs cracked.

'Get us out of here, and find me some salts.' Franny's request was made to no one in particular and for no real reason. None of them had any desire to remain in the dark hall longer than necessary. The footmen were already shuffling back in the direction from which they'd come.

'Who is this hysterical creature?' asked St Germain. 'Surely not my unflappable older sister.'

'Pah. I remain steady largely for your benefit. I've found you and Anabel, who, if I'm being honest, I thought quite dead. Now I may reasonably succumb to the fit of the vapours which has been teasing me since she first disappeared.'

This speech brought them into her room, a sight she had never fully appreciated until that moment. Vivienne rushed forward and embraced her in a hug so fierce, the pressure threatened to kill her just as soon as she'd been found. The force ripped her hand from St Germain's, a comfort from which she had not yet been ready to part.

Franny dismissed the footmen with instructions for bathwater to be brought up. Harriet was waiting off to one side, worrying the cross that hung from her neck. Anabel had never seen the stout woman so close to fainting, but she recovered quickly and came to fuss over her mistress.

'Let me see you.' She turned Anabel this way, and that, smoothed her hair back, lifted her chin. Then the woman tsked with the vivid disappointment reserved for and mastered by lifelong retainers.

'Out. Everyone out,' she said, at her most unyielding.

Anabel wished to protest, but she couldn't very well request a single gentleman remain with her, particularly while she bathed. She swallowed the lump in her throat that formed when he reached once more for her, held her trembling hand in his, and kissed the back of it.

'You will never know how relieved I am to have you here before me.'

She nodded, bereft of words. He departed with a last look over his shoulder, and Franny just behind him. Her chin began to quiver the instant he was gone.

Vivienne kissed her cheek and took her leave. 'I'll let you bathe in peace, but send for me at any hour.'

Soon the room was quiet, the bath filled. Harriet helped her disrobe.

'Don't suppose they ever dusted in there,' the maid remarked, holding up one very dirty sleeve of her dressing gown.

Anabel stepped into the bath and sank to her neck in the hot water. She pushed her wet fingers to her eyes where they burned with tears.

'Our hostess will have put everyone's mind at ease, and I'm guessing his lordship will have your dinner sent up before I can ring for it myself. You scrub this very bad day off you, and then we'll get you tucked in tight.'

Harriet was right.

By the time she was dried and in a fresh nightdress, a tray had been brought up. Harriet removed the cover. Anabel stared.

'This is what was served for dinner?' On it were all her favourites, along with a slice of apple pie.

'Not at all.' Harriet said nothing else as she bustled about the room tidying while Anabel nibbled on bacon.

The weariness of relief enveloped her before she finished eating, and she struggled to keep herself from tipping head first into the plate. She called for Harriet, who removed the tray. A short time later, the maid bid Anabel a good night and left the room entirely.

In the yawning stillness, even sheer exhaustion couldn't triumph over the fright Anabel felt. Every time she closed her eyes, she was sunk once again into a darkness from which she could not escape. She gulped and bit her tongue, willing herself not to cry again, lest she relapse once more and become a watering pot to rival Lady Marrow.

The hours moved too slowly for her liking. For a stretch of several minutes, she heard people in the hall, doors opening and closing. She glanced at Pip, who was curled on the bed next to her, and when she strained to look at the clock, it was almost midnight. Careful not to disrupt the kitten, she slipped from under the counterpane, picked up the candleholder, and walked to her door, cracking it open with care. Sticking her head out, she looked one way and then the other. The house had gone quiet.

She padded down the hall, counting the doors as she went, till she came to the one that had carried her out of her bed. Her fingers settled on the knob for a deliberating moment, before she straightened her shoulders and pushed in.

'Anabel.' St Germain sounded astonished, and his brows nearly disappeared into his dusky blond hair when she shut the door with a gentle but unmistakable snap behind her.

There was a vigorous fire burning in the grate, and he was sitting up in his bed, unencumbered by a nightshirt, with a book in hand. She stared at the grooves carved between the muscles of his torso, the line of fine hair running down his chest and disappearing into the bedcovers folded over at his waist. Heat spread up her neck, down into her stomach, and lower still. She swallowed several times in quick succession.

'I—I can't sleep.'

He marked his page and set the book aside.

'Whenever I shut my eyes—' Her voice wavered, and she couldn't finish the sentence.

He was out of bed in a trice, pulling her into the safe circle of his arms. His skin was hot under the hands she pressed against his back, and the soft hair on his chest tickled her cheek.

'Take a deep breath for me.'

His words rumbled through her on a current of care and concern. She filled her lungs and nuzzled her nose into the comforting firmness of his body. On his skin, the lingering scent of the woods at twilight. A subtle pressure settled on the crown of her head as St Germain rested his cheek there.

'Tell me how I can help.'

Her cheeks flushed, and her mouth went dry. 'I was hoping—that is, I thought I might—is it possible, may I just lie next to you for a little while?'

A cold fury of disappointment flowed through her when he unfolded them from one another and set her at a little distance.

'Anabel.' His tone held a warning.

Her lips trembled. Terror hovered just inside her mind, waiting for the moment she closed her eyes.

He rubbed his jaw and sighed. 'Come.'

She followed him to his bed, and he handed her up, wrapping the bedcovers tight around her.

To her dismay, he wandered from the room before returning in a nightshirt. Anabel watched him trade the book he had set down when she entered in favour of another before climbing on top of the silk counterpane.

'Would you like me to read to you?'

'That very much depends on the book you've selected. Nothing prosy, if you please.'

When he replied, she curled into the warmth of his voice. 'Imp. You'll approve of my choice, I think.' He opened the cover and began. '"After so many months of uncertainty, the most extraordinary thing has happened. My happiness is not so far distant as I once assumed."'

She gaped. The turmoil of her last few days had eclipsed every thought of Lady Cecelia's journal. He glanced from the page to her and continued reading through a slight, satisfied grin.

'"I brought with me this empty journal, the pages within as vacant as the vast, hollow expanse of my soul, certain each thin sheaf would soon bear the weight of my deepest torments—those ceaseless rivers of agitation and despair threatening to consume me whole since I last visited this place and met the man who would bewitch and bewilder me. However, the clouds which have overshadowed my heart for an unfathomable duration have finally begun to lift, and I scarcely dare do more than commit this unexpected joy to paper, in case the Gods feel it right to tear such unearned happiness from me once more. After our sorrowful parting the year past, I held no hope for a reunion, knowing his duties called him further afield than I have ever dreamed of going. Alas, he is here."'

'Gracious. Lady Cecelia was touched by a hint of the theatrical. Have we many pages of the same?'

He flipped through the journal. 'Indeed. Ah. Her aunt, apparently a guest here in the distant past, came upon the secret passageway and told her of it. Lady Cecelia used the private room to hide the journal, should a curious maid discover and subsequently thwart her plans.'

'Yes,' Anabel huffed impatiently, burrowing a little further beneath the counterpane. 'But what plans?'

He made a humming noise and turned several more pages. 'Here we are. "My heart beats wildly at the very thought of what I am about to write. I am resolved to cast aside all that is familiar and take flight into the unknown, with nothing more than the promise of freedom. Tonight, cloaked in darkness, I shall slip away with James, loyal valet to Lord F—who, despite his station, has proven himself the most noble of men, and who will carry me far from the constraints that have so long suffocated my spirit.

"Within me, a tempest rages: fear, guilt, and an almost overwhelming sense of liberation. The consequences of our actions fail to find a foothold in my mind when the whispers of new beginnings call to me, and my heart, for the first time in many years, feels safe in the hands of the man who has, against all odds, become my salvation."'

He looked ahead another page. 'They planned to sail to Canada, where James had family.'

'How odd she should choose to leave her journal behind.'

'An act of finality, I suspect. The journal was her last testament to her life in England.'

Anabel twisted up the corner of her mouth. 'Do you

think she found the happiness of which she was in such great expectation?'

'I hope very much that she did. The future offers no guarantees. However, we might make choices which increase the likelihood of achieving our heart's desire.'

'Indeed,' Anabel replied, rather absently.

He leaned over to his bedside table. 'Shall we try this next?' He held up another book. 'A satire of gothic novels. Ellena's suggestion. I was on chapter four when you came in, but I'll start from the beginning.'

She nodded into the pillow on which her head rested, her heavy eyelids fluttering.

He read with an elegant, natural cadence and, much to her delight, created different voices for each of the characters.

Anabel curled into the centre of the bed, as close as she could get to him, and before he came upon his previous stopping place, she had drifted to sleep.

Harriet's voice was an unwelcome intrusion. While she adored her maid, Anabel hadn't finished savouring the sound of St Germain impersonating a silly young lady.

She drew a sharp inhale and flung herself up. Harriet wasn't in St Germain's room. Anabel was in her own bed. The one she'd left last night. A vague memory of being carried flitted around in her mind. Her eyes darted around the room. On the end table near her bed, a small piece of folded paper with just one word written upon it. The letters were spaced a little apart from one another, the bottom of each weighing a bit more than the top. Anabel read it without trouble: *cottage.*

33

An unsettling sense of familiarity overwhelmed Saint as he paced the cosy cottage. The sameness of his morning compared to the one the day before made him irrationally concerned for Anabel. So much so, he was contemplating returning to the house to ensure she was there, just as her lovely face appeared in the doorway, lit by the temperate autumn sun. She greeted him with a happy little lilt of her lips, but dropped her gaze in an unusual show of diffidence.

'You snore.' He stifled a laugh at her dramatic gasp. 'Don't rip up at me. The sound is delicate enough to be charming.'

She closed the door and leaned back against it. 'Count yourself fortunate to have discovered so before we are married.'

He instinctively took a step towards her. 'Before we are—'

'Married.'

His breath bottled in his chest, and his eyes burned as they studied her, looking for any sign he'd misheard her.

'If you will still have me, Valentine Matthias Ainsley, I'd very much like to be your wife.'

Saint ate up the remaining space between them in a few eager strides. He bundled her hands in his and held them over his thundering heartbeat. His forehead dropped to hers.

'Tell me how I came to be the luckiest.'

'The stretch of time spent in that small room, although short when measured against a long life, rearranged the very molecules of my being.' She shifted to better see him. 'The candle burned out, leaving behind darkness and silence so tremendous, I imagined I could hear the moon rising. Having no wish to bear witness to my own grim end, I closed my eyes, but a deeper blackness never appeared. For hours, I watched a beautiful life unfold: a small wedding in the chapel here at Sylvancliffe, a dusting of snow on the ground; my hand on your arm as we ascended the steps of Vivienne's home in London, for the party she wished to host in our honour; the blessed sound of our first child crying as she entered the world.'

Saint's stomach twisted with the familiar mix of guilt and failure. A single tear slid over the sharp cut of his cheekbone.

Anabel freed a hand to trace the wet trail. 'Come now, you dear man, it's not so bad as that.'

'If I'd done more—' His head dipped, but she demanded his attention with a finger under his chin.

'You have trampled me, compromised me, and trapped me in your home. I think you have done quite enough.'

He chuckled and brushed the tip of her nose with his, admitting, a little ruefully, 'I'd a whole speech prepared for this very moment. Something about a hundred remedies for every concern but only one you. A bit trite, even more so when eloquence escapes me in my unmitigated happiness.'

There was a slight smile on her lips but a glimmer of concern in her eyes. 'In the dark, I resolved to choose the path that would lead me where I most wished to go if given the chance, but I still harbour some small doubt—fear that with time you will know regret.'

'What I meant when I said, "you are perfect because I love you", is "you are perfect *because* I love you". We come to one another with our own individual strengths of character but also ways in which we might grow. If you desire to improve the proficiency with which you read and write because doing so would influence *your* happiness, I will collect every star from the night sky so you will always have light by which you might practise. With respect to my own feelings, I have recently come to discover the joy of reading aloud.'

She leaned into him with an airy chuckle, snaking her arms around his middle. 'And the accounts and inventories and invitations?'

'My household has managed without a mistress thus far, you may choose your responsibilities and leave the rest. I will follow your lead. We may tell the staff and whomever else whatever you like.' His hands ran long and languid over her back, and he hoped she could feel the truth and assurance behind every word he spoke. 'I do think you'll find more care than you anticipate should you decide to welcome more people into your confidence, but we might pass it off as some imagined complaint if that's your preference. Ah! I have it. Excessive Penning Disorder—extremely rare but not unheard of, and the natural result of an abundance of intelligence which causes the sufferer to experience physical pain when trying to constrain their writing to the prescribed space or read the dull words of others. Naturally, you may hire someone to accomplish both on your behalf.'

The way she tipped her head back to catch his look, the fine lines of amusement at the corners of her eyes, the broad smile she bestowed upon him, was a triumph.

He palmed her cheek. 'I cannot promise a perfect life, Anabel, or the absence of frustrating days ahead. I can only vow to love you and champion you through whatever trials the future may bring.'

'If future is another word for choice, then you are another word for future, Saint.'

The husky way she said his name sent a thrill through him. 'You have guided me to a path of reconciliation, connection, and teased me back into being like no one else could. Call me something no one else does.'

'Have you an appellation in mind?' She traced aimless lines and small circles along the back of his neck. Rough shivers ran down his body.

'Valentine.' He bent his head to kiss the hollow behind

her earlobe. 'Love.' He felt the quiver of breath in her belly where it touched his abdomen. 'Husband.'

'Hus—' The word wavered in her throat '—band.'

Saint's lips curled up. 'How did that feel?'

She repeated the title with soft insistence, enthralling him with the way her lips wrapped around the word, making it sound celestial, divine, sublime. With a primal groan he dropped his hands to her buttocks and lifted her up, pulling the fabric of her dress to her knees and wrapping her legs around his waist. A soft fire burned in her eyes that had nothing to do with the one aflame in the grate. She ran her palm over his biceps, flexing her grip around the tense muscles.

Pressure built in Saint's chest, and he claimed her mouth with gentle demand, like a man who had searched a lifetime and found ambrosia. Anabel kissed him back, warm and eager. He traced the seam of her lips with the tip of his tongue, urging her to open for him. When she parted the petals of her mouth, he deepened their connection, devouring her gasp on a hungry moan.

One hand held her firmly between his body and the door. The other sought the supple swell of her hip, tripped up the curve of her waist, and grazed the subtle roundness of her breast. He traced a slow line from collarbone to collarbone and down into the valley between her breasts, leaving a trail of gooseflesh as he went. His fingertips skimmed the delicate sweep of her neck, and tangled in the soft hair at her nape. He pulled gently, skipping kisses along her jaw and nipping at the smooth exposed flesh of her throat. Her needy, guttural sound vibrated in his mouth. A flood of heat surged beneath his skin and swept between his thighs. The breeches he wore struggled against the growing evidence of his arousal.

He needed to see more of her, to explore the map of her body until she was euphoric with pleasure, and slipped his hands around her back to undo the four buttons on her dress. With a gentle tug, the sleeves dropped from her shoulders, the fabric of her bodice bunching at her waist. Anabel arched toward him. He held her glittering stare as he pulled the ribbon of her stays.

The stiff garment eased around her bust. Saint palmed her breast through the thin cotton of her shift, her nipple coming to a hard point under his hand. He bent his head and grazed her bottom lip between his teeth. When he lightly pinched the taut peak of her breast between his thumb and forefinger, she moaned on his tongue. The wanting pulse in the sound spread fire to his heart. He forced himself to ignore the agonising throb of his cock, pressed hard and heavy between her legs, and lifted his head from hers.

'We ought to return to the house.' Restrained desire turned his voice raw.

She tilted her pelvis, shifting herself along the hard ridge of his arousal and working him quickly to the edge of oblivion.

'No.'

He kneaded her buttocks while she rocked into him, experimenting with her pace and drawing a guttural sound from the deepest point of his desire.

'Anabel,' he whispered, breathless with longing. 'I do

not trust myself. This time, I will not be satisfied spending in my breeches.'

Her nails dug into his shoulder. 'What is my trust in you worth? You see, for the whole of my life, I have loved none other. Since the very afternoon I fell from the tree and you blew on my two scraped knees and carried me back to Woodruff.'

Her confession stilled him, and he blinked in startled confusion.

'Someday soon, I will answer every inquiry I can see already forming in your eyes. In this moment, what I most desire is to give my heart that which it has quietly ached for, long before it could even comprehend the word: you.'

Saint groaned as she began to move in his arms once more. A dozen questions coalesced in his mind, but the only one he wished answered in the moment was how to make his beloved happy.

'Please.' She traced a thumb over his brow, the hollow of his cheek, the defined curve of his bottom lip.

He kissed her finger, resting on his mouth, and spun them away from the door.

34

Anabel's whole being trembled with want. The night in the pantry, his ardent gaze had unravelled her all the way down to her pulsing centre, and his playful, tender ministrations provoked the first stirrings of an unfamiliar boldness in her hammering heart. She wished to once more feel that hum of pleasure, to begin her life with him before another day passed, to know she had not stumbled into a dream from which she might wake.

St Germain—Valentine as he would forever be to her—released her from his grip. His hands ran up her back, the heat of his palms burning through the nothingness of her shift as she slid down his body, every inch of her furious for more.

When her feet were firmly on the ground, the backs of her knees grazing the soft edge of the sofa, he pushed the rest of her dress down to the floor and helped her step from the puddle of silk. With aching slowness, he peeled away her stays, his light caress cresting along her shoulders and down the length of her arms. Gooseflesh prickled where he touched her, her skin pulling taut with sensation.

'Sit,' he instructed, sensual and commanding.

The fine cotton of her shift grazed her nipples as she settled on the sofa, the slight tease unbearable against her hard peaks.

He sunk to one knee and drew her kid leather boot to rest on his lean thigh, then undid the laces and slipped off the shoe. She was struck breathless by the intimacy of her stockinged foot in his hand, his thumb massaging her arch. He reached under the garment, roving over the sensitive flesh of her thigh and perilously close to the crease of her groin. Her legs drifted further apart. With a flick of his hand, he undid her ribbon garter and rolled down her stocking with unhurried, delicious purpose.

Her body felt as though it could burst into flame. When she finally spoke, desire choked her voice. 'Now you.'

She stood and slipped her hands between the fine wool of his coat and his moulded shoulders. He shrugged off the garment, his muscles rolling under her grip. She dropped down in front of him, working through fastenings on his waistcoat, her anticipation building with each one. He grabbed the fabric of his shirt and jerked it over his head. The ridges in his abdomen tensed. With reverent movements, she followed the dip from the centre of his chest to his navel, her short nails raking his exposed skin. He quivered, and she revelled in her newfound power.

He watched with heavy, glazed eyes, as she unfastened

a button on his buckskin breeches and then another, the side of her palm brushing his rigid hardness with light strokes. There was a slight tremble to her hands. The last button fell away. His manhood seemed to swell under her appraising gaze.

Her hand twitched at her side. Following an instinct, a craving, she curled her fingers tentatively around his hot flesh, surprised by the silky feel of his tight skin.

He tipped his head back and groaned her name, a tremor shivering his body. She licked her lips and worked her hand along his stiffness in tentative, unhurried strokes. He thrust his hips to her rhythm, and heat pooled in her core.

'Not yet. Not like this. Not before you,' he said, placing a stilling hand on top of hers.

Anabel tipped her head in question.

He brought them both to standing. 'When you come undone with pleasure, I will follow.'

Her centre clenched at the promise in his voice.

He pulled off his boots and stockings and breeches. When he'd finished with himself, he slipped off her shift. They both stood bare, every inch of her flesh burning under the greedy satisfaction in his eyes.

Running his thumb along the crease of her breast and feathering the very tip of her nipple, he said in a sensuous, simmering tone, 'I've never seen anything so exquisite.'

She arched into his touch as he lowered himself to the ground in front of her, and flushed when he nuzzled the patch of curls at the juncture of her legs. His warm palm savoured the journey from ankle to thigh, and he applied slight pressure just below her centre, opening her to him. She jerked when the pad of his thumb rolled the bud above her entrance. He kissed her then, in the same spot, his tongue warm and firm and demanding something from her she ached to give.

Her legs shook, and when his finger teased her folds, she put both hands on his shoulders to keep herself upright. Tension coiled inside her, fierce and unrelenting, and she pushed against his mouth. He moaned into her. She panted, releasing a little cry when his lips pulled suddenly away from her.

Valentine rose from the rug and grabbed her hand. He sat back on the sofa. His strong legs fell open, his erection rising from dusky blond curls to rest thick and hard on his stomach. Guiding her closer, he said, 'Put one knee here,' gesturing to the outside of his hip, 'and one here.'

Anabel crawled up to straddle him, placing her hands on the taut tendons running from his neck to his shoulders. He gripped her thighs and urged her forward till she hovered just above his cock. When her sex settled upon his hard length, he rolled her hips. A little surge of delight pulsed through her.

'Like so. You have all the control. If you wish to stop—'

She pressed her open mouth to his, her tongue searching and needy. His palms grazed up her sides to cup her breasts, small in his masculine hands, and with a gossamer touch his thumbs brushed her sensitive nipples. He teased her on his length until she whimpered his name with the longing of a seed waiting for spring.

'Please,' she begged, the throbbing between her legs

had grown painful as exquisite sensation began to pull her apart.

He lifted her hips a little away from him.

'Come to me slowly.'

Anabel frowned in confusion. Understanding dawned when the hot, firm tip of his insistence stroked her entrance. She was slick with wanting, and her whole body quaked when she pushed down, taking only a very little bit of him inside her. The sensation jolted a gasp from her lungs. She withdrew from him entirely before sinking onto the head of his arousal a second time. She paused, aching with awareness and the slight discomfort of an unfamiliar fullness as she took more of his length.

'Just so. As much or as little as you wish.'

She edged herself off, feeling the tip of him slip out of her entrance. He held the base of his cock firm in his hand and drew small circles at her opening with the head, eliciting a low hiss of want from her lungs. Her nails dug into his shoulders, and she slowly glided herself back down, her sex tightening with an instinctive grip of pleasure. His groan made her muscles grip hard around the inches of him sheathed inside her.

'God, Anabel,' he rasped out, his eyelids drifting closed a long moment.

She rocked her hips away, intoxicated by the exhilarating demand of his hard tip at her opening, and sunk down on him till the head of his erection met her natural barrier. There was an uncomfortable strain of pressure from the resistance in her core, and a nervous sound lodged in her throat.

His eyes were clouded with desire when he met her own heavy gaze, but still he repeated, 'The control is yours. We may stop at any moment.'

Anabel wasn't certain she could extract herself from his embrace, even if she weren't endlessly and infinitely in love with him. Her body craved what he had to give. She bowed forward, her mouth seeking his. He kissed her, slow and thoughtful and drugging. His fingertips skimmed the channel down her back, and the warm, soft palm caressing small circles over her peaked nipples elicited a feverish moan.

Sweat gathered in small beads at her hairline. Her legs trembled with exertion and need and restraint, and her body shuddered with every touch. He raised her up, dragging the wet tip of his desire from her entrance to the bud nestled in her curls, sliding himself back and forth over the bundle of nerves. Dizzying tremors wracked her body.

Her hand closed around his. She settled his head at her opening and sank down with gentle but determined force. A quick twinge constricted her muscles, but she only stopped once her patch of curls met his. With him inside her, there was no room for anything else. The breath in her chest seized. She pressed her fingers to her low abdomen, surprised she couldn't feel his stiffness pushing back, and dropped her head to stare at where they joined, spellbound that he was hers and she was his.

'Are you all right?' He swept over her with a look of affectionate concern.

She nodded, even her throat feeling too full for words. His thumb caressed her parted mouth. Tears welled in her eyes but vanished when he leaned forward and took her nipple lightly between his teeth, flicking the swollen point with the tip of his tongue.

His hands found her hips, and he rocked her back and forth at an easy pace, the constant friction where her centre met his pelvis driving her to the precipice of something divine.

'Valentine,' she cried, tipping into a feeling too intense to be named.

He lifted her, pulling out till only the tip of him remained inside, and eased up into her with slow, wicked strokes. Violent tremors shook her whole body.

'Anabel,' he said in his low, caressing way, the whisper of his breath cool on her flushed neck.

She moaned in response.

'I want to feel you come for me, on me.'

Anabel understood the desire in his voice, the command if not its name, and would have agreed to anything he asked to release the coil of need growing impossibly tight within her. He brought her down his length with tormenting slowness, burying himself to the hilt of his cock. Pinning her hips to his, he began to roll against her, each undulation ruthless and demanding. Her hands found the sharp angle of his jaw and her lips closed on his as the sensations mounting inside her became too much to bear.

She jerked in his arms, her centre gripping his hardness in frenzied spasms and her whimpers of pleasure dissolving on his tongue. He held her, supporting her spent, quivering body between his two hands, and thrust into her with urgent, hungry strokes. He groaned her name again and again, and she felt him swell within the walls of her core before warmth suffused her from the inside out.

Her breath came in ragged gasps, his own heaving chest rose to meet her frantic rhythm. Unable to do anything but, she folded into him.

'You cannot sell this place,' she panted, 'but I daresay you have already come to the realisation on your own.'

His laugh lifted her weary form, and he dropped a kiss on the top of her head. 'As it happens, yes. Although if I hadn't, you now know how to persuade me to your way of thinking, any time, on any subject. I fear I'm already quite addicted to your taste, your scent, your feel.'

Anabel pinked, the full stretch of her skin pressed to him growing hot. She hid her face in the curve of his neck, tasting the salt of his sweat on her lips.

'What's this, beloved? Dauntless when faced with a haunted manor but bashful upon the discovery I am yours to command? That will never do.' There was gentle amusement in his tone, and his hands roamed over her in relaxed, soothing caresses.

'Only a little conscious, to talk so.' The abstract ideas she had formed with regard to laying with a man had always precluded speaking—nay, teasing—about her pleasure or his.

He encouraged her eyes to meet his and brushed rushes of damp hair from her face. 'I hope it becomes the most natural thing in the world for you, to tell me what you like, what you want.'

She gave a small nod, and the parts of her body still warm with pleasure throbbed.

He touched her lips with a solemn, reverential kiss before slipping himself from her, the evidence of their coupling wet and hot between her legs.

'Let's set you to rights and return you to the house, lest we send both Harriet and Franny into a fit of the vapours.' He nicked her chin, then stood and spun around in search of something.

Anabel swallowed hard when faced with the curve of his firm buttocks, the dip in each cheek just right for her hands. He retrieved a handkerchief from his discarded coat pocket and kneeled in front of her, pressing the soft cotton to the dampness on her thighs. His careful, attentive movements challenged her belief that coupling was the most intimate act two people could share and convincing her, rather, it was all that would come after.

He set aside the handkerchief and picked up her stockings. When she reached for them, he wagged his head, slipping them over her foot and up her calf, teasing the sensitive skin behind her knees. Her breath, having just recovered a normal cadence, wavered on her exhale. By the time he'd slipped her final button through its loop, her body was humming, her centre craving the feel of him inside her. She turned to face him. He was hard again, his erection bobbing under her captive attention. Her tongue skimmed her lips.

An intimate smile curved his mouth as he pulled up his breeches. 'When the guests depart, I'll secure us a common licence. I can follow you to Woodruff, if you wish to be married from there, or we can remain here for a time—although snowfall is still a way off. Franny will be thrilled with the match. Doubtless she'll be agreeable to acting as chaperone as long as necessary.'

'I'd like to remain here.' Every joyful memory at her family estate had an equally distressing counterpart, and home to Anabel had come to mean any place where she could curl into the warmth and safety of Valentine.

Dressed, he held out his hand to her, bringing her knuckles to his mouth for a quick kiss before leading her outside.

The slice of woodland between the cottage and the house was a world of its own. Sun dappled the path through a canopy of orange leaves, clinging tightly to the branches before winter's cold forced them away. Under their feet was the soft grind of fallen foliage already becoming something new. Anabel released a content sigh into the wind, spreading her happiness out over the sea, all the way to the edge of the world.

They broached the treeline and were starting across the lawn when Franny came frantically towards them.

'She's vanished, Saint, vanished!'

He peered down at Anabel, his brow furrowed.

'Who?' he asked, when his sister was nearly upon them.

Franny put one hand to her chest and the other to her hip, gasping for air. Her agitated, wide-eyed focus settled on the space between them where their fingers remained intertwined.

Anabel couldn't stop a shy smile from forming when his hand squeezed hers.

'Why, I never—'

'Who's missing?'

Franny's gaze sharpened, and she cast a suspicious, scrutinising look from one to the other. 'Where have you two—?'

'Franny,' he said, his voice rising with impatience. 'Who is missing?'

'Of what are you speaking?'

A laugh bubbled up through Anabel's chest, and she tried to smother the sound behind the back of her free hand.

'Oh, yes, of course.' Franny recovered her thoughts and straightened her cap. 'Lady Hester.'

Anabel's betrothed fixed his keen stare on her. She peeked up at him, her lips scrunching up against a guilty grin. 'I may—or may not—but very definitely had been made aware of her plans to elope,' she said. 'The intelligence escaped my mind. My thoughts have been turned in another direction for some days, through no fault of my own. Dare to disagree, but I have it on excellent authority I can persuade you to my way of thinking, any time, and on any topic.'

His skin was stained with sun and joy. His lips curved in an intimate smile.

He beamed. 'Imp.'

EPILOGUE

The hushed sound of his wife reading the menu to herself made Saint smile. Mrs Crane, likely as not under the influence of Mrs Bates, had developed a decided soft spot for her new mistress and would have learned Greek, had Anabel asked it of her. The woman, when given an example of the unusual way in which to write the menus henceforth, commented only on her excitement at having a lady of the house once again and desired to know what more could be done to ensure Anabel's comfort in her new home.

He glanced over to the desk in their private sitting room where she was seated, admiring the pleasing shape of her mouth as it moved and attempting to ignore the subtle tightening of his breeches.

'A packet for you, my lord,' said Grimm from the open doorway. 'The last we'll be getting for some days, if my knee has anything to say on the matter.'

Saint took the wrapped parcel, thicker than the letters he was used to receiving, and noted the quiet that had settled over the space. As the butler retreated, he looked at his wife. Her eyes were focused on him, wide and a touch nervous. Taking the packet with him, he first closed the door then went to her side, depositing the parcel upon the desk before kneeling in front of her.

'Whether we open this is entirely dependent on you.' Saint had been corresponding with the physician in London studying reading blindness. The man had offered to send materials he'd discovered helpful in his efforts to improve comprehension among his patients.

He could see her chest expand with a breath. Anabel nodded, and pride curled the edges of his mouth.

Standing, he said, 'The letter opener, if you please.'

She opened a drawer and handed him the slim piece of brass, watching his every move. Wrapped in plain brown paper was a short missive, a longer sheaf of instructions, and papers of varying shapes and sizes.

He picked up the note and read it aloud: '*Do not be discouraged by the simplicity of the lessons. From what your letters have revealed to me of your wife, I've no doubt she will advance quickly. My professional recommendation is always to begin with the most basic units of language. Nothing will be so important as consistency. When she is near to finished with what's enclosed, send word. It will be a great pleasure to observe her progress first hand upon your return to town for the season.*'

'Well, my darling, what say you?'

'It feels as though my very bones are shaking.'

'You must learn to trust yourself the same way you trust me,' he said, nicking her chin.

She reached out and caught his hand, touching his knuckles with a lingering kiss.

Saint ran his eyes over the instructions. 'According to his research, understanding the structure and patterns of syllables is critical to building the correct foundation for both spelling words as well as making sense of them when reading, so we ought to begin there. He's included everything we need, as well as a short poem, which we are to recite together.' He hummed. 'I think I'll quite like that.'

She sent him a mock glare, rose from her chair, and brushed past him. 'If I'm to exhaust my wits and spend who knows how long fending off frustration, I'd like at the very least to be comfortable.'

He trailed his wife to the sofa in front of the fire, where she removed her slippers and curled her feet under her.

'After,' she said, 'for my patience and perseverance, you may read to me the letter Lady Hester sent. I will forever remain impressed by and commend Lady Marrow for her stoicism, once she realised what was afoot. I'd not thought such a thing possible.'

On that fateful day, by the time Saint, Anabel, and Franny had reached the house, a maid had come forward with a letter entrusted to her care by the absent lady, for delivery to her aunt.

According to the maid, Lady Hester had been out for a very early walk and come upon an express rider. Offering to take the missive to the house, she noticed it was addressed to herself. Some other aunt had taken ill, and

Lady Hester was certain the one present with her at Sylvancliffe would not begrudge her going. Not wishing to upset her aunt or the house at large, Lady Hester departed as soon as she was able, commending most of her trunks to Lady Marrow's care for their safe return home.

Several people present had known the tale to be a lie, none of whom were willing to contradict the narrative, however. Lady Marrow, both confused and concerned, *had* demanded her salts, but when Grimm entered to announce Sir Marcus has been called away unexpectedly, before a fresh vial could be procured, the woman had shuttered like a house before a storm, praised her niece as the most thoughtful creature, and excused herself with a serene, regal smile.

She had, according to Franny, known of the partiality between the pair as well as her own brother's opposition to the match. But as Lady Hester was as dear to her as a daughter and her brother not yet forgiven for the slight against her raiment, she declined removing from Sylvancliffe when Sir Marcus appeared as a guest, or to write, with any sense of urgency, to the duke regarding his wayward child.

With Anabel nestled to his side, Saint picked up the slips of paper they were to begin with. After a half-hour, he said, 'I think it won't be long at all till you are the one reading to me.'

'You say so because you love me.'

'I say so because I know no other as brave or determined.'

Pip jumped up, rolling around on the neatly organised

pile upon the sofa and sending sheafs of paper floating to the floor.

'You never told me why you were tearing through the hall that first night,' replied Anabel.

'And you have yet to reveal to me a single detail about your sustained *tendre* for me, despite my manifold requests,' he replied with a challenging grin. Getting his wife to answer his questions on that particular subject had proved near impossible, no matter the methods he had employed.

Anabel pinked and dipped her head before looking at him. 'Because 'tis embarrassing, when I have loved you forever and you have loved me hardly six weeks complete.'

''Tis true I have loved you in shorter duration, but I'd argue with greater feeling.'

She swatted at him.

'Very well,' he said on a chuckle. 'I'd heard a noise in the hall and thought it was some spirit—my father's, or Lady Cecelia's or some other. Quite certain now it was only this mischievous biscuit.' He swiped a hand over Pip before she jumped down to lay in her basket.

Her eyes twinkled. 'I do so enjoy the feeling of being right.'

'Your turn.'

'It seems in addition to my difficulty with letters, my memory has also failed me.'

'Anabel.'

She shivered. 'Do not say my name in such a way if you've any desire for me to continue speaking. In truth, I recall the day you first came to Woodruff and know I decided then you were the best of men based solely on your simple kindness, but the years after were largely absent specific moments, at least with regard to myself. On my way to becoming grown-up, I witnessed your loyalty to those most important to you, your careful concern, not just of your intimates, but of anyone existing in your sphere at any given moment. Characteristics learned from your papa, no doubt, that our children will learn from you.'

He pulled her onto his lap and kissed her, long, hard, thankful she'd chosen him.

Anabel snaked her fingers into his hair and caressed the seam of his mouth with her tongue, moaning against him when he parted his lips.

'I challenge anyone who knows you not to love you. Indeed, I suspect I'll be the object of any number of pointed glares and hushed whispers passed behind gloved hands when we go down to London.'

'Will that trouble you?' There was nothing he would protect so fiercely as his wife's happiness.

'Hardly,' she laughed. 'Indeed, I'll be so disappointed if our union, and at such a place as Sylvancliffe, stirs no gossip, I'll be forced to drop inadvertent mentions of being caught mid-embrace or mention how lucky we were not to be rained upon when we accidentally fell asleep on the beach, just to set tongues wagging myself.'

'Imp,' he chuckled, hands sliding up to unbutton her dress before he flipped his wife onto her back.

ALSO BY GEORGINA NORTH

Painting the Duke

The Gentleman Spy

The Rake of Tamarix Hall

ACKNOWLEDGMENTS

Nothing about this book has come easy, and I can't be certain it would have made its way into the world without a bit of help.

To my beta readers, Helen Davis and Ann Peterson, you two were a dream. Your thoughtful feedback and suggestions reignited my excitement for this project, and I hope you both love the final result.

I owe a heartfelt thank you to my dear friend, Amy Barron, who spent days mired in handwritten chapters, decoding my messy scrawl and typing up those pages so I could continue drafting.

Another big thanks goes to my editor, Amy Scott, and my proofreader, Helena Fairfax, both of whom ensure no Americanisms of mine slip through. And to Jennifer Therieau, who designed this cover with the patience and forbearance of a saint.

To Joanna Hinsey and my Auntie Reen, who between them split several dubious honors including having a front row seat to every book-related meltdown and listening to me discuss (certainly not whine or moan about) the many lessons I have learned while working on this book.

Thank you to my wonderfully kind and supportive

husband, Keola, who shoulders more of everything without a word of complaint, particularly during those long stretches of time where I am little more than a ghost in our house.

And as always, the biggest thank you goes to you, my dear reader, for choosing to spend your valuable and finite time with this book. I hope you found something special between the pages.

ABOUT THE AUTHOR

Georgina North lives in Southern California with her husband and their two cats. When she's not curled up with her laptop and a cup of coffee, you can find her daydreaming in her favourite chair, eating In-N-Out, or adding more books to her to-read pile.

Be the first to know!
Sign up for Georgina's newsletter
to receive updates
on new releases and more.

www.georginanorth.com

www.ingramcontent.com/pod-product-compliance
Lightning Source LLC
Chambersburg PA
CBHW030517310726
48979CB00010B/1706/J

* 9 7 8 1 9 5 9 7 9 4 1 0 3 *